ABDUCTED!

As Kerry stepped into the shabby cab she suddenly felt her wrists seized. She was so frightened she could not make a sound at first. But as the driver slammed the door and sprang to his seat, she remembered Ted and screamed for help.

She was not sure that her voice had been heard for it was almost immediately smothered in a dusty woolen cloth that was stuffed into her mouth. She tried to struggle free from the hand that held her, but she accomplished nothing.

"God! Father-God!" she cried in her heart. "I'm yours! Won't you please take care of me? You've promised! I'm trusting you!"

Grace
LIVINGSTON HILL

AMERICA'S BEST-LOVED STORYTELLER

KERRY

LIVING BOOKS®
Tyndale House Publishers, Inc.
Wheaton, Illinois

This Tyndale House book
by Grace Livingston Hill
contains the complete text
of the original hardcover edition.
NOT ONE WORD
HAS BEEN OMITTED.

Library of Congress Catalog Card Number 88-51598
ISBN 0-8423-2044-X

Printed in the United States of America

01 00 99 98 97 96 95
11 10   9   8   7   6   5

KERRY Kavanaugh thought when her beloved father died that the worst that could had come upon her. The day her mother told her, six months after her father's funeral, that she was going to marry again, and that she was going to marry Sam Morgan, the multimillionaire, Kerry knew that there were worse things than death.

Sam Morgan had been a youthful acquaintance of Mrs. Kavanaugh's—a sort of skeleton in the closet ever since Kerry could remember.

"If I had married Sam Morgan," Mrs. Kavanaugh would say plaintively as she shivered in a cold room, "we wouldn't have had to stop at such cheap hotels."

And Kerry's father would say in a tone as nearly acid as his gentle voice ever took:

"Please leave me out of that, Isobel. If you had married Sam Morgan, remember, *I* would not have been stopping at the same hotel."

Then Kerry's mother's blue eyes would fill with tears, and her delicate lips would quiver, and she would say:

"Now, Shannon! How cruel of you to take that simple remark in that way! You are always ready to take offense. I meant, of course, that if *I*—that if *we*—That I wish we had more money! But of course, Shannon, when you have finished your wonderful book we shall have all we need. In fact, by the time you have written a second book I believe we shall have more than Sam Morgan has."

Then Kerry's father would look at her mother with something steely in his blue eyes, his thin sensitive lips pressed firmly together, and would seem about to say something strong and decided, something in the nature of an ultimatum. But after a moment of looking with that piercing glance which made his wife shrink and shiver, a softer look would melt into his eyes, and a stony sadness settle about his lips. He would get up, draw his shabby dressing gown about him, and go out into the draughty hotel hall where he would walk up and down for awhile, with his hands clasped behind his back, and his gaze bent unseeing on the old ingrain carpet that stretched away in dim hotel vistas.

On one such occasion when Kerry was about ten, she had left her weeping mother huddled in a blanket in a big chair, magnifying her chilliness and her misery, and had crept out to the hall and slipped her cold unhappy little hand into her father's; and so for a full length and back they had paced the hall. Then Father had noticed that Kerry was shivering in her thin little frock that was too short for her and too narrow for her, and he opened wide his shabby dressing gown, and gathered her in close to him where it was warm, and so walked her briskly back another length of the hall.

"Mother was crying," explained Kerry. "I couldn't listen to her any longer."

Then a stricken look came into Father's eyes and he looked down at Kerry solicitously.

"Poor little mother!" he said. "She doesn't always understand. Your little mother is all right, Kerry, only she sometimes errs in judgment."

Kerry said "Yes" in a meek little voice and waited, and after they had taken another length of the hall, her father explained again:

"She is such a beautiful little mother, you know, Kerry."

"Oh yes!" assented Kerry eagerly, for she could see that a happier light was coming into her father's eyes, and she really admired her frail little mother's looks very much indeed.

"She's always the most beautiful mother in the world, you know, Kerry."

"Oh, yes!" said Kerry again quite eagerly.

"You see," said Father slowly, after another pause, "you ought to understand, little daughter, I took her from a beautiful home where she had every luxury, and it's hard on her, very hard. She has to go without a great many things that she has been used to having. You see I loved her, little Kerry!"

"Yes?" said Kerry with a question in her voice.

"And she loved me. She *wanted* to come!" It was as if he were arguing over and over with himself a long debated question.

"But, Father, of course," bristled Kerry, "why wouldn't she want to come with you? You're the bestest father in the whole wide—"

Then Kerry's father stopped her words with a kiss, and suddenly hastened his steps.

"She might have had the best in the land. She might have had riches and honor!"

"You mean that ugly fat Sam Morgan, father?" Kerry had asked innocently with a frown.

"Oh, not that man!" said her father sharply. "He is a—a—*louse!*" Kerry remembered how her father had spoken the word, and then seemed to try to wipe it out with his voice.

"I mean, Kerry, that he was not worthy of your mother, your beautiful mother. But there were others she might have had who could have given her every thing. It is true I thought I would be able to do so too, some day, but my plans haven't worked out, not yet—. But Kerry, little Kerry, Beautiful

Mother gave up all her chances in life for me. We must remember that. We must not mind when she feels the lack of things. She ought to have them. She was made for them. She is your beautiful little mother, Kerry, you will always remember that?"

"Oh yes," caroled Kerry for she could feel that a different tone was coming into her father's voice, the tone he wore when he went out and bought Mother a rose, and made jokes and laughed and cheered Mother so that she smiled. Kerry was glad the cloud was passing, so she promised. But she always remembered that promise. And she never forgot the tone her father used, nor the look of his face, when he called Sam Morgan a *louse!* That was a word nice people didn't say. It was a word that she had been taught not to use, except when it applied to rose insects. It showed that Father felt very deeply about it that he would use the word, and she could sense that there had been apology to her in his eyes when he used it. She would never forget the thought of that great big thick-lipped Sam Morgan as a louse crawling around. Even as a rose louse he acquired the sense of destructiveness. Rose lice spoiled roses, and her beautiful little mother was like a rose.

After that Kerry's father worked harder than ever on his book. He used Kerry's little bedroom for a study, and his papers would be littered over her bed and small bureau, and Kerry never went in there except when she had to, to get something, while Father was working; and then she went on tiptoe. He was always deep into one of the great musty books he brought from the library, and he must not be disturbed. He told her one day that he was going to make Mother rich when his book was done, but there was still much work to be done on it, much much work, for it was to be the very greatest book of its kind that had ever been written, and it would not do to hurry, because there must be no mistakes in the book.

Kerry's mother read a great many story books, and ate a

great deal of chocolate candy. Sometimes she gave some to Kerry, but most of the time she said it wasn't good for little girls.

Kerry went to school whenever they stayed long enough in a place to make it worth while, for Father had to go to a great many different places to be near some of the big libraries so that he might finish his book sooner. And then when they would think he was almost done with the book, he would find out there was some other book or books he must consult before he would be sure that his own was complete, and so they would journey on again to other cheap hotels.

In this way they spent some years in Europe and Kerry had wide opportunities of seeing foreign lands, of visiting great picture galleries, and wonderful cathedrals, and studying history right in the historic places. For often Kerry's father would stop his work in the middle of a morning, or an afternoon, and take her out for a walk, and then he would tell her about the different places they were passing, and give her books out of the library to read about them. He taught her Latin also, and to speak French and German and Italian. As she grew older, she would go by herself to visit the galleries and great buildings, and would study them and delight in them, and read about the pictures, and so she grew in her own soul. Sometimes, on rare occasions, her beautiful mother would go with her to a gallery, dressed in a new coat, or a pretty hat that her father had bought for her, and people would always turn to look at the beautiful mother. Once Mother told her that she had been called the most beautiful girl in her home town when she married Father.

And once, when Mother and she had gone to the Louvre together, Sam Morgan had suddenly turned up.

Kerry had not seen him for several years, and he had grown puffier and redder than before. There were bags under his eyes, and he wore loud sporty clothes. Kerry's mother was rapturously glad to see him, but Kerry hated his being there. He tried to kiss her, though she was now sixteen, just back from school in Germany. Kerry shied away, but he did kiss her full on her shrinking mouth with his big wet lips, and she hated it. She looked at him and remembered that her father had called him a louse! She took her handkerchief out and opening it wiped her lips, *hard,* and then she walked away and studied the pictures until her mother called her and said they must go home. Even then Sam Morgan had walked with her mother down the street till they reached their own hotel, but Kerry had walked far behind!

Kerry had never mentioned this to her father, but somehow he always seemed to know when Sam Morgan had been around and Mother had seen him.

For two long years Kerry had been put in a school in Germany, while her father and mother went to Russia and China and some other strange countries because it had been found necessary for the sake of the book. They had been long years to Kerry, and she had worked hard to make the time pass. Her only joy during those two years was her father's letters. Her mother seldom wrote anything except a little chippering postscript or a picture postcard. Kerry sensed that her father had promoted even those. Yet Kerry loved her mother. She was so very beautiful. Sometimes Kerry took delight in just thinking how beautiful and fragile her mother was. It seemed somehow to make up for all the things she lacked, like not being well enough to keep house and make a home for them, and not being able to eat anything but the dainties, never any crusts. Kerry had been brought up to really like crusts.

The money to pay for Kerry's tuition ran out before the two years were over, but Kerry won a scholarship which carried her through to the finish of her course; and she stuck to her study in spite of her loneliness and longing to be with her father—and her beautiful mother.

When she joined them again it was in London, and she was startled to find that her father had been growing old. There were silver edges to his hair, and lines in his face that had been there only occasionally before she went away. Now they were graven deep.

The book, he told her, was almost done. It needed only copying. He must look up a typist. But first he must try to write something for the papers that would bring in a little extra money to pay the typist. They really had spent a great deal that season because the mother had not been feeling well, and had to have a better hotel, and luxuries now and then.

Then Kerry surprised her father by telling him that she had learned typing at the school so that she might help him, and they only needed to look out a cheap second-hand machine to rent and she would begin the work at once.

It was a great joy, those days she spent working with her father. Neatly the pages mounted up, page after page, with all the little notes put in so carefully, just where her father had marked them on his diagram. She even managed to sketch a couple of diagrams for him and her cheeks glowed at his praise.

All the little scraps of paper on which he had written his notes, all the bits of yellow paper, white paper, blue paper, backs of business letters, even brown wrapping paper that had been scrupulously saved and used in the precious manuscript were marshaled, number by number, scrap by scrap, until they were all there in orderly array, the fruit of his labor and scholarship. Her father! How proud she was of him.

She was almost seventeen when she began to help her father in the final stage of his book. It was about that time that Sam Morgan had appeared on the scene.

But nothing could take away her joy in the life she was living with her father. Not even a louse! She brushed him off from her thoughts as she might have whisked away an insect.

Her mind was opening up now. She saw, as she copied day after day her father's great thoughts, how really wonderful he was. She began to comprehend what a stupendous work he had undertaken. She began to take a deep personal interest in it, and its success. She even ventured a suggestion one day about the arrangement of certain chapters, and her father gave her a quick proud look of admiration. Kerry had a mind. Kerry had judgment. He drew a sigh of quivering delight over the discovery.

"Kerry," he said to her one day, "if anything should ever happen to me you would be able to finish my book!"

"Oh Father!" Kerry's eyes filled with tears of terror at the thought.

"No, but dear child, of course I hope nothing will happen. I expect fully to finish it myself. But in case the unlikely should happen, you could finish it. You have the mind. You have the judgment. You understand my plan, you can read my notes. You could even talk with the publishers and if there were any changes to be made you could make them. In a technical book like this there might be changes that would have to be made under certain circumstances, and it would be disastrous to the work if the writer were gone, if there were no one else by who could understandingly complete what had to be done. Listen, Kerry. There are some things I must yet tell you, and then I can go on with my work less burdened, knowing that if anything happened to me, you and little Mother would have plenty to keep you in comfort. Because, Kerry, I have assurance from other men in my line that such a book as this is going to make its mark, and to be profitable."

Then Kerry, with aching heart, listened to his careful directions, even took down notes and copied them for future reference, "if anything happened."

One day Kerry's father looking up casually between dictation, said:

"Kerry, I'm leaving the book to you. Understand? If anything happens to me Mother will have our income of course. That is understood. But the book will be yours. I've filed a will with my lawyer to that effect. I think Mother will not feel hurt at that. She rather regards the book as a rival anyway, and she will understand my leaving you something on which you have worked. You see, Kerry, Mother would not understand what to do with the book. Her judgment is not—just—well—she is all right of course, only I would prefer your judgment to be used in the matter of the book. And you will understand that whatever comes from the book in the way of remuneration is to be all in your hands. You are not to hand it over to Mother to handle. She is a beautiful little mother, and we love her, but she would not have the judgment to arrange about the book, nor handle any money."

Then Kerry put down her work and came over to her father's side.

"Father, are you feeling worse than you did last summer?" she said anxiously. "Did you go to the doctor the other day when you went out to walk alone? Tell me the truth please."

"Yes, I went to the doctor, Kerry, but only to ask him to give me a thorough examination. I always feel that is a good thing once in a while. I wouldn't like to get—high blood pressure or anything—at my age, you know."

"And did you have it?" Kerry asked anxiously. "Tell me what the doctor said. Father, please! I've got to know."

"Why, he assures me that I am doing very well," evaded the father glibly. "Says I'm ninety percent better off physically than most men who come to him."

She was only half reassured, and went back to her work with a cloud of anxiety in her heart.

Six months later her father lay dead after a sharp brief heart attack, and the world went black about her.

The world went black for Kerry's mother too, in a material sense. She insisted on swathing herself in it in spite of Kerry's strongest protests.

"Father didn't like people to dress in mourning, Mother!" pleaded Kerry. "He said it was heathenish!"

"Oh, but your father didn't realize what it would be to us, Kerry, to be left alone in a world that was going gayly on, and not show by some outward sign how bereaved we were! Kerry, how can you begrudge me the proper clothes in which to mourn your father. That was one thing about him, he never begrudged me anything he had. He always spent his last cent on me! You must own that!" And the widow sobbed into a wide black bordered handkerchief for which she had that morning paid two dollars in an expensive mourning shop in London, while Kerry sat in the dreary hotel apartment mending her old glove to save a dollar.

"But, Mother, we haven't the money!" said Kerry patiently. "Don't you realize it's going to take every cent of this three months' income to pay for the funeral? You've insisted on getting everything of the best. And violets too when they're out of season and so expensive—and such quantities of them! Mother, Father would be so distressed for you to spend all that on him now that he is gone! You know he needed a new overcoat! He wore his summer one all last winter through the cold because he didn't want to spend the money on himself—!"

"Oh, you are cruel! A cruel, cruel child!" the mother sobbed. "Don't you see how you are making me suffer with your reminders? That is just the reason I must do all I can for him now. It is all I have left to do for him."

It was on Kerry's lips to say: "If you had only been a little kinder to him while he was alive! If you had not thought so much about yourself—"

But her lips were sealed. She remembered her father's words:

"She is the only little mother you have, Kerry! And you will always remember that she was the most beautiful little mother in the world, and that she gave up everything she might have had for me!"

Well, she might have done it once. Kerry almost had her doubts. But she certainly had lived the rest of her life on the strength of that one sacrifice!

But the indignation passed away as her mother lifted her pitiful pretty face helplessly. Kerry turned away in silence, and the mother went on ordering her black. Satins, crepes, a rich black coat, a hat whose price would have kept them comfortably for a month, expensive gloves, more flowers, even mourning jewelry and lingerie. Now that she was started there seemed no limitation to her desires. As the packages came in Kerry grew more and more appalled. When would they ever pay for them?

But over one matter Kerry was firm.

"Of course it is your money, Mother, and I've no right to advise you even, but you shall not spend it on me! Get what you want for yourself, but I'm not going to have new things! I know Father would tell me I was right!"

There was a battle of course, but Kerry could not be moved, though later she compromised on a cheap black dress of her own selection for the funeral. But the mother battled on every day.

"Of course, Kerry, I don't blame you for feeling hurt that your father only left you that old book. It was such a farce! He knew that we both knew it was worthless. I've known it for years but there wasn't any use in saying it to him! He was hipped on it, and wouldn't have been good for anything else till it was out of the way. But it must have hurt you to have him leave it as a legacy, as if it were a prize. If I were you I would throw it in the fire. You'll have to eventually of course when we pack, and it's only around in the way, a lot of trash!"

"Mother!" Kerry's indignation burst forth in a word that was at once horrified and threatening.

"Oh, well, of course! I know you are sentimental, and will probably hang on to the last scrap for awhile, but it is perfectly silly. However, you don't need to feel hurt at your father for leaving you nothing but the old trash. He knew I would look after you of course, and he would expect me to spend on you what ought to be spent to make you respectable for his funeral. Your father, my dear, while a great deal of a dreamer, had the name in his world of being a very great scientist. You must remember that. Whatever we suffered through his dreaming, at least he had a fine respectable name, and we must do honor to it."

It was of no use to argue, and Kerry, sick at heart, finally compromised on the one cheap dress for herself. In truth she really needed the dress, for her wardrobe was down to the very lowest terms.

Sam Morgan did not come to the funeral. Kerry was always glad afterwards to remember that! She could not have stood his presence there. It would have been like having vermin in the room, a desecration.

But other men came, noble men, some of them from long distances. Professors from the nearby universities. Telegrams poured in from practically all over the world, noted names signed to them, scientists, literary men, statesmen, great thinkers, even kings and presidents. The noble of the earth united to do him honor, and his widow sat and preened herself in her new black, and ordered more violets, wondering that her simple-hearted husband should have called forth so much admiration. Why hadn't she known in time that he was such an asset, and managed somehow to turn his prestige to better account financially?

Sam Morgan did not turn up for three whole weeks after the funeral, and it was even some days after that that Kerry discovered he was in Europe.

Kerry was hard at work on the book. Carefully, conscientiously, she had gathered every scrap of paper on which the wise man had jotted down the least thing, and they were under lock and key except when she was working on them. She did not trust her mother's judgment. In a fit of iconoclasm she might sweep the whole thing into the fire.

Kerry foresaw the day when creditors would come down upon them for georgette and crêpe and gloves and hats and furs and jewelry, for now a fur coat had been added to the extravagances. Her mother was spending money like water and would not realize until it was all gone. Kerry's father had laid her beautiful little mother upon her as a care, and when the income was gone, then Kerry must be ready to pay the bills. So she worked night and day, and shut in her room did not notice how often her mother was out for the whole morning or afternoon. The book was almost done. When it was finished, Kerry meant to take it to America to the publishers with whom her father had been corresponding. She knew there would be a battle with her mother, for Mrs. Kavanaugh hated America. She had grown used to living abroad and intended to stay there. She had even talked about the South of France for another winter, or Italy.

Kerry let her talk, for she knew there would be no money for either going or staying. She was much troubled in mind where the money for their passage was to come from, for she doubted being able to restrain her mother's purchases, and it was still several weeks till another pittance of their small annuity would arrive. Yet she determined that nothing should delay her trip to America as soon as her work of copying was completed, even if she had to get a job for a few weeks in order to get the price of passage.

Then suddenly Kerry became aware of her mother's renewed friendship with Sam Morgan.

Kerry had retired to her little room and her typewriter as usual after breakfast, but found after copying a few pages that she had left a newly purchased package of paper out in the sitting room, and came out to get it.

Her mother stood before the small mirror that hung between the two front windows, preening herself, patting her hair into shape, tilting her expensive new hat at a becoming angle, and something glittered on her white hand as she moved it up to arrange her hair.

Kerry stopped where she stood and an exclamation broke from her.

Mrs. Kavanaugh whirled about on her daughter, and smiled. A little bit confused she was perhaps at being discovered prinking yet quite confident and self-contained.

"It certainly is becoming, isn't it?" she said and turned back again to the glass.

A premonition seized upon Kerry. Something—something—! What was her mother going to do? And then she caught a glimpse of the flashing stone on her hand again.

"Mother!" she said helplessly, and for a second felt a dizziness sweep over her.

"Why, where are you going?" she managed to ask, trying to make her voice seem natural.

In a studiedly natural tone the mother answered:

"Why, I'm going out to lunch, dear," she said sweetly. "You won't mind, will you?" as if that were an almost daily occurrence.

"Out to lunch?" Kerry could not quite tell why she felt such an inward sinking of heart, such menace in the moment.

"Yes, dear," said Kerry's mother whirling, unexpectedly round and smiling radiantly, "Mr. Morgan telephoned me that he wanted me to lunch with him. Would you have liked to go? He meant to ask you, I'm sure, but I told him you were very busy and would not want to be disturbed."

"Mr. Morgan!" repeated Kerry in a shocked voice. "You don't mean you would go out to lunch with that—that—" she wanted to use the word her father had used about Sam Morgan but somehow she could not bring herself to speak it—"with that man my father so despised!" she finished bitterly.

"Now, now, Kerry," reproved her mother playfully. "You must not be prejudiced by your father. He never really knew Sam Morgan as I did. He was just a little bit jealous you know. Of course I am the last one to blame him for that. But you know yourself your father would be the first one to want me to have a little pleasure and relaxation after the terrible days through which we have lived—"

Kerry put out her hand almost blindly and wafted away her mother's words; impatiently, as one will clear a cobweb from one's path.

"But Mother, you—you—*wouldn't* go anywhere with that—that—" she choked. She was almost crying, and finished with a childish sob—"that great fat *slob!*"

"Kerry!" her mother whirled on her angrily, "don't let me hear you speak of my friend in that way again. You must remember you are only a child. I am your mother. Your father always required respect from you."

"Oh, Mother!" cried out Kerry helplessly, "don't talk that way. I am eighteen. I am not a child any more. You know that man is not fit—" And then suddenly she noticed the diamond again and her eyes were riveted to it in a new fear.

"Mother, you haven't been buying diamonds! Mother, are you *crazy?* Don't you know you've already spent more money than we have?"

The mother glanced down with a sudden flush, and laughed a sweet childlike trill.

"No, you're wrong, for once, Kerry. I didn't buy that diamond. Sam gave it to me. Isn't it a beauty? Even an amateur must see that."

"Sam!" the word escaped Kerry's horrified lips like the hiss of a serpent as she stood like a fiery, flaming, little Nemesis before her mother. But Mrs. Kavanaugh paid no heed to her now. In a high sweet key she went on:

"Yes, *Sam,* dear! I may as well tell you the whole story now, though I had meant to wait and prepare you a little first, but you might as well know everything. Mr. Morgan has asked me to marry him and I have accepted. He has been most kind in every way. He has even offered to make *you* his *heir!* My dear, you don't know what luck we are in! He has castles, real castles, three of them, and all kinds of places in America besides. And a yacht that is the envy of royalty. We can live where we like, and travel when we please, and there is nothing, simply nothing, that we cannot have. My dream for you is going to come true. Last night he was planning to have you presented at court. My dear, he is simply crazy about you. He *loves* you, he really does! He will be a *real father* to you—"

"Stop!" cried Kerry flashing her eyes like blue lightning, her face a deathly white. "Stop!" and then with a great cry she burst away from her mother, shut herself into her room and locked the door.

2

KERRY stood behind that locked door, a flaming, furious, frantic young soul, desperate, helpless, bound by the submission of years.

Her mother! Her beautiful mother! Going to marry that awful man! It could not be true. It must be some awful dream! It must be a nightmare that would pass!

She put her cold trembling hands over her eyes, and brushing away the vision of the present, tried to conjure up the dear dead past.

She heard her mother moving about the other room, little familiar movements, in her gentle, deliberate way. Mother was a perfect lady always, nothing impulsive or unconsidered about her habits. The shoving of a chair, the clink of the handglass as she laid it down on the old-fashioned marble shelf under the mirror. Kerry could almost vision her turning her head critically before the mirror to get one more glimpse of herself in her new hat before she went out.

And she could do that, when her child was suffering so on this side of the closed door! But that was an old hurt, almost callous now.

Now—! She was stepping across the floor. That was the board in the middle of the room that creaked!

She had picked up her bag and gloves from the table, and now she stood a moment to put on her gloves, turning again to get another glimpse of the new hat.

Kerry's eyes were closed, and the door against which she leaned was locked, but she could see it all, every motion. Now, she had turned and was walking toward the hall door. She was going! In another instant she would be gone! Gone with that awful—!

"Mother!"—

Kerry fumbled with the key frantically. It came out in her hand and had to be fitted in again! Oh, why had she locked her door! She would be gone—hopelessly—forever—perhaps!—It must not be! She must stop it! She *must!* Father would expect her to do something—!

The key slid into its hole again and she broke out into the sitting room wildly, the tears splashing unheeded down her white cheeks.

"Mother!"

The hall door was just closing, but it halted on the crack, and slowly swung open a couple of inches.

"Well?" said a cold voice, cold like icicles.

"Oh, Mother!" sobbed Kerry, her voice full of love and pleading. "Oh, Mother! Come back!"

The door opened a trifle wider and Isobel Kavanaugh's delicately pretty face appeared.

"What is it you want, Kerry? I'm late now, I cannot come back!" Her voice was haughty and unsympathetic.

"Oh, Mother, just a minute. Come in! I *must* speak to you!"

Mrs. Kavanaugh stepped inside and drew the door to.

"You'll have to hurry!" she said coldly.

Kerry was like a bright flame as she went rushing toward her mother. Her hair was red gold and as she crossed the room a ray of sunlight, the only ray that could get inside that dark hotel room, caught and tangled in its wavy meshes. It set a halo about the white face, with the great purply-blue eyes set like stars, wide apart. In her earnestness, her awful need, her face shone with hurt love and tenderness.

"Oh, Mother! Mother! You're the only mother I have, and you're so beautiful!" It was like a prayer, that form of words that had become a habit through the years—

Unconsciously Kerry had chosen the only mode of approach that could possibly have halted this vain woman a moment longer. For an instant she was almost mollified. Then she looked startled into the lovely illumined face of her daughter and saw her beauty as she had never seen it before. Saw that it was beauty even deeper, and more wonderful than her own, for with its delicacy was mingled a something of the intellect—or was it spirit?—they were all one to Mrs. Kavanaugh—that made it most unusual. Then too, there was that red-gold hair—or was it gold-red?—that the mother had always regretted and called plain red. She saw like a revelation that it made a startling combination. Kerry, in her trouble had suddenly grown up. Kerry was *beautiful!*

Then with the first throb of pride that made her look again, came another thought more powerful. Kerry would be a *rival!*

Perhaps Kerry already was a rival! Sam had been most insistent that she should bring Kerry along. Almost rudely insistent! Had there been anything back of that? Of course not! But—

All this in a flash of thought. Then:

"What a perfectly ridiculous child!" she said coldly, "to call me back at such a time just to say that! But of course, you were always just like your father!"

"But, Mother, you will stay! You will not go with that bad man! For I'm sure he is bad, Mother, or Father would not have said what he did about him. I'm sure Father knew!"

"What did your father dare to say about my friend?" flashed

the mother angrily. "Tell me instantly. You've no right to keep anything back like that. Your father had no right to say anything behind my back—"

"But Mother, he was only sorry about you. He was talking of you so lovingly," pleaded Kerry.

"What did he say?" demanded the now furious woman.

"He said—" struggled Kerry, wildly casting about for some way to answer without telling all— "He said—he was not—worthy—of you!"

The fury went out of the woman's eyes. She lifted her chin vainly with a little smile of self-consciousness.

"Oh, well, he would," she answered half sneeringly. "You know my dear, your father thought no one was worthy of me, not even himself, I'll say that for him. Not even himself. He was always humble enough. He knew his limitations, your poor dear father did!" Her tone was amused, reminiscent of a past which she scarcely seemed to regret.

A great anger surged over the girl, her vivid face flamed, and her dark eyes burned with unspeakable emotions.

"Mother! Oh, Mother! Listen. You don't understand! He didn't mean just that. He used a word—!"

"A word! What word? What do you mean? I insist on knowing!" The cold voice beat on the girl's consciousness like shot.

"It was a word—that showed he did not—respect him—"

"Tell me this instant!"

Kerry brought it out reluctantly, and in the great silence that followed for an instant she could hear her own heart beating.

But the echoes of the room were broken by a harsh laugh.

"Is that all?" laughed the woman. "Now, I know you are lying. Your father would never have used a word like that. It is ungentlemanly. Your father was always a gentleman, whatever else he was not. Well, I think it is about time this useless conversation came to an end. I'm going!"

But Kerry caught her as she threw open the door, and

pulled her in with a strength born of her great need. Flinging back the door with one hand she dropped upon her knees before her mother, her clasped hands uplifted and pled:

"Oh, Mother, *dear,* you're all I've got! Won't you give this up? Won't you? *Won't* you? I'll take care of you. I'll work hard! I'll buy you beautiful clothes. I know I can. I shall have the book ready now in a few days and Father said it would give us all we needed—"

But Mrs. Kavanaugh, deeply stirred for the instant by her daughter's pleading, was stung into contempt by the mention of the book. With a curl of her lip she froze into haughtiness, and swept Kerry aside almost fiercely.

"Oh, that book! You and your father are crazy together!" she muttered as she stepped over the prostrate girl and hurried down the hall.

The tone and the look she cast back at her child wounded Kerry as if she had struck her. Covering her face with her cold hands she crouched by the door until the sound of her mother's little high heels had clicked away into silence, and she knew that she was actually gone. Then she gathered herself up heavily, and shut the door, dropping into the chair and sitting for a long time with her face in her hands.

"Oh, Father, Father, what shall I do?" she murmured, and was still again, as if listening for her father's earthly voice with its gentle tender accents. "What *can* I do?" she wailed. "She will not listen to me! She does not care—! *She does not care!*"

A long time she sat there, trying to think, trying to still the wild rebellion of her heart, trying to find a way out of the terrible maze that life had become.

At last she rose and went swiftly into her own room and began to work at the book, feverishly, frantically. If she could only get it done! If she could only get it to the publisher and prove to her mother that it was going to be worth something! If she could only do this in time, perhaps, *perhaps* she might be able to persuade her mother not to do this dreadful thing; not to tie herself for life to that dreadful man! If Mother was sure of plenty of money to spend she would listen to reason. Mother was afraid that they both would be penniless. That was the matter. Poor little, beautiful, judgmentless Mother!

Thus Kerry tried to excuse her parent, and salve the wound that last cold look of Mrs. Kavanaugh's had inflicted. Thus she worked with bright red cheeks, and bated breath, her fingers flying over the keys of her machine as they had never flown before, trying to beat time and finish the book before her mother should wreck both their lives.

But all the time as she worked with tense brain, there was that undertone of hurt, that running accompaniment of excuses for her mother—her dear beautiful mother. The only little mother she had! The mother whom her precious father had loved so deeply—so tenderly.

Poor Father! Where was he now? Did he know of this awful thing that was threatening her life? What would he tell her to do?

And her fingers flew on.

She did not stop to eat. The thought of food was distasteful. She had but that one purpose—to get done.

There came an interruption. A knock on the door! A man from the undertaker's had come with a bill. He wanted to see her mother. He said Mrs. Kavanaugh had promised that he should have his money that afternoon, that he needed it to meet a note. He had been several times on the same errand, but she had promised to have it ready for him if he came this afternoon.

Kerry stood with the bill in her hand staring at the figures, a great wave of indignation surging through her. Fifty dollars was all that had been paid on her father's burial! And she had thought that it was all covered by the money which their lawyer had sent two days after her father had died. There had been enough, even to cover the expensive clothing that Mrs. Kavanaugh had insisted upon. What had become of the money?

"Mrs. Kavanaugh is not in at present," Kerry managed to

say, out of a throat and lips that had suddenly become hot and dry. Her voice sounded hollow and unnatural to her own ears.

"She said she would be here this afternoon," urged the man looking around suspiciously. "I have to have it. You sure she didn't leave it for me anywhere?"

A ray of hope sprang into her heart.

"I will go and look," said Kerry quickly.

Yet with sinking heart she turned toward her mother's bedroom door, knowing even against her anxious hope that she would find nothing.

There was a little wooden box of carved work inlaid with ivory in her mother's drawer where she kept her special treasures. If there was any money in the house it was always kept there. Kerry found the key, fitted it into the ivory keyhole, and threw the lid back, but found nothing there but a picture of Sam Morgan, and a couple of thin letters in scrawled bold hand, tied together with silly blue ribbons. From the upper side of one glared her own name coupled with the word "love."

Kerry snapped the lid shut, clicked the key and closed the drawer, her face drained of every semblance of color.

Somehow she managed to get back to the other room and dismiss the undertaker with a promise about tomorrow. But when he was gone she sat down and groaned.

She was still sitting there in helpless sorrow when a few minutes later her mother applied her latch key and entered.

"You don't mean to say you've been sitting there sulking ever since I left?"

The mother's voice was amused, half contemptuous, as she breezed happily in, filling the tawdry room with the scent of violets from a great bunch pinned to her coat.

Then she caught sight of the somewhat familiar bill lying on the floor where Kerry had dropped it, duplicates of which had been coming to her at brief intervals ever since her husband's burial.

Kerry lifted haggard eyes.

"Mother!" she condemned yet with a caress of hope behind the words, "haven't you paid for my father's funeral yet?"

"Oh, mercy!" said Mrs. Kavanaugh in a bored tone, "Has that tiresome man been dogging my steps again? I certainly would never go to him again if all my family died. Well, you needn't be so tragic about it. I've got the money to pay for it now, any way, and then we'll be done with him. Look, Kerry!" and she displayed a great roll of bills, fluttering her white fingers among them gloatingly, the diamond glistening gorgeously.

"You can't say Sam is stingy!" she caroled. "He gave me twice as much as I asked for—most of them hundred dollar bills! Just think of it, Kerry! We shall be rich! We can buy anything we like! Just take it in your hand and see how it feels to hold as much money as that all at once!"

But Kerry dashed the roll of bills to the floor and caught her mother's white hands in her own frantically, gripping them so tightly that the great diamond cut into her own tender flesh like a knife.

"Mother!" Kerry cried, "you shall never pay for my father's burial with a cent of that man's money! What have you done with the money Father left with the lawyer for that purpose? Where is it? I know there was plenty. I saw it myself. What did you do with it?"

"Well, if you must know, you silly, I paid for my fur coat with it. The man wouldn't let it go on a charge because of that trouble we had about the bill there last year, so I had to pay for it or let it go, and it was too good a bargain—!"

"But, Mother! How did you think we would ever get the undertaker paid?"

"Oh, I thought he could wait till the next annuity came in. Those undertakers are all rich!" said the woman carelessly, beginning to preen herself at the mirror again.

"This hat is certainly becoming, Kerry, isn't it? And these

violets. What a heavenly smell! I declare I've just been starved for flowers all these years. Come, Kerry, get out of that grouch. Pick up that money from the floor. I'll pay that bill to-night if that will satisfy you. Come, sit down. I want to tell you what a wonderful time I have had!"

But Kerry held her head high and looked her Mother sternly in the eyes.

"You will *never* pay for my father's burial with money from that man!" she said in a low steady tone.

Then she marched straight over those loathsome hundred-dollar bills to her bedroom door, and with her hand on the knob stood watching her mother.

Mrs. Kavanaugh laughed disagreeably and gathered up her money.

"Of course you would make a scene!" she said in a high excited voice, "but you'll come to it. You'll be glad enough of the money some day. You must remember that this is a matter about which you have nothing to say!"

Then Mrs. Kavanaugh went into her bedroom and shut the door.

Kerry stood in front of her own door, her face white and set, staring at the door that had shut her mother away from her. It seemed like the closing of an eternity between them.

A long time she stood there trying to think. She heard her mother going about her room, putting away her things, even humming a little tune, a gay little air she must have heard out in the world where she had been that day. The girl looked bitterly toward the undertaker's bill lying on the floor. One thought burned within her soul. Her father's burial must not be paid for with money furnished by Sam Morgan. There might be humiliations to come, but *that* should never happen. She knew that he would have chosen rather to be buried in the potter's field than to have had such a thing happen. Of course, one amount of money was the same as another equal amount, but she could not stand the thought that her mother could have done such a thing—spent the burial money on herself, and then be willing to use Sam Morgan's money in its place.

Kerry stood there staring at her mother's door, until she heard her mother lie down for her nap. She stood there while a great purpose grew within her, and until her limbs began to tremble and her feet ached. She must do something about it. She must prevent her mother's paying that bill with unholy money!

Quietly she went into her room and got her hat and coat. Cautiously she stole back through the sitting room, picking up the bill as she passed, and opened the door to the cloak closet. Yes, the big brown box was still there on the shelf, the cord lying in a snarl on the closet floor. Mrs. Kavanaugh never was known to put anything away.

Kerry lifted the lid of the box to make sure the coat was still inside. It had been too warm to wear it. Mrs. Kavanaugh had had it out only once since its arrival, and Kerry's questions and anxiety about the price had caused her to put it out of sight again. Yes, it was there safely, lying in velvety lovely folds under the tissue paper.

Kerry felt like a thief as she lifted the big box down from the shelf, tied the string firmly about it, carried it out into the hall and closed the door cautiously behind her. Yet this thing was right that she was doing. It was just. Her mother had no right to take the money that her father had left for his burial and buy luxuries for herself, and then force his enemy's money upon her husband. She would take the coat back where it was bought and beg them to return the money. If they would not do that she would sell the coat for what she could get and pay that bill. But her mother should not be allowed to do such a monstrous thing as that to her dead husband. Even though it might be only an idea, it was an idea that the loving daughter could not endure.

Kerry's heart was beating wildly, and there was a set to her lips that reminded one of her father, as she stepped out into the street carrying the great box.

She trembled as she climbed into a tram car and paid her

fare. She trembled more as she got out at the corner near the fur store and started toward the door. Now that she was here it seemed a preposterous thing she was about to do. Sell her beautiful little mother's coat! Sell it without her knowledge! The habit of the years clutched at her throat and tried to detain her, but her loyal feet carried her straight inside the door, and her brave voice, though it trembled, gathered courage to ask for the proprietor.

She was told he was busy, and she was left to wait in a dark little corner of an office. That half hour seemed a century, and she went through tortures as she schooled herself to meet a scornful proprietor, and become a humble suppliant. Over and over she conned the words of a speech she had thought out, fearful lest she should forget; reminding herself constantly that she must in no wise reflect upon her mother, her beautiful little mother. Father would not like that. Father had told her to remember—!

Was it the thousandth time she had said that to herself when the man appeared, a tall, dark, frowning creature with black angry eyes and a hurried air.

"You wanted to see me?"

Then his eyes sought the box which stood at her feet as she rose.

"What is wrong? You have brought back a coat?"

Then Kerry lifted her wonderful purply-blue eyes under her shabby little hat, and unconsciously put her soul into them.

"It is my mother's coat," she spoke bravely. "I have come to ask you to take it back. My mother has not worn it. It is just as it came from the store. My father is dead, and we cannot afford to keep it. We have no money to pay for his burial."

The man eyed her through with his little coal-black eyes that were like knives they seemed so sharp. When he saw that she was telling the truth his face took on a cunning look.

"Let me see it," he said pointing to the box, his voice in no way softened, just sharp and hard as if he did not believe her.

Kerry took the coat out of its wrappings and handed it to him. Its soft folds fell luxuriously over his hands. A glint of avarice came into his eyes. It was one of his best coats.

Carefully he examined it in every little inch, inside and out. He saw it was not hurt. He could see it had not been worn. But his face was still hard.

"I can't take back a garment at the same price," he said in that icy tone. Hope sprang up in Kerry's heart.

"But it has not been worn at all," she pleaded. "It has not been out of the box except a few minutes when it first arrived."

"How do I know that?" his voice raked itself over her tender sensibilities.

"Oh!" she said, and was very quiet, then reached her hand out for the garment.

"I have to sell it for second hand!" went on the proprietor, ignoring the outstretched hand.

"What would you give for it?" asked Kerry quietly.

The man continued to look it over, carefully examining pockets and lining.

At last he pierced her with his keen little cunning eyes again.

"I'll have to take off fifty dollars," he said narrowing his eyelids. "It's a rule we have—"

Kerry made a quick calculation.

"All right," she said at last with trouble in her eyes. "If you will give me the cash right away I'll have to let it go at that. We must pay the undertaker at once."

The man went away quickly and returned with a roll of bills. His manner was suddenly cordial. He pressed the money upon her, counting it out rapidly. He almost hurried her away.

Puzzling, troubled, wondering if she should have stood out for the other fifty dollars, Kerry hurried down the street, grasping the shabby little bag that held the money. It occurred to her that perhaps he thought she had stolen the coat, and wished to get rid of her as soon as possible before the theft was discovered. Or perhaps he feared that her mother might come and demand the whole of the price. As matters stood he had his coat, and fifty dollars to the good, and now he would probably sell it again at the original price. Well—it was done now. She must not think about that other fifty dollars. She was only glad to have money enough to cover the bill and a few dollars over. A great burden had rolled from her heart with the feeling that her father's own money would pay for the last that they could do for him on earth.

She was very tired when she reached the undertaker's place for it was a long walk, and her mind was weary beyond words. She had felt that she must save even the few cents her car fare would have cost.

Kerry could see that the undertaker seemed surprised and relieved when she paid the bill. Was the whole world tangled up in worries about money? Even the fur man. Surely he had more than enough and to spare. And yet how eager he had been to keep that fifty dollars! Who knew but that he too had his perplexities? Well it was a troublous world. She wondered why any of it had to be at all. How good it would be if she might have gone with her dear father where there were no more of earth's problems. Or were there other problems, there, wherever he was gone?

Kerry came away from the undertaker's with a sense of freedom and of having been washed clean from a soil that had been upon her. That bill was paid, anyway, and honestly paid. If her mother was angry about it she would probably have to suffer, but she was glad she had taken the coat back, glad that the man had been willing to take it even at a discount; glad, glad, glad that the bill was paid with honest money intended for the purpose.

When Kerry reached the hotel rooms her mother's door was still closed, so she laid the receipted bill and the few remaining dollars on the table where she knew her mother would see it as soon as she came out. Then she crept away behind her own locked door feeling age-old and very tired.

It was her mother's knock upon her door that roused her.

"Kerry! What is this?" her mother asked when she came to the door. Her mother was standing by the table where the receipted bill and the money still lay.

"That is the bill," said Kerry in a weary voice. "It is paid. I took that fur coat back!"

"You took my fur coat back!" exclaimed her mother with a curious mixture of amusement and fury in her voice. "You— took—it—*back*—!"

"Yes, Mother. You had no right to buy it. That was not your money. That was Father's money and he had a right to be buried with it! I could not let you bury him on charity!"

There was fire in the girl's eyes, tired and infinitely sad though they were.

The mother faced her for a moment, quite furious, then she suddenly turned childishly away and laughed.

"What a ridiculous infant you are! As if one dollar was any different from another! However, I'm not sure but I'm just as well pleased. I saw a coat to-day in another shop that I believe had better lines. But what have you done with the rest of the money? Did the man try to cheat you?"

"No, Mother, he took off fifty dollars because it was being returned. He said it was a rule they had."

Kerry's voice was tired and patient.

"The old fox!" said Isobel Kavanaugh. "He knew better. He told me himself that I might return it if I found I did not want to keep it. Well, I shall go right back to him to-morrow and get that other fifty dollars! I'll take Sam with me, and he'll make the old liar stand around."

Kerry looked at her mother hopelessly and turning went back into her room.

That night she lay awake long hours trying to plan some way to make her mother see reason, and awoke with dark circles under her eyes, and a wan, drawn look on her face. She had determined to finish the manuscript as soon as possible.

She felt that it was imperative that she get her mother away from Sam Morgan. With the book really done and ready to present to the publishers perhaps Mrs. Kavanaugh would begin to have some faith in it, and get interested in going back to America to have it published. For it was with an American publisher that her father's past dealings had been, and to whom he had promised the publication of his greatest work.

But Kerry was not left to a quiet day of work as she had hoped. Instead her mother was up bright and early and hurried away on an errand. Kerry surmised that she was going as she threatened after the fifty dollars, and she tried to turn her mind away from the thought of it all, and settled down to her important task. She had not however more than got out her papers, before she heard her mother coming back and calling her.

Mrs. Kavanaugh had on her new hat, and a fresh bunch of violets. She wore an excited air, and her eyes were sparkling. She began to speak rapidly, vivaciously, as soon as Kerry appeared in the doorway.

"Get yourself dressed up, darling. Put on that little green silk dress that your father always liked so much, and my hat with the chic brim, the green felt. I'll lend you some gloves too, and you must wear my fur neck piece. We're going out!"

Kerry's face suddenly took on a suspicious, stony look.

"Going where?" she asked dully.

"Why, we're going out, dear. Come, quick!"

"Just you and I alone, Mother?" There was a wistful ring to the girl's voice.

"Well, no, darling, Sam is going too! You see he is taking us."

"No!" said Kerry, drawing back into her room, "I can never go with him!"

"Well, but you must, precious; I say you must, and I'm your mother you know. Don't you remember what your father always used to say? He always said I was your only little beautiful—"

"Stop!" cried Kerry. "You're not that when you go with that man. You're not being my mother when you would do a thing like that! I will *never* go with that man *any*where!"

"But, Kerry, darling, listen!" said Mrs. Kavanaugh putting on her sweetest smile, "you simply must this time. I suppose I'll have to tell you, though I meant it for a surprise when we get there, but we're going out to get married, darling child. Mother's baby wouldn't desert her on her wedding morning, would she?" The tone was sweet and wheedling, one that had never before failed to touch the sensitive daughter's sense of duty.

But Kerry stood unmoved, looked stonily at her silly parent.

"Mother! You couldn't do that! You wouldn't do that! You wouldn't do that to my father!" she kept repeating in a toneless voice.

"Watch me! See if I won't!"

Mrs. Kavanaugh flashed angry eyes at her child, and turning pranced out the room, down the hall out of sight, and Kerry was left alone with her horror.

3

KERRY stood for an instant listening to her mother's retreating footsteps. Then she suddenly sprang to the window and looked down to the street. Yes, there was a cab waiting at the door, and while she looked she saw her mother come out and Sam Morgan help her into the cab. They were going, then, to get married. She felt the inevitable settle down upon her like a great awful weight that would crush her.

Frantically she threw up the window and leaned out shouting "Mother! Mother!" but the crowd of the city surged by and her voice was drowned in a myriad of noises. A stray passer-by glanced up, and wondering, watched her waving her hand, but the cab disappeared in traffic.

Lost! Lost! Lost!

Kerry's beautiful little mother was lost to her!

Even if she dashed down the stairs without waiting for hat or coat and flew down the street after her it was too late to do anything now. She had no idea where they were going! She could never find them in that great city!

She closed the window suddenly and dropped back into a chair to cover her face with her hands and groan aloud. Oh, this was worse, infinitely worse than death. If she could see that lovely face of her little mother lying dead in a coffin over there in the room where her father had so recently lain, she would not feel such sorrow as surged over her now. Such righteous horror and indignation! The man that her father despised, after a few short weeks had taken his wife—had stolen her mother away! But worse than all, she had *chosen* to go with him of her own free will. The thought was almost more than the young heart could bear. Like one who has received a sickening blow she writhed under the first sharp pain.

But soon there came a prodding thought. What was to come next? Would they return? Here? Soon?

She must not be here when they came! She must get away quickly or it would be too late. She must never be caught in the power of Sam Morgan. She and her father's book must get safely away where he never could find her.

She shuddered again as she remembered his hateful kisses on her lips, his coarse flabby face near to hers, his bold pop-eyes looking derisively into hers.

She staggered to her feet and went frantically to her room, half dazed, scarcely knowing what to do first.

Her papers and notes caught her glance, scattered in orderly array over her bed and table. Well, they were the first things to think of. They were like a part of her sensitive father; his work, the child of his brain, to be protected.

Hastily she went to work, schooling herself to be calm, to try to think coolly, dashing the unbidden tears away from her face, pushing back her red gold hair, she gathered the papers, each into its separate envelope as she had been trained. She put them all in the little brief case in which her father had kept them, locked it securely and dropped the key on its narrow black ribbon around her neck and inside her dress. Swiftly she put the cover on her typewriter and fastened it for carrying. Then she changed into her black dress.

A glance around her room showed very few things that were dear to her: some of her father's books she cherished and had meant to keep always, especially some few rare bindings, and old first editions that he prized, and had told her were very valuable. Now she looked at them with infinite sorrow in her eyes, but went to them steadily and took them in her cold hands. She loved them, but they must be sacrificed. Beside them she had only five dollars in the world. They must be made to help her in this greatest emergency of her life. They must be turned into money for her immediate necessities.

Swiftly lest her heart should fail her she put them into a big bag of her father's.

The rest of her packing took scarcely ten minutes.

She drew out the little trunk that had been hers when she was away at school, and which had been small enough to be stored under her bed. Into it she put her meager wardrobe, and the few little possessions that she prized most, all of them trifling gifts from her father at one time or another. There were a few snap shots they had taken when they ran away to the seashore for a day now and then, and one very good one of her father that she had taken with her own small camera. As she was about to close and lock her trunk she hesitated, then went out into the sitting room and got the large handsome photograph of her mother in its silver frame that stood on the desk in the sitting room. She packed it down beneath her garments. Then she locked her trunk and sat down to write a note. It was not an easy task. Love and indignation still fought in her breast. The tears streamed down her face and blistered the paper as she wrote.

Dear, Beautiful Little Mother, Good-by!

I am going away. You have driven me to do this. I can *never* be where that man is! You have done a dreadful thing! But Oh, I love you for you were the only little mother I had!

You must not try to find me for I will never come to be with you *and him*. But if you ever are in trouble and need me, write to Father's old lawyer friend in London. When I know what I am going to do I will let him know how to communicate with me.

> Your broken-hearted
> Kerry

Kerry slipped fearfully into her mother's room and laid this note on her mother's bureau. Then she went down and got a man to come up and get her trunk and other baggage. Holding in her lap the precious brief case containing her father's book, she rode away in the cab, her trunk behind her, her typewriter at her feet, and the big bag of rare books on the seat beside her.

It was to a railway station she went first, where she checked her trunk and typewriter, and then taking another cab she drove far uptown to a little old book shop where her father had an old friend. Getting out with her two bags she paid the man, dismissed him, and went fearfully into the shop. Now, if her father's friend were not in, what should she do next? And if he were not in and would not or could not buy her books, how was she to go any farther?

She opened the door and stepped into the sweet dim twilight of the book-lined shop. In the shadows of the book stalls, she saw three figures, one of the old man whom she had often seen when she came here with her father, the other two younger men. They were standing at opposite sides of the table each with a book open in his hand. They looked up as she entered.

The old man turned and came to meet her.

"Well, well, and whom have we here?" he said graciously. "Bless my soul if it isn't Shannon Kavanaugh's little lassie. Well, I'm glad to see you my child, glad to see you! And it's a sorry day to see you in black! I can't tell you how my heart aches for you! I miss your father coming in more than you would think. He was my friend for long years."

Kerry gave him a wistful smile, and felt the tears coming to her eyes, but she held them bravely back.

"Oh, thank you, Mr. Peddington," she said, "I was afraid perhaps you would not remember me."

"Remember you! Remember you? How could I ever forget that bonnie face? How could I forget those eyes so like your great father's? Oh, he was a great man! How proud I was to call him my friend! And his wonderful book that he was writing! He told me how you were helping him. Tell me, did he get it finished before he was taken away? Or will the world lose all that knowledge?"

"Yes, it is done, Mr. Peddington," answered Kerry eagerly. "He had it practically done several weeks before he died. We were going over it making corrections, finishing diagrams and rearranging some chapters, but it was practically just as he wanted it, and he had told me everything he wanted done. I have been copying the last things, and getting it ready for publication."

"And so it will soon come out, will it?" asked the old man eagerly.

"I hope so, Mr. Peddington, I'm planning to go to America to Father's publisher within a few days now."

"Oh, you are! How fortunate he was that he had some one to carry out his wishes and finish his work. Is there any way I can help you? I would be only too pleased. Your father was often good to me."

"Oh, Mr. Peddington! I thank you so much!" said Kerry gratefully. "Father always told me what a friend you were. And so I came to you to-day. I have here a few of his books that he loved, and he told me they were valuable. He told me if I ever needed funds to sell them, and to come to you to find out how to dispose of them. So now I've come. Would you mind looking at them, and telling me if I can get enough out of them to help me to get to America?"

She opened up the bag, and the old man took out the books

one by one, handling them as if they were delicate flowers, caressing the old bindings with his slender white fingers.

"Oh, a first edition! Very rare. Yes, I know a man who would buy that for his collection! And this? Ah! That is worth a great deal! Yes, I remember the day he brought that down to show it to me. Some one gave that to him. It is a pity you have to part with it, child. Perhaps I could advance you something on it and keep it for you until you can redeem it."

"Oh, no, Mr. Peddington, that would not be fair to you," said Kerry wistfully. "It would probably be a long time before I could ever redeem it, and you might have opportunities to make a good sale. I do not want you to be hampered by such a promise."

So they went on from book to book. Some were of course less valuable than others, but the old man received them all with great eagerness and acted as if they were volumes for which he had been searching long.

In the end Kerry's big bag was empty and such a sum of money in her shabby little hand bag as she had not dreamed could be realized from those dear old books, valuable though she knew them to be.

The two young men at the farther end of the book shop had gradually edged nearer and nearer to the other customer, watching her furtively. Long slant rays of sunlight touched and haloed her red-gold hair where it broke forth in soft little wavy strands about her face. Such a sweet young customer, with such a sweet low voice, that had nevertheless penetrated to their dim corners!

Shannon Kavanaugh! Ah! A name to conjure with! They both looked up at that. They neglected the volumes in their hands and sidled around pretending to reach for other volumes nearer to the old proprietor of the shop. The taller of the two, the one with the deep gray eyes and firm pleasant lips, ventured to walk around in front of the old man and the girl, and go to the other side of the book table. As he passed them he turned and looked full in the dark eyes of the girl. But the

other young man with the coal black eyes and the little pointed mustache over his full upper lip, edged nearer and nearer,
until at last he stood almost back to back with old man
Peddington, where he could overhear every word that was
spoken.

Shannon Kavanaugh! Shannon Kavanaugh's new book of
which the world had heard hints now and then in magazines,
and scientific articles by great men. *Ah!*

"How soon do you sail?" asked Peddington as Kerry was
about to leave the shop.

"Oh," gasped Kerry, a shadow of anxiety crossing her face,
"I wish I could go to-day. Now that you have helped me out
so wonderfully I'm only anxious to get started. I'll have to
find out about a boat. I don't know just how to go about it.
Father always attended to traveling arrangements."

"Well, why not start at once?" said the old man kindly. "I'm
sure there's a boat going to-morrow. It would only be a question of whether you could get reservations. Suppose I look up
the sailings in the morning paper."

At this the taller of the two young men, the one with the
deep gray eyes, lifted his voice.

"Pardon me, but I could not help overhearing. There is a
boat leaving at noon to-morrow from Liverpool, sir," he said
courteously. "I'm sailing on it myself. I don't know of course
if there are any reservations left."

"Oh, thank you!" said Kerry gratefully. "Could you tell me
where to go to find out about it?"

Kerry left the book shop with full directions about ships
and what to do if she could not get accommodations on that
boat. She signaled a cab for she felt that every minute might
be precious and it was important for her to get away from
London to-day if possible. She had a timorous fear that Sam
Morgan might turn London upside down to find her. If she
lingered she might never be allowed to go. She was not yet
quite of age. She was not sure how much power a step-father
would have over her. And there was no one in the wide world

to whom she could appeal who would have the right to help her. She longed to put the ocean between herself and the man she feared.

Thinking her frightened thought she arrived at the office of the steamship company, only to be told there were no reservations left for a lady alone. As she turned away, a woman came hurrying up. She was elegantly clad and in haste. She wanted to give up her reservation. She had found friends going on another steamer four days later and wished to go with them.

The agent called to Kerry just as she was leaving and she went back, but when she heard the price of the lady's reservation she gave a litle gasp.

"I ought not to pay so much," she said with a troubled look.

"Oh, very well," said the agent coldly, and turned away. Troubled and feeling as if she was about to break down and cry Kerry opened the door and went outside. She tried to think what to do, but a great fear seemed hounding her on every side. If she spent so much money she might starve when she got on the other side. On the other hand—

She had walked a whole block away from the place and was trying to cross the street when traffic interfered. From the curb stone where she had been jostled by the crowd she caught a whiff of violets, heavy and lovely, penetrating the myriad smells of a London street. Unconsciously she turned toward the shining limousine from which the perfume came. To her horror she saw that it contained her mother and the man from whom she was fleeing!

For the instant she was too horrified to move, too stunned to even take her eyes from the little scene that was being enacted before her, right there in the open street where any one might gaze.

Her mother, her beautiful little mother, had drawn the expensive glove from her shapely white hand and was admiring the glitter of the rings on the third finger. And Kerry saw that another had been added to the great white stone that she had worn that morning, a circlet of platinum set with diamonds and sapphires. A wedding ring. Then they were really married! The sight was burned into her soul. For days after she could see those rings whenever she closed her eyes.

There was a kind of finality about the sight that was like another blow. Yet there came a time when she was thankful that she had seen it. For, how else would she have known surely that they were married? That after all she had not run away too soon from a little mother who had grown repentant before the actual deed of marriage was consummated.

And there before her eyes, that unseeing mother turned toward the great heavy-faced, coarse-featured man, lifted up her pretty lips, apparently in response to his request, and let him kiss her! Before assembled hurrying multitudes!

Kerry sickened at the sight, and almost reeled. Then caught her breath and turned away as the traffic suddenly broke, and the car passed on.

She stood still on the curb watching it pass, unmindful of the crowds that were almost pushing her into the street, unmindful that she had been in haste and this was the time to pass on unless she wished to wait another turn of signals. She watched the shining car threading its way through the London street, as one might watch the pall of a beloved pass. When it was out of sight she knew such utter loneliness as only a young soul can feel who is entirely alone in the world.

Suddenly Kerry realized what she must do. She must go back and get that reservation if it was still to be had!

She turned so quickly that she almost knocked over a small person behind her, but when she had righted herself and apologized she fairly ran back the block to the steamship office, and hurried up to the desk.

"I'll take it!" she said, all out of breath, and waited anxiously watching a young man who was looking over the ship's diagram.

"Beg pardon," said the clerk apologetically to the young

man, "but this lady was here before! I don't know just which of you—"

The young man flashed a pair of coal black eyes at Kerry and touched his hat politely.

"That's all right with me," he said, "I'll take that upper berth in the other stateroom."

Kerry thanked him and wondered why those black eyes seemed strangely familiar as if she had seen them not long ago. But she was too engrossed in paying her money and getting the details of her passports and other arrangements settled to follow up the thought, and as soon as she could she hurried away to get herself and her baggage off to Liverpool.

Kerry sat in the station all that night. She was afraid to hunt lodgings. She was afraid to go about at all. She kept herself hidden in a corner, and pulled her hat well down over her face whenever people entered the room where she was sitting. She did not know Liverpool very well, having always been hurried through to a boat or a train when she came that way.

As early as she dared in the morning she went to her boat, and hid herself in her cabin. She felt more and more nervous as the time for sailing drew near lest she might be caught even yet. Of course her mother would make a great fuss when she found the note, and she had probably wept a great deal and made a most unhappy time for her bridegroom. He would likely have started detectives on her track. Would her mother think of her sailing to America? She did not know. Isobel Kavanaugh had shown herself so little interested in the great book on which father and daughter had been counting so long, that they had seldom talked about it before her. The matter of a publisher in America would not perhaps occur to her. She had always preferred Europe to America and sneered at her husband for calling himself American. She liked to have people think she belonged abroad. She would not have understood her husband's earnest desire to have his book published in America because he wished what glory should come from it to reflect upon his native land.

Still, though, she feared, and kept herself hidden.

As the morning wore away she reflected that a detective would not need to know about the book or an American publisher, he would search all possible outlets from the city of London, as well as London itself. And it would be an easy thing to find her, because her name would be on the passenger list. Oh, if she only might somehow have managed to get that other woman's reservation without telling her own name!

Trembling, she sat in the corner of her luxurious stateroom and stared at its appointments with unseeing eyes while time passed, and she was left unmolested. Now and again she would look down at her shabby garments, her threadbare coat, and her scuffed slippers, and realize that these were not the garments that belonged in such a deluxe apartment as she was occupying. Of course she had no business there! But it came to her that the very cost of her refuge made her safe. Her mother would never fancy she had the money to pay for a passage on one of the better boats. Her mother would expect to find her serving in some humble position somewhere in London. She might be even now huddled in a corner of the hotel sofa prettily moaning her child's "low-down" nature which would prompt her to become a humble servitor rather than accept the bounty of a man to whom she had taken a dislike. Mrs. Kavanaugh had been wont to taunt her thus whenever Kerry tried to suggest any kind of economy.

But in spite of her hopes, and of all the arguments in favor of her safe escape Kerry sat in her stateroom anxiously as the minutes slipped away toward high noon.

Breathless she listened to the call for all not sailing to leave the boat at once. She heard the sound of thronging feet along the decks, the chatter of eager voices in last farewells, the staccato of a sob here and there. She heard the long blast of the whistle, and felt the throb of the engine and the shudder that went through the great ship.

Outside the wharf hands were shouting to one another.

She stole to the porthole, keeping well out of sight, and peeked out. Snarls of colored paper ribbons were fluttering down across the opening. Others were unreeling from the dock now moving fast away from the side of the ship, and one little pink strand rasped out and whizzed past her face straight into her porthole, landing on the floor. She stepped back with her hand on her heart, her face white and startled. Then realizing that it was only a stray, meant for the deck above her, she stepped closer to the porthole and looked out again. Now that she could feel distinct motion under her, now that she had seen a narrow space of water between her and land, she took courage.

The water was a rod wide now, and growing wider. She drew a deep breath and came nearer, looking out, her eyes sweeping the dock. And suddenly she saw a bulky figure, head and shoulders above most of the throng, come elbowing through the crowd. The sun shone down upon his uncovered red head, and glinted on a red mustache, as he pushed the throng aside, elbowing his way to the front, and wildly waving his hat as if he expected the boat to stop for him. Could that be Sam Morgan? She got only that one glimpse of him, for a woman began to wave a handkerchief and it fluttered up and down between his face and Kerry's vision. In her excitement she could not be sure.

Kerry shrank back in new fright, but could not keep from peering out, trying to see if her fears had real foundation. If that was Sam Morgan he had probably seen her name on the passenger list in London and followed her at once. Failing to reach the boat in time he would probably send a message by wireless or radio to the captain of the boat and she would be detained when they reached the other side. Would there be any way to get free again? What would be the law in the United States about the rights of a mother and such a step-father?

Just then there came a sound at her stateroom door. The rattle of a turning key. She saw the door slowly open and a florist's box was thrust in. Then the stewardess saw her cowering by the window, her eyes large with fright mingled with defiance.

"I beg your pardon, Madam," said the woman, "I thought you were on deck. I thought everybody was on deck. These flowers just arrived, as we started, and I wanted to make sure they wouldn't get lost."

"Flowers?" said Kerry trying to steady her voice, "But there must be some mistake. No one would send flowers here to me. My friends do not know what ship I am taking."

"The box has got your name all right, and the number of the stateroom," affirmed the woman consulting the label. "Aren't you Mrs. Winship?"

"Oh, no," said Kerry with relief, and laughed a nervous little laugh, "that must be the lady who gave the stateroom up yesterday. I just got it at the last minute."

"Oh," said the stewardess, "well, then you'd better take the flowers. It's too late now to send them back. I'll have the steward attend to sending word to the florist, but you might as well have the flowers as throw them into the ocean. Here, I'll put them in water for you."

So, presently the small stateroom was filled with the splendor of orchids and gardenias, and Kerry was left to look about her and wonder. Kerry Kavanaugh with orchids. She almost laughed. Then she sobered and sat down to think.

So then, the stewardess had not known about the change of name. Pehaps there was some chance that the change had not yet been made on the ship's list, had not been sent down from London. Yet how would Sam Morgan have known to come to that dock if he had not seen the name on the list of passengers? Was it really Sam Morgan? Perhaps her eyes had deceived her. Well, she might be out on the ocean, but she was by no means sure that she was free from the man she dreaded.

She breathed more freely as the afternoon wore on and no one came to molest her. She had not gone down for lunch; she had the stewardess bring her a tray. Later in the afternoon she crept up on deck and went about a little, trying to find a secluded place where no one would see her, for even this much of a glimpse at her fellow passengers told her that her wardrobe was unfit for mingling with theirs. She resolved to keep utterly to herself, and to this end found a comparatively lonely spot where she might watch the gulls dip and sail, and look off at the horizon line, trying to feel that over there beyond all that water somewhere there would be a place for her, where she might work out her little drab life, and get to the end of it honorably. There were no dreams of gallant lovers within her young disillusioned mind. Her one ambition was to complete the work of her great father and see that he had his rightful meed of glory. Beyond that, and keeping out of the reach of her undesirable step-father, she had no present wish.

It was the steward who presently sought her out, called her Mrs. Winship, desired to show her where her steamer chair was located and where he had placed her in the dining room. He was all deference.

Kerry, aware of her own shabbiness, in spite of the new black funeral dress, shrank back and tried to explain that she was not the person he supposed her to be. She was just plain Miss Kavanaugh who had purchased the reservation that Mrs. Winship had given up.

The steward eyed her glorious red-gold hair that had slipped from its moorings beneath the little black hat and was waving gorgeously about the girl's delicate face. He decided it would be just as well to leave the arrangements as they were. Her name might not be Winship but she had the look of a perfect lady.

So Kerry, having sat for a few minutes in her steamer chair and contemplated her shabby little slippers, decided to get herself back into shelter and see what she could do toward furbishing up her scanty wardrobe for the occasion. Her one evening dress was a dark green chiffon which she herself had fashioned from an old gown of her mother's, and there was a rip in it that needed attention.

Kerry came shyly to the dining room that evening in her simple green chiffon, with a tiny string of pearl beads around her neck and her red-gold hair fastened with a little gold comb that had belonged to her great grandmother. Three gorgeous golden-hearted orchids leaned from the mossy green of her dress. She found she was no longer "Mrs. Winship." She had somehow blossomed into "Miss Kavanaugh," the daughter of the great scientist of whom everybody in the scientific world had heard. She could not understand how they had learned who she was, and she trembled inwardly all through the meal, wondering if there had been a message about her sent to the captain by her step-father, and if perhaps the captain already had orders from Sam Morgan to detain her when they reached the other side.

On Kerry's right there sat a tall young man with clear gray eyes and a nice voice. He reminded her vaguely of something pleasant and he spoke to her as if he had met her before, though he did not explain why he was so friendly. He seemed to know all about her. He spoke of her father and of having heard him lecture once. It warmed the lonely girl's heart to talk with one who held her father in such reverence and spoke of his mind and his work in such a tone of deep respect. She found his name was Graham McNair, and she heard the man across the table call him Doctor. She wondered if that stood for medicine or philosophy.

There were several other women at the table, all older than Kerry, two of them wives of professors in American Universities. Kerry was the only girl at the table.

The women looked upon her with great favor. As she listened to them she perceived that somehow her father's fame had preceded her and given her a prestige that her simple self and her shabby garments could never have claimed in such surroundings. It surprised her to know that her quiet, unassuming father had yet commanded so much enthusiasm from people of the world. She knew that among scientists he was beloved, but he had never sought wide popularity.

She would not have been so much surprised at her reception if she could have heard Graham McNair before her arrival at the table. Her heart would have glowed at the wonderful things he told about her noted father—though she would still have wondered where he gained some of his information, unless she had happened to hear him mention the name of Peddington.

"Peddington, you know, the old book shop in London. He knows everything about the great men of to-day, especially the scientists, and he was a personal friend of Shannon Kavanaugh!"

If she had heard that she would perhaps have remembered the clear gray eyes that had searched her as she passed him in the book shop yesterday morning, and the nice kind voice that had given the information about the ship's sailing. As it was her memory only hovered vaguely about something pleasant and indefinite, and she was glad to have such a friendly neighbor at the table.

Across the table sat a young man with very black eyes and a sulky mouth who was introduced as Professor Henry Dawson. His eyes and the careless slump of his shoulders, as well as his half disgruntled expression, seemed strangely familiar, also, to Kerry.

She would certainly have been amazed if she could have known that his presence at the table was due to the fact that he had professed to be an intimate friend and associate in the same line with her father, and that he had spent time trying to bribe the steward to seat him next to her.

The steward had arranged that he should sit at the same table, but his own insight into character as well as his desire to please the owner of the clear gray eyes had stopped at that, and Henry Dawson Ph.D. sat across the table, down a little way, not even exactly opposite to the daughter of the great man. Henry Dawson, Ph.D. might be the friend of Shannon Kavanaugh, and Shannon Kavanaugh's daughter, all he liked, but he was not going to get the chance to monopolize the girl with the red-gold hair during that voyage, not at the table, anyway!

So Kerry Kavanaugh, shabby little daughter of a dear dead scientist, running away into the world to hide, found herself unexpectedly among friends. And many discriminating people in the dining room turned to look and ask: "Who is that girl with the red-gold hair? Isn't she quaint? Quite a style of her own, hasn't she? She's so distinguished looking!"

4

SAM Morgan was one of those who think they are possessed of all knowledge and can handle any problem with the greatest possible efficiency.

Therefore, when Sam Morgan's bride of a few hours descended upon him from the hotel room whither she had gone to bring down the presumably repentant step-daughter, and with open note and streaming eyes had proclaimed the flight of that daughter, he wasted no time in idle talk.

"H'm! Gone, is she?" he said, his little slit eyes growing narrower. "Alrighty, you just run back up and stay there till I see what I can do. There, there, baby, don't you cry! She'll come back. You wait till I get after her. What's that? Oh, no, she won't drown herself. No, she won't kill herself. She's got too much sense! Besides, you see you went at this thing in the wrong way. I told you. But there's no use crying over spilt milk. You get back up there, Isobel, and just be calm, in case she comes in."

"But suppose she doesn't c-c-c-come!" wailed the mother, always a petted half frightened child.

"Well, never mind, you just be calm in case she does come,

and leave this thing to me. Money'll do anything! Money'll find her alrighty. You leave this to me! Get a book and read a story and leave it all to me!"

So Isobel, greatly relieved, went smiling back upstairs and settled down to a book, after having carefully gone over her own possessions to see if Kerry had taken any of them with her, and also ascertained what of Kerry's belongings were missing.

Yes, Kerry's clothes were gone, and the little old school trunk was gone, and Shannon Kavanaugh's papers and manuscripts were gone, and his books. How like Kerry to take those old books! Not worth carting around! Then the child had really intended her going to be something more than a mere gesture!

The mother gazed around with troubled gaze, for she really was fond of Kerry. Kerry was a habit that she would not know how to do without. It half frightened her to think of getting along without Kerry.

But when she noticed that her own lovely photograph in its silver frame was gone too, the picture that Shannon had loved so much and upon which he had spent such an enormous sum even when they were poor, her eyes took on unwonted starriness. Ah! Kerry had taken her picture! Then Kerry still loved her and Kerry would come back, as Sam Morgan had said; Kerry would come back and they would all be happy. They would live in castles and yachts and travel a lot, and buy new clothes in Paris whenever they liked, and it would be heaven below!

So Kerry's mother sat down to finish the last three chapters of a most exciting novel.

Sam Morgan betook himself at once to his lawyer whom he ordered to do something about this newly acquired stepdaughter of his.

"And make it snappy!" he said as he rose to leave the office. "I've got my plans made to leave London, and I don't want to be hung up around here waiting for a spoiled child, see? Get your best detectives on the job and make it snappy! She can't have gone far. She hasn't got a cent that I know of, or if she has it can't be many. She's likely sitting around in some park crying her eyes out for her mother by this time. She isn't much more than a kid. But she's a humdinger! Yes, I said it. She's got the looks alrighty! Now get to work. Yes, you can leave a message at the usual address. If she's roaming the streets put her up at some decent hotel till morning. The Missis and I are out on our honeymoon. See? And we don't wantta be bothered. But you keep an eye on the young one. She's a little bit slippery. Even if you have to put bracelets on her, don't let her give you the go-by. Because I wantta get out of this little old dirty town. Got my yacht waiting out in the harbor for a week, waiting for the Missis to make up her mind, see? And I don't wantta wait a day longer. So, make it snappy!"

Having thus delivered himself Sam Morgan slammed the door of the office breezily, and went his way, stopping to see a few old friends, getting himself jovially drunk, and then more and more unpleasantly drunk, until he was in a noisy frame of mind when he returned to his waiting bride.

Isobel Morgan had finished her book, and her last box of sweets, and was sitting curled up on the sofa pathetically weeping into her lace bordered handkerchief. She was blaming Kerry as usual for trouble she had brought upon herself. Between sobs she occasionally took time to admire her white hand with its flash of diamonds, and to put it up gracefully and pat her fresh marcel into shape. Just to think, now she could have her hair attended to by a professional, always! And Kerry too! Kerry must have more attention and begin to dress and groom herself as the rest of the world did!

Isobel had never seen Sam Morgan drunk before. She was not used to seeing anyone drunk. In the old days at home in her dear old South, when Sam Morgan used to take her on surreptitious rides behind his fiery pair of Kentucky bays, her father used to hint things about Sam Morgan's habits, but

Sam had never been drunk in her presence. He knew better.

But now, she was *his!* He had married her good and tight that morning. Her father was dead, and her mother was dead, and her fool of a book-worm husband was dead, and her pretty little puritan of a daughter had run away, and she was *his!* What could she do about it if he was drunk? So Sam came noisily into the room where his wife awaited him weepily and breezed up to her, giving her a good resounding smack on her prettily painted lips.

"Hello, Baby! Bawling again? I didn't know you were one of those sob-sisters. I didn't marry you to furnish you a wailing wall. Get busy and mop up, and let me see a little sunshine! 'Let a little sunshine in!—Let a little sunshine in—!'" he chanted noisily, tripping a clumsy step or two to his own measure. *"Get me?"*

He suddenly brought up fiercely in front of her and glared into her face.

Shannon Kavanaugh had kept Isobel most carefully from sights and sounds that might disturb her. And before that her father had protected her young eyes from sights that were not fit for her. She had smelled liquor on his breath of course when he had kissed her, but for the last two or three weeks Isobel herself had been sipping a little from a wine glass now and then just for politeness, when she went out with him to lunch or dinner. She had been brought up to disapprove of drinking on general principles, but she could not be rude, and she had intended when they were married to gently draw him away from it. Men by themselves fell into habits, but everything would be different when they were married. So had she reasoned, if Isobel Kavanaugh could be said ever to have reasoned about anything at all.

So now, when Sam Morgan brought up before her with his ugly red face scowling into hers, and his ugly coarse voice howling "Let a little sunshine in!" she sat up and mopped her eyes and began to giggle. The giggle was perhaps a little frightened, but as it grew in strength the fright vanished:

"Oh, Sam! How funny you are!" she giggled. "You're so really witty, you know! But you oughtn't to sing that way! You really ought not, you know. I think that's something sacred you're singing, isn't it, Sam? One of those queer new American jazz-hymns? I'm quite sure it is, Sam, and you *oughtn't!* You oughtn't to make fun of sacred things."

Sam stared and then guffawed.

"So! You're doing the pious act, Baby!" he roared. "I wouldn't, Baby! It's not your line! You're not heavyweight enough for that. Do the violet act, and be my pretty Baby Bell! *Iso*bel, *Baby*-Bell! And get a hustle on, will you, old lady? I want my dinner. We're going to a swell joint to-night to celebrate, and if you don't get a hustle on I'll go alone! See?"

He fell into swing and chanted:

"On my wedding night, when the moon shines bright, I'll dine ah-la-lo-o-one!"

Isobel got herself off her sofa and stared at him half frightened and then giggled again:

"Oh, Sam, you're so funny!" she gurgled. "I'll be ready in just a minute. I must powder my nose."

She emerged from her room in a moment serenely with a question in her eyes.

"But Sam, what did you do about Kerry? Is she coming with us?"

He whirled upon her viciously:

"Look here now, you leave Kerry to me. I said I'd see to her, didn't I? I said I'd do it, didn't I? Do you trust me, Baby, or don't you trust me? That's a question for you to decide right here and now. Of course if you don't that's the end—" he looked at her like a lion about to eat her.

"Oh, certainly!" she fluttered.

"Well—now that sounds more like it! You trust me! Well, I knew you did, so I've attended to that matter, and it'll come out alrighty. See? I've put it in the proper hands."

"And did you find Kerry?" asked Kerry's mother eagerly, beginning to brighten.

"Well—it's all right. I've put it in the proper hands."

"Is she going out with us this evening?" asked Isobel anxiously.

Now that she had carried her point and married her rich former-lover she longed most of all for Kerry's approval. She was not used to doing anything without consulting Kerry. It went against her spoiled yielding nature to have to depend upon her own decisions and suffer the consequences of her own acts. Some one else had always protected her from consequences all her days.

"No. She isn't going with us to-night," responded Sam with a twinkle in his eye. "It's our wedding night, see? And she isn't going this time. I've arranged to give her a little lesson. A much needed lesson! Next time she won't run away and hide from her dear new papa. Next time she'll be glad to do what she is told."

"You're not hurting Kerry in any way?" asked Isobel anxiously. "Shannon would never forgive me if we hurt Kerry in any way."

"Shannon! What's Shannon got to do with it? Shannon's out of the picture! Dead. Buried. He can't do any squawking! But I'm not doing any harm to Kerry. Didn't I tell you I loved Kerry? Fact! I didn't know but I'd wait a year or so and marry Kerry instead of you but you see I didn't. Now, you needn't begin to bawl again! I didn't, did I? Come on, let's get a hustle on. All set? Alrighty! Alrighty! Le's go! I want another drink! I'm parched!"

More than half frightened now Isobel started to put on her hat.

"But where have you left Kerry?" she asked as they started out the door. "Will she be here when we get back?"

"Well, no, perhaps not that soon, Baby. You see I want her to have a real good lesson. But she'll be around before we sail to-morrow on our yacht. You needn't worry. She'll be around, *glad* to come, and no more monkey shines. See? Now, come on!"

Somewhat reassured Isobel followed her husband out of the door, and tried to give herself up to the gayety of the evening, albeit an undertone of uneasiness kept cropping up in her spoiled heart.

So while Kerry crouched in her corner of a dingy Liverpool station, and drowsed the night through, her mother in gala attire was going the rounds of night clubs, and learning what her bridegroom's idea of gayety really was, sipping, too, at his bidding—*more* than sipping as the hour grew later—at the wines her husband ordered, and simpering to him radiantly:

"Oh, Sam, how funny you are! You always would have your little joke!"

Sometime along about one o'clock the next day, Sam awoke to his genial, easy-going, unprincipled old self.

Kerry? Oh, yes! He'd forgotten! Kerry! Of course, *Kerry!* He'd see about it right away. There must be a message down in the office right now. He'd left orders to that effect.

They had come home to Sam's more luxurious apartments, and Isobel was preening herself before a mirror more worthy of her beauty than the one in the cheap old hotel. Isobel was thinking how she would show Kerry all the luxuries of the new place. Kerry would come and see it all. And Kerry would be repentant for all the hard words she had said the day before as Kerry always was, and would kiss her and pat her, and call her her beautiful little mother, the only little mother she had. And then everything would be lovely.

That was probably the cause of this unwonted headache she was having now, her worry about Kerry! Kerry had made a scene! Kerry somehow was apt to make a scene when people didn't go her way. She must speak to her about that! She must let her know—oh quite gently of course, and after she had been back an hour or so—how she had been the cause of her dear only little mother's headache. And Kerry would be sorry. Isobel just doted on seeing Kerry repentant. She had such a sweet look in her eyes when she repented, and made Isobel feel oh so righteous and worthy!

Sam Morgan returned in a couple of hours. He said that his lawyer had inquired at all the hotels in London and could find no such person registered. They had also questioned the people of the hotel where the Kavanaughs had made their residence for the past nine months and could get no information beyond the fact that Miss Kavanaugh had left in a cab with her baggage. They had been unable so far to locate the cab, as it must have been one of the cheaper sort, perhaps run by some private individual operating on his own account. The lawyer had appealed for more definite information before further search, and Sam Morgan found himself unable to give any beyond the fact that the girl was a "humdinger" for looks, and had hair like a yellow flame.

Isobel, when questioned by a detective, was most indefinite herself. She produced a snap shot or two of Kerry, and a list of places where Kerry enjoyed going, the art galleries, the libraries, a cathedral or two and museums. But when they asked for a list of her young friends Isobel had to own that Kerry had no friends either young or old. She had always been her father's close companion, and had not seemed to need friends—at least she never seemed to speak of it. Of course she had acquaintances among the girls who were in school with her.

There followed days in which telegrams were sent in various directions. One to the school she had attended in Germany. One to a pension where they had stayed for a time in Paris, one to a little villa in the south of France where they had gone once for Isobel's health. Isobel unearthed all their past almost gleefully and brought it forth from her memory day by day to spread before the lawyer and the detective, and grew excited and fascinated by this new game of hide and seek. She was almost proud of Kerry that she had remained so long successfully hidden. Kerry was clever. She had always said Kerry was clever.

Day after day they lingered, the yacht waiting for their

coming, Isobel being kept happy by much shopping, between visits of the detectives.

Kerry's note fell into the hands of the detectives, and the lawyer mentioned in it was searched for, but proved to be taking a trip through Italy and Switzerland. Correspondence with him brought no light on the subject. Kerry had not yet found her job and settled down. Kerry had meant what she said and would not communicate with the lawyer until she was safely settled on her own. But how was Kerry getting on without money?

"You don't think anything terrible has happened to Kerry, do you, Sam?" Isobel asked anxiously one morning. "I can't think she would stay away from her only little mother so long unless something had happened. Of course, Kerry was always clever—"

"Kerry is a little devil!" said Sam crossly. "She doesn't want to be found! But I swear she shall. She can't double cross us much longer. We've got the best detectives in London and I'll tell you what, *they know their onions!*"

"Then why don't they find Kerry?" wailed Isobel beginning to cry. "I want Kerry! If you hadn't made me be so pre-cip-i-tate she wouldn't have run away! I t-t-told you she d-d-didn't like me to m-m-marry so soon after Shannon—!"

"There! Now you can cut that out, old lady! Hear that? I'm not going to be haunted with Shannon Kavanaugh. He's dead and you can let him stay buried. If I had thought you were so stuck on him I'd have married that woman you saw me with that day at the art gallery. She would have taken me in a minute if I'd asked her, and she didn't have any dead husbands to bawl about or any brats to play hide and seek with. And I can tell you right now, if Kerry doesn't turn up within the next twenty-four hours you and I are going to cut loose and go on the yacht! I've waited long enough! There are plenty of other pretty girls I can get to go with us if Kerry is so high-hat she has to keep out of sight. Let her get left behind then! Let her eat a little humble pie! *There*—you go bawling again! What did I get married for anyway?"

"Oh, Sam! Don't talk that way!" pleaded Isobel in new horror. "You said you *l-l-l-oved* me!"

"Well, so I did, Baby, but I wasn't counting on your being a sob-sister. Come, mop up and we'll go for a ride, and mebbe we'll stop at a shop or two and buy Kerry some pretty togs for the yachting trip. How so, Baby, will you like that?"

So Isobel was appeased, wiped her eyes, powdered her delicate nose, and went prettily off to enjoy a morning shopping for Kerry, with a few more trifles for herself thrown in. So easily was Kerry's mother reassured. She was having a delightful time doing the things she had always wanted to do, spending the money she had never hoped to have, buying the things for which she had always longed. She really felt too as if she were being most forgiving and gracious to rebellious Kerry, buying her lovely sports clothes and evening gowns, and velvet wraps fit for a princess.

That night when they came back to Sam's hotel after a noisy and exhausting round of pleasure they found a note from the lawyer saying that they had discovered Miss Kavanaugh's name on a sailing list of a ship bound for the United States. They had cabled but could get no information about the young lady after she landed—

"That settles it!" said Sam more than genially drunk as usual, "We'll start for the yacht to-morrow morning. Get a hustle on, Baby! We're not waiting any longer. Our search is ended!"

"But I don't understand," said Isobel anxiously.

"No, you wouldn't, Baby, but I do!" wagged Sam Morgan. "I said our search is ended!"

"Oh, do you mean we will catch the ship and get Kerry?"

"There you go, Baby! You haven't the sense you were born with. Don't you know that ship landed in New York yesterday? How are we going to find Kerry in New York? We got to put the whole thing in the detectives' hands and just go off and have our honeymoon. Kerry is a little devil, I tell you and we can't be bothered waiting around for her any longer. See, old lady? We're going on our honeymoon in the morning!"

"But you said we would find Kerry!" wailed Kerry's mother with a deluge of tears.

"Yes, but you held out information on us, old lady!" said Sam Morgan solemnly. "You never mentioned Kerry's going to America. You didn't say she had friends in the United States."

"But she hasn't!" wept Isobel. "She hasn't been there for years. Oh, my poor little Kerry! She won't know what to do. Shannon never let her travel alone—!"

"There you go again! Shannon! Shannon! Shannon Kavanaugh is DEAD!" roared her husband mightily. "If you mention him again I'll go off and get a divorce! I'm sick to my soul of him and his notions. Besides his dear little, poor little, Kerry is a dear little, poor little devil! She can take care of herself alrighty! Oh, yes, she's clever alrighty! She's clever! She's a devil!—"

And with this gallant reply Isobel had to be content and to go weeping to her couch.

The next morning Sam Morgan was his genial self again, but very determined.

"We're going yachting!" he announced. "We aren't wasting any time, see? How soon can you get your stuff together? Better just let the maid pack up this truck you've been buying. Telephone and have a trunk sent up, that'll be the easiest way. Anything down at that other hotel you need to get or are you just going to chuck it all? We'd better close up that deal. No use hanging on any longer now we know Kerry's gone for good."

Isobel gasped and suddenly realized that here was a matter in which she must depend upon herself. There was no kind good Shannon to take all the burden of packing and sorting. There was no Kerry to do her bidding while she lay resting and reading her endless novels and magazines.

How sordid and dreadful the dull shabby rooms looked when she entered alone and remembered the place where Shannon's body had lain before they took him away to the undertaker's. How with even this short absence the rooms seemed to be haunted and fearful. Shannon gone! Kerry gone! No one to depend upon. Sam already a broken reed, although she had not fully realized that as yet. The power of his money blinded her, the anticipation of her new position as his wife still held its glamour.

She shuddered and drew back as the shut-up air of the deserted rooms struck her like a human hand and smote all her senses harshly.

Quickly she forced herself to walk across the room and pull open the curtains which had been drawn down that last evening she had stayed there. The bald sunshine slanted a thin shiver of light across the faded carpet, and grim old furniture. The scuffed upholstery glared out in all its defects. How she hated it! If any shadow of doubt about the course she had taken with regard to her marriage had dared to hover around the door of her mind it quickly scuttled away in the face of the sordidness of the old life.

She went into her old bedroom resolved to work rapidly and get away. She would not look toward Kerry's door, which stood wide and showed an empty room, from which the housemaid had already stripped the bed covers and taken down soiled hangings.

Isobel attacked her clothes closet first. Those old cheap clothes that had been such a trial! How quickly she disposed of them, the rusty black satin, the old blue chiffon that had seen so many summers—and winters; the green velvet that would have made such a lovely little frock for Kerry, only she never had been quite willing to give it up herself, her one velvet! How shabby it looked now in the glare of the common little lodging room! Her old dressing gown and the feather trimming that Shannon used to like her to wear because he said it reminded him of the ermine and velvet in which he would like to dress her if he could. Dear old Shannon! She wondered if he wasn't glad that she was living in luxury now! He had always wanted her to have nice things, and while he hadn't of course approved of Sam any more than her father had in her youth, still Shannon would be glad to have her taken care of.

All the old things in the closet she took down and abandoned; threw them on the bed in a heap. She would give them to the housemaid. Kerry would have objected and wanted to keep them. Kerry always liked that brown foulard with the little buff daisies scattered over it. But Kerry wasn't here, and Kerry would have far finer things now. She remembered the green suit with the ermine collar and the eggshell satin blouse that she had bought for Kerry yesterday and flung the whole armful of her formerly cherished garments onto the pile.

There was nothing left in the closet but a little orchid silk, cheap and thin and flimsy, trimmed with soiled and tattered lace, but that was a dress that Shannon used to love to see her in. He used to say sometimes when he had worked hard all day, and his head was aching and things were discouraging:

"Put on your little orchid silk, Mother—pretty little Mother—and sit over there where I can look at you. It will rest me!"

And when she had dressed to please him, vain enough herself to enjoy the little by-play, he would say:

"Now, turn your head and look over there and smile. Yes, that's the way—beautiful little Mother, that's the way I will have you painted by a great artist! Some day I'll do it! Don't throw away that dress, Isobel. I'll have you painted in it yet! Some day when my book is done and I get money that'll be the first thing I will do, while you still look young and lovely. Not that you'll ever be anything but lovely to me, my love, but of course we must grow older some day, and I want your portrait painted while you look just as you do now!"

A wild thought seized Isobel as she fingered the flimsy silk and tattered lace. Shannon was gone but she was now in a position to have the portrait done by any artist she chose. Why not save the dress and have it done? A freak of course, but Sam would gratify her in anything she asked for, and perhaps it would please Shannon to know that she was carrying out his wish, if dead people could see what was going on in the world they had left. It pleased Isobel's vanity too, and she folded the flimsy silk carefully and wrapped it in tissue paper, and locked it into the little lacquered box along with Sam Morgan's three love letters, finding no incongruity in the assortment.

Then she turned her attention to her bureau drawers, and an old trunk that held her winter clothing. Short work she made of that, too, clearing the trunk, and laying in it such few things as she felt she would like to keep. Pictures of herself and Shannon, dance programs from her girlhood days, an old fan a dead lover had given her.

The pile on the bed for the house maid was enormous, and the trunk was nearly full when Sam arrived blustering, and found Isobel seated on the floor beside the half packed trunk with a baby's shoe in her hand, crying gently. The shoe belonged to Kerry's little three-months-old brother who had died of pneumonia before Kerry was born. Isobel was weeping lovely tears over the little shoe, and in her lap lay three photographs of Shannon Kavanaugh when he had been young and handsome and came acourting her.

Sam Morgan when he saw them stamped his big expensive shoe and swore at his bride. He swept her off the floor, tossed the shoe into the trunk, the pictures across the room, and ordered her to put her hat on.

Isobel, a little frightened, and a good deal relieved to be thus summarily lifted out of her sentimental gloom, got herself ready.

"But what about Kerry?" she asked sweetly, "have you heard anything more?"

"Kerry's in New York somewhere," replied the millionaire. "We're getting over to our yacht as fast as we can get there. We'll take a little skip out around the Mediterranean for a few weeks, and then if we feel like it we'll trip over to the States. I want to run down to my plantation for a few days and see how the cotton crop is this season, and then we can step up to New York for a day or so and see if Kerry has come down off her high horse yet. How's that? Alrighty, Missis?"

Isobel looked troubled.

"But I don't like the idea of not knowing how Kerry is getting along all this time. I couldn't really enjoy much with her on my mind, you know."

The bridegroom scowled.

"There you are!" he said, "that's just what I thought! Marry a widow with a child and you only have half her mind. She's got no thought for you, just for her child! She comes and bawls over a baby's shoe, and moons over her dead husband's picture, when she knows he couldn't give her butter on her bread half the time when he was living."

"But Sam, dear, aren't we going to hear from Kerry at all, all that time?"

"Oh, sure! We'll have a radio on board the yacht. Talk to her every day if we like. Send out messages, you know, and all that sort of thing. Come on, old lady. All set? What are you going to do with all this junk on the bed? Stuff it in the trunk?"

"No, I'm going to give it to the maid. I was just going to send for her."

"Well, I have a bell boy out in the hall. I'll send him. Come, get that trunk closed up while I'm gone."

Isobel cast a hasty glance around the room, located Shannon's photographs and stuffed them hurriedly into the trunk underneath the other things, shut the lid with a click and locked it. She straightened up with a guilty look as Sam came back.

"Here's the maid. Come, now, get a hustle on!"

"Oh, I'm quite all ready, Sam," said Isobel sweetly, beginning to put on her gloves. "You're sure we can talk with Kerry over the radio all the way, aren't you, Sam?"

"Sure!" said Sam heartily. "All set, Baby? Well, get a hustle on then. I need a drink!"

5

KERRY'S first dinner at sea was most reassuring. It almost made her forget for a few minutes that she was a fugitive on the earth, and that her future was most uncertain.

Graham McNair suggested that they go out and watch the end of the sunset, and Kerry, going to her stateroom for her coat, came face to face with Henry Dawson approaching from the other end of the corridor with his overcoat.

"How fortunate!" he said smiling, "I was coming in search of you. I do so want to have a little talk with your father's daughter. I knew him so well, years ago, when I was a mere cub in science. I wonder—would you like to take a little turn on the deck? And then we might find a sheltered corner somewhere and get really acquainted."

Kerry thanked him, but told him she had just made other arrangements for the evening. "Sometime of course—!" She hesitated because somehow she had taken a dislike to the coal black eyes, and the oily voice of the Ph.D. He did not look like a man whom her father would choose as a friend. There was something about his face that she distrusted. And where had she heard his voice before?

"Oh, well, then, how about to-morrow morning? Shall I

look you up on deck? All right, we'll call that a date, please,"
and he went away with a courteous bow. But just as he
turned to pass on it suddenly came to Kerry where she had
seen him. The slump of his shoulder, a certain assurance, an
arrogance of attitude reminded her. Wasn't he the man who
had been looking over the shipping list when she came back
to say she would take Mrs. Winship's reservation? Why
should that make her uneasy? Or was it only that she shrank
from talking over this man's memories of her blessed father?
Why did she take dislikes this way, unreasoning prejudices?
He was perhaps one of the finest men that walked. A scientist
also. One who evidently revered her father. She must put
down all such silly reactions and be a woman. She must remember that she was no judge of men. She had always been
sheltered from the world and taken her coloring and ideas
from her father. She must try to shake herself free from prejudice, and take things as she found them. She must remember
that she was now on her own, and must cultivate a sound
judgment.

It was pleasant to be walking with Graham McNair. She
had a sense that he had not noticed the shabbiness of her little
brown coat, and her scuffed slippers. He walked beside her
with the gracious deference he might have given to a queen.
She felt that it was not for her sake of course, but in honor to
her great father, and her heart rejoiced that she was given the
joy of seeing how others honored her father. She had always
resented and grieved over her mother's low estimate of him.

There were many colors left over from the sunset, spread in
soft radiance upon the water, which was smooth as glass, for
the evening was a quiet one, and the loveliness of the hour
unsurpassed.

Kerry felt a joy rising in her troubled soul, a kind of ecstasy
of enjoyment in the coloring of the evening, and the stretch of
bright empty water. The vast space reaching away on every
side seemed to shut her in and protect her. For the time being
at least she was safe; and for this little hour she might enjoy the

scene and forget that there were perplexities and loneliness, and perhaps fear, at the end of her journey.

Kerry was glad that her companion did not seem to think it was necessary to keep up a continual chatter. They could stand and look at the beauty about them, the peace and loveliness, and just enjoy it without an obligation to voice their delight in words. She seemed to know his pleasure in it without a word being spoken.

They had walked several times back and forth, and stood at various places to look and look again, when suddenly, as they were watching a great star blaze out and burn, and signal like a new arrival, Graham McNair spoke:

"I have sometimes thought," said he quietly, "that it might be something like this when the Lord Jesus comes back again. A quiet evening, hushed in twilight, as if waiting in expectancy, a great star burning, just as when He came before, only a more wonderful star than any we can see now! Have you ever felt that way?"

He spoke so quietly, in such a matter of fact tone, tenderly, as if he were speaking of mothers' prayers, little children's laughter, and beloved homes, that she was not quite sure if she had heard him aright. She lifted startled eyes, and when she saw that he was looking at her as if he expected an answer, she spoke hesitatingly:

"I—am not sure—that I understand—just what you mean. Do people—do *you*—expect God—that is Christ, to come back again?"

"We certainly do!" The voice was very clear and low, with a kind of ring of triumph in it.

"With a star?" she asked wonderingly—

"With a silver trumpet!" said the triumphant voice quietly. "Possibly with a star too, though there is nothing said about it. But certainly with a trumpet!"

"Nice night!" said Henry Dawson Ph.D. suddenly coming up behind them.

They turned, let down with a jar to earthly things.

"Yes," said McNair taking up the burden of the conversation after a decided pause.

"But it can't last!" said Dawson in his flat voice. "Not this time of year. We're due for a storm before we get across."

"How many times have you crossed?" asked McNair politely, studying the other man with narrowing gaze, and getting a very good view of Kerry's delicate profile with the side of his eye.

Dawson launched easily into detailed accounts of the various ocean storms he had encountered on his trips.

Kerry watched the opal tints die away from the water, and McNair watched Kerry while Dawson talked. Hadn't the man any sense of the fitness of things, or was he really as he seemed to imply, an old friend of the Kavanaugh family? McNair couldn't be sure, but he stood his ground.

The orchid and rose and green died, the purple and gold blended into gray. The sea became a sheet of beaten metal lit with a full moon, and still McNair stood his ground. Kerry, her eyes far away to the bright horizon, was not listening. Perhaps she was wondering about that silver trumpet.

Suddenly she moved, and turning to McNair with a weary look said:

"But I must go in. I really am very tired. It's been a long day. Thank you for all this—!" her hand fluttered a little motion toward the panoply of silver and gray. "And—" she hesitated, "for the star and the trumpet. It was interesting. I shall think about it!"

Dawson eyed them jealously, his last sentence about a simoon he had once experienced in the desert, suspended in mid-air. Then he spoke in a vexed detaining tone which struggled to be playful:

"Don't forget our little conference in the morning, Miss Kavanaugh. It's really quite important, you know."

"Conference?" asked Kerry turning back with a surprised glance. "Oh!" and she laughed and went on her way.

McNair looked keenly at the other man, but refrained from questioning him, though his tone seemed almost to invite it.

"You were speaking of the simoon I believe, Mr.—excuse me—Professor Dawson. It must have been an interesting experience."

"Knew her father well, you know," explained Dawson, his eyes following Kerry with a gleam in them that McNair did not like.

"Indeed!" said McNair with a lack of interest in his tone.

"It was most stimulating to come into contact with such a man in the world of science," went on Dawson. "We did not always *agree* of course, but I found him a man quite open minded and amenable to reason."

"Ah?" responded McNair. "About how long ago was that?"

"Why, about nineteen-thirteen I think."

McNair studied the other man again with that almost suspicious narrowing of the eyelids.

"H'm! In Russia, did you say?"

"Oh, no, in England, I—"

"Ah! I had understood he was in Russia during that period," said McNair disinterestedly, "but I must have been misinformed. Did you say you studied with Dr. Kavanaugh?"

"Oh, no, I said I was *associated* with him. We, I—was doing some experimental work at that time on my own account—I—"

"If you will excuse me," said McNair suddenly, "I think this friend may be looking for me," and he vanished courteously after a man who had just strolled by.

"Now," said McNair to himself an hour later as he stood alone on the forward deck looking off to sea, "what can that pup be about? Something mean I can pretty well wager. I wonder if I can do anything about it?"

Kerry kept pretty well to her own quarters the next morning. She had no mind to have a conference with that strange, black-eyed man who was so offensively intimate with her father.

She had not slept very well her first night out at sea. There were too many things to think about! Her mother far away by this time in the London she had left, hunting for her perhaps, and crying. Yes, she would cry! That hurt to think of and she could hear her father's voice almost reproachfully, "The only little mother you have, Kerry! Your beautiful little mother!"

Then her young heart burned hotly, and her own tears flowed. "She's all right only she hasn't any judgment, Kerry!"

That was it. Mother had not used good judgment in marrying Sam Morgan, and there had been nothing Kerry could do about it but go away and leave her mother to her fate! Had she been wrong in leaving her? Oh, but it was impossible to stay!

Then Kerry's mind turned breathlessly toward the book that was to be her salvation both mentally and financially. She must fill her mind with her work, and not think or she never could go through this hard hard time. In the morning she would get up early and work, work, work. Three days hard work ought to put that manuscript in perfect order. Just a few pages to be recopied where her father had made some last corrections. Just a few more notes to be incorporated in the appendix, and she would be ready when she landed to go at once to the publishers. She must get it done! She must not let herself be beguiled into spending time idling on ship board. She must work!

Then a great ache came into her heart and her tears flowed anew! Oh, why had life been so hard upon her? Why had she had to live at all? When she came to think about it she had always been a little lonely child. Only the last two years when she had been her father's close companion and helper had she had any joy in her life. And now that was all gone! What was it all for? She wished she had asked her father. He was wise. He had thought of things like that. He was patient. He must have had some idea of why life was, or he would never have had those sweet patient intense lines about his mouth and eyes. Oh, Father! Dear Father! If you only had not gone away!

And then her mind came back to the evening and the silver sea, and her brief talk with the gray-eyed man who talked about a trumpet and a coming Christ. What did he mean? Was he just talking poetry or was it something real in his life? If she ever had another opportunity she would ask him, for it seemed as if there must have been a meaning behind it, a meaning that might ease the awful hunger of her soul.

And then she fell asleep.

When Kerry awoke the next morning she could not tell where she was. At first she thought she had been dreaming, and that she lay in her little hard bed in the cheap hotel in London, with a fog outside, a burden on her heart, and a day of perplexity before her.

Then the monotonous lash of the waves, and the motion of the boat made themselves real to her dreamy senses, and she had the whole sad story of the last two days to go over again. She experienced once more the shock she had first felt.

So does sorrow undo the work of sleep by one sharp thrust with the first waking breath, when one is passing through the valley.

Kerry opened her eyes and saw a gull sweep by her porthole; saw the interminable passing of the sea outside lit with sunlight sharply gay and blue, yet felt its beauty was not for her. There could be no joy in sky or sea or journey, for she was all alone, and the world was full of sadness. Why did she have to live? Oh, Mother! Oh, Father! Why was such a heartbreaking thing as life ever brought about?

By and by she conquered the awful sorrow that kept swelling into her throat, stinging tears into her eyes, and crept from her berth.

A breath of sea air from her porthole brought a sudden

longing to get outside and drink in the beauty and the brightness, and throw off this gloom that was upon her for awhile. But she resisted it. For there was that unpleasant person with the bold black eyes and his insistence for a "conference" whatever that might mean. And there was her work that she must do.

So she dressed quickly and let the stewardess bring her a tray. After eating her breakfast she took a few long breaths at her open porthole and then sat down to her typewriter, working diligently until her head began to swim, and the back of her neck ached.

She put her papers carefully away, stowing the brief case in which she kept it far back in a drawer of the wardrobe, made one or two little changes in her simple costume, and throwing her coat over her arm opened her door into the corridor.

As she did so a paper fluttered past her from under a chair and rustled out ahead of her. Kerry, recognizing it as one of the sheets she had just copied, sprang to catch it but the draught from the open porthole wafted it on, and it fluttered a step or two down the corridor and landed at the feet of Dawson, Ph.D., as Kerry had already begun to call him. He always seemed to be just arriving whenever she went out!

Dawson stooped and caught it, and quite rudely, Kerry afterwards remembered, put his gaze upon it, as one who would eagerly devour its contents. Then, after an instant as Kerry stood with outstretched hand, he lifted an absent-minded gaze and apologized:

"Oh, can this be yours?" he asked, and handed the paper to her almost reluctantly. "Or is it just waste paper?" he added as an afterthought.

"Thank you!" said Kerry, stepping back to her own door and throwing the paper on her bed. She closed and locked her stateroom door, and went on down the corridor.

Dawson had lingered waiting for her.

"Are you going to the dining room now?" he asked. "May I walk with you?"

There was nothing for Kerry to do but assent, and together they went to the table.

They were the first of their table to come to lunch. Dawson seated her politely and then went to his own place. But as soon as some of the others came in he made excuse to go to his stateroom for a magazine in which he said he found a joke he wanted to read to them all.

When he returned a few minutes later with the magazine they all listened politely to his joke, and made out to laugh quite creditably, but Kerry found herself wondering why he cared to take so much trouble to hunt up that vapid little joke. Was the man utterly devoid of any sense of humor?

McNair came late to the table, and Kerry was just rising to leave as he entered the dining room.

"Oh, are you going so soon?" he said as she passed him, "I've been hard at work all the morning, and did not realize I was being so late. Well, perhaps I'll see you on deck this afternoon."

Then he caught Dawson's eyes upon him balefully, as he rose from his seat.

"I'm coming, Miss Kavanaugh," said Dawson much to Kerry's annoyance, for she had risen with one of the other women, hoping to avoid his undesired company.

"Now," said he bustling ahead in his brusque way, "we're going to find a quiet place where we won't be disturbed. I know the very spot. I've been guarding it all the morning hoping you would come, but you didn't appear."

He looked at her for an answer, but Kerry had been taught long ago by her father to keep a quiet tongue in her head whenever a stranger who might be troublesome was about.

Kerry did not answer. Instead she smiled off at the sea and pointed to a gull that was dipping and circling above the deck.

Her companion looked annoyed at the gull as if it were intruding.

"Now, if you'll just come over here," said Dawson eagerly, "I think we shall not be disturbed."

Dawson led the way to a corner where he had prepared two seats for a tête-à-tête.

Kerry looked at her watch and hesitated.

"I can spare you ten minutes perhaps," she said doubtfully. "You see I'm very busy just now. I have certain work that I must do before this voyage is over, and I must keep to my schedule or I won't get done."

"Work?" said Dawson eagerly, "well, perhaps what I have to say will help a little in that way."

Kerry looked at him surprised.

"How could what you have to say have any possible bearing on my work?" she asked with a ripple of laughter.

He looked annoyed.

"Well, suppose you tell me what your work is and then perhaps I shall be better able to explain to you," he answered cunningly.

Kerry felt a hot antagonism against the man. He was presuming greatly on an intimacy to which he had no right.

"My work? Oh, a little reading, a little writing, some letters and odds and ends, and quite a lot of mending. I came away in a great hurry, you see. Are you good at mending, or darning stockings, Professor Dawson?" Kerry ended with a laugh that was so like her father's she almost recognized it herself. Her father had been good at throwing people off the track. She had always admired the skill with which he evaded the inquisition of curious newspaper men and visiting scientists who wanted to pry knowledge out of him for their own ends. Kerry had a feeling that here was one of the same brand and instinctively she took her father's way of self-defense.

Dawson's reaction to her answer was embarrassment and annoyance, but he held himself in check and summoned a smile.

"I see you are witty like your father," he remarked dryly, "and you know how to keep your own counsel," he added with a bit of a snarl at the end of his tone.

Kerry sobered and looked at him gravely.

"I don't undestand you, Professor Dawson; what is it you are trying to say to me?"

She was not yet quite eighteen, but she suddenly felt ages old. She sensed vaguely that a battle was ahead, and she must fight single-handed. There was no one living to help her.

"I want to talk to you about the thing that interests you most in all the world!" he said eagerly. "You know what it is, but you are afraid to trust me. But you needn't be. I am your friend and I was your father's friend. I stand ready to help you in every way possible. And Miss Kavanaugh, I want you to know that of all your father's friends I know no one better fitted to help you than I am because of my deep interest for years in the things that your father was studying."

He paused and pierced Kerry with that cunning beady black gaze of his.

"Yes?" said Kerry coolly, almost choking over the word in her dry little frightened throat, but voicing the syllable with a sangfroid worthy of a woman of the world. She looked him back with a cool inscrutable gaze in her purply-blue eyes that had somehow turned a deep amber, the friendliness all shut out of them.

"Do you believe that I am ready to help you in your great work?"

"What work is that?" asked Kerry sweetly, feeling herself growing more and more angry now. Why, this man was almost impertinent! He was almost in a class with Sam Morgan! Was there any abominable animal or insect to which she might compare him that would rank even lower than a louse?

"I mean the great work on which you are now engaged!" he announced with a meaningful look, and lowering his voice he added huskily, "Your father's great book!"

He studied her face a moment and then went on.

"I can understand how you must be hampered, not being a scientist yourself. There will be things of course that should be altered to bring them up to the times. Your father was an older man and quite conservative. And I, knowing your father's general trend, would be able to make suggestions to you without in the least changing his style—"

But Kerry had suddenly risen, and as she stood for an instant looking down upon the small sharp little man she seemed to have grown taller by several inches, and to have acquired a new poise. She smiled quite freezingly as a queen might have done to a presuming courtier, and answered him with steady voice in which the rising anger was quite held in abeyance:

"Mr.—Professor—Dawson, you are making a great mistake! You seem to be under the impression that I am trying to finish or rewrite or reconstruct some work of my father's for publication. That is not the case. Whatever my father wrote was entirely finished and complete and contracted for with his publisher before he died. But if it had not been, I certainly should never allow *any* man whether he thought he was a scientist or not, whether he professed to be a friend or a foe, to add to or reconstruct or delete a single word from anything my father had ever written. Certainly not you, Professor Dawson. Now, if you will excuse me, I have something else to do."

And with her red-gold head held high she marched away from the place and stumbled down the companionway straight into the arms of a man who was coming up.

Graham McNair caught her as she would have fallen, and she looked up and gave a little sob of a laugh as she recovered herself, but he saw that there were tears upon her cheeks.

"Can—I do anything for you?" he asked, a little at a loss to know whether to laugh it off or go deeper into facts.

"No thank you—Or, yes—there is. There's a man out there on the deck—I wish you'd throw him overboard for me please. Not quite drown him, perhaps—but—just give him a *good scare!*"

Her face was dimpling with smiles, but he could see that the tears were not far away from the blue eyes lifted so bravely. The red-gold hair caught the sunlight in a full blaze as she looked up and he looked down upon her.

His eyes twinkled back to her smile, but his face grew suddenly grave as he answered:

"I'll do that!" he said earnestly. "I'll take pleasure in doing it. I think I know just whom you mean."

Then he flashed her a smile to cover his own gravity and they went their ways.

When Kerry reached her stateroom she looked at once at the bed for the paper she had thrown there before going to lunch, but it was nowhere to be seen. She looked on the floor under the bed, and down behind the mattress, but she could not find it. She even sent for the stewardess, but the stewardess said she had not been there since early that morning. Then Kerry got out her papers and went all through them carefully, but the page numbered seventy-five, one of the pages she had recopied that morning, was nowhere to be found!

6

AFTER Kerry had gone over everything in the room three times, the last time slowly and unhurriedly, with a calm conviction growing in her mind that it was positively gone, she sat herself down to discover what had been on that missing sheet.

Indelibly she found stamped on her brain the vision of Dawson as he held it in his hand and scanned it avidly. She was sure from his brief absorption, his absent-minded gaze as he handed it back to her, that he had seen something there that more than interested him.

She took out her papers and went over the previous page, and the following one with the notes in little bunches fastened neatly with clips and duly numbered. Yes, that was the page that mentioned the Einstein theory in connection with the new ideas that Shannon Kavanaugh had worked out! It was the page of all the others perhaps that she would least have wished to have seen by an alien before the book was safely under copyright. It contained the crux of all the argument in brief form. What ill wind had worked against her that it should have been just that page that had strayed out into the corridor when the enemy was passing?

For now she had unconsciously come to call this Dawson person an enemy. Kerry felt as if an evil force were specializing on her incompetent self just then.

With a heavy heart she sat thinking. How often her father had warned her that she must not open her mouth about his book, must never even speak of it, nor answer any question about it no matter how insignificant. He had told her of enemies in the profession, thieves also, who would steal not only thunder, but glory that did not belong to them. She felt that Dawson Ph.D. was both a scientific enemy and thief.

It was plain to be seen that he had planned in some way to use her or the book for his own purposes. His proposition on deck just now angered her beyond words. What did he think she was? A child to be led about by bland words? Did he think her father so much of a fool as not to have left his affairs complete, and in hands that were competent to look after them?

And yet, had he? How careless she had been that she had allowed a single sheet of the precious paper to slip out that door!

She tried to think of the possibilities for the thief.

He might use the subject matter in an article, or as a basis in a book of his own, if indeed there was enough to base his argument upon in that single page. Of course if he was a bright man—and he must be, in the sense of having cleverness, cunning—he would quickly understand and supply all that the stolen paragraphs implied. Even if he wrote only an article in a magazine using the material he had—and of course he must have got it somehow! There were such things as skeleton keys—would that be enough to hurt the contract with the publisher of the book?

Kerry was well versed in book contracts. Her father had talked this one over with her. Had in fact showed her some of his other contracts, discussed each separate item and helped her to understand what she should agree to if it fell to her to sign the contract for his book. Dear Father! He must have known months ago that he would never live to see the book published. His great life work!

Kerry brushed away a tear and went on with her intensive thinking.

She knew all about that paragraph in all author's contracts that bound the author with an oath that there was nothing in the manuscript libelous, or that could infringe upon another author's writings. She realized there might be ground for suit in such a matter if an article should appear before the book came out.

Somehow she must get hold of that paper. If it was in the room it must be found. If it had been carried away carelessly when the room was put to rights, it must be found. If it had been stolen *it must be found!* But how to go about it. That was the thing!

But the thought carried her still further. Even if she found the paper, she would never be able to erase its message from the mind of the man who had read it, if indeed he had taken it and read it! Oh this was dreadful! Actually descending to charge a fellow being with such an ugly crime! And for such sordid reasons. But what else could she think? Her father had warned her.

However, whatever the outcome, this should be a lesson to her. She must put the rest of her precious manuscript where it could not be found, at least until she was positive that man had not somehow managed to enter her stateroom and taken that paper. Of course if he had entered it once he could do so again. She must not leave it unguarded, not for a single minute! Suppose it should all be stolen, notes and copy and all! Where would she be? And the world would lose the book her great father had written. All her father's life and hard work would have gone for nothing! Another man would profit by it—if indeed his jealousy did not cause him to destroy it before it ever came to the light of day.

But the more she thought about it the more she realized she

could not just stay here in her room the rest of the trip. For one thing she would have to pay extra for her meals to be sent to her, and her store of money was already much reduced. When it was gone she would be absolutely penniless, with nothing left to pawn. No, she must husband her money, and she must guard that book with her very life, but she must somehow manage to do it without letting anybody suspect that she had anything to guard.

The first thing that she did was to carefully copy from the notes once more that seventy-fifth page with its changes, as exactly a duplicate of the lost page as it was possible to make.

Then she set to work to gather the notes of the whole book, as far as she had completed it. They were fastened together by little clips but now she carefully removed the clips and sewed the sheets with thread, a few in a group. These she laid smoothly between the leaves of a magazine. Hunting out a tube of paste from among her working materials, she carefully gummed the margins of the magazine together, with the notes between the pages, removing every other page to make it less bulky, until all the notes were put away except the few which were left for changes in the last twenty pages. Those she would finish copying that afternoon, and then if anything happened, she would have all the notes safely in one magazine.

But what about the manuscript itself? Could she work the same scheme with it? Would it be too bulky for her to carry around with her in one of those pretty bags that all the women carried? The bags were for sale in the main cabin. She would buy one. Perhaps they were expensive, but a fancy bag could be carried even to the table, and slipped beneath her chair, or in her lap.

Her fingers flew rapidly over her typewriter keys all that afternoon, and before it was time to dress for dinner she had copied all the changes, and was through with the last of the notes.

It took only a few minutes to paste the remaining papers

between the leaves of her magazine. The notes were ready to put away, and she decided to put them in the bottom of her trunk, under everything else. Nobody would think of looking into an old magazine packed carefully between two framed pictures. It would look as if it had been put there to protect the glass. She even wrapped an old apron carelessly around the frames, leaving visible the back of the magazine where the name was printed. She replaced her things smoothly, fitted in her tray, and locked her trunk feeling that the notes at least were reasonably safe.

But there still remained the manuscript and an envelope containing instructions for her interview with the publisher. This envelope was sealed and she had never opened it. Her father had written it in his last days, and told her about it, but somehow she dreaded opening it, and had put it off till the last minute. She knew it contained a letter of introduction to the publishers, with whom her father had had some communication from time to time as the book progressed, and she knew that letter was important, for without it she would not have identification.

It was getting late. The coast would be clear for a few minutes, for everybody would be dressing for dinner.

Kerry wrapped the manuscript and the long envelope in a piece of soft paper, and throwing her coat carelessly over it on her arm she hurried to the cabin where expensive trinkets of all sorts were on display. Not again would she leave that precious manuscript behind her. As she had hoped there were very few people about, and she made her purchases unhindered and hurried back to her stateroom.

She bought a couple of new magazines, and an attractive little bag of hand woven wool with gay little strap handles. It was large and soft and would amply hold all she needed to put in it.

She slipped hurriedly into her one little evening frock, put the manuscript into her new bag, stuffed a soft little silk shawl on top of it, with a magazine sticking out behind it and was ready to go. The shawl was of green, with long silk fringe. It was the one beautiful relic of her childhood, a gift her father had brought her from China while she was still in school. The fringe hung carelessly out and made a lovely touch of color in her somber costume. She slung the bag over her arm and went out on deck for a few minutes as if she were going to read, and so sauntered into the dining room quite naturally, carrying her new bag. No one would suspect she carried a treasure that she was afraid to leave behind her.

She held it in her lap during the meal, in constant fear lest it would slide off to the floor, but greatly assured to have the precious book where she could touch it all the time.

Sitting there at the table with the voices of friendly people all around her, and her special aversion sitting diagonally across from her eating his dinner like any sane Christian, Kerry reflected that she had been very silly and foolishly frightened, to spend her money for the bag. It was absurd in the extreme for her to imagine that man wanted her book, or had any dishonest intentions against her. Probably that missing page was even now lying under her trunk, or perhaps a whimsical wind had fluttered it out of her porthole and it was swashing about somewhere in the great ocean right now. Probably Professor Dawson Ph.D. had only kind intentions after all when he offered so assiduously to help her with her father's book. At most he was only seeking a little fame; he wanted to be able to say "I helped compile that book! I was associated" etc. Well, at least she was glad that she had taken the safer course, for she never could have made herself sit through a meal and act like other people if she had left it behind her. And absurd or not she was going to enjoy that lovely bag! It was the first pretty thing she ever remembered to have bought for herself.

"Oh, thank you, no. I can carry the bag. It is only a light little thing," she found herself saying to McNair as he helped her up the companion-way and asked her to walk awhile on the deck.

She slipped her hand deftly through the soft straps, tucked the bag under her arm, and flung the green shawl about her shoulders. The long fringe hung down and the bag was out of sight.

They walked the deck together for a while, watching the dying colors on the water as they had done the night before, and Kerry felt again that peace that had possessed her in the young man's company.

She longed to asked him some questions, yet dared not break the sweet quietness of their friendliness. At last, as the same star burned out again she said shyly:

"I wish you would tell me what you meant last night, about the silver trumpet. I've been puzzling all day to know about it. Was it real, or was it some book you have been reading, a poem perhaps? I may be stupid. I haven't read much of the modern literature."

He looked down at her and smiled, and even in the dusky twilight she thought she saw a light of eagerness in his eyes.

"Yes, it's real!" he said. "The realest thing there is in the world. But it's a Book too. Wait! Let us go over yonder and sit down where we shall not be interrupted and I'll tell you all about it. But—" and he looked down at her critically, "you're not warmly enough dressed for sitting out here. The wind is coming up. Wait! I'll get you some rugs! But no, suppose you come with me. I'm afraid your friend might spirit you away before we have our talk."

"My friend?" she questioned with a look of annoyance in her eyes, "I have no friends on board."

"You're mistaken," said McNair smiling. "You have *one* at least in myself. But isn't Dawson your friend? He gave me to understand that he was quite an intimate of the family, and closely associated with your father in his work."

"I never heard of him before," said Kerry earnestly. "I doubt if my father ever did. He usually talked to us of those he met. I never heard this man's name, although that professor's wife at the table told me that Mr. Dawson had written several scientific books which had been favorably received. But he is not *my* friend. The fact is I have taken a most violent dislike to him, which of course is all wrong, and I'm struggling hard to forget it. But don't call him my friend, please."

"I'm greatly relieved," laughed McNair, "I shan't be afraid to monopolize you then as often as you will let me. Now, here we are, just wait a moment, and if Dawson turns up we'll run and hide behind those life preservers."

He laughingly unlocked a door, disappeared and re-appeared almost immediately with an armful of rugs, steering her back to the deck once more.

There was some kind of an entertainment going on in the cabin, and crowds were assembled there. McNair led her by a deserted way to a sheltered spot on the upper deck where they seemed to be alone with the stars. He produced a big soft coat of camel's hair.

"Here, I brought this for you," he said, "put it on. Oh, I have another for myself." He laughed as she lifted eyes of protest. "You'll find it's quite chilly when you have sat for a few minutes."

He tucked her in with a rug, and arranged a cushion at her back. She wondered where he found all these comforts so easily, as if he had prepared for the necessity.

It was wonderful up there among the stars. For a few moments they sat and looked.

At last he spoke.

"Where do you want me to begin?"

"At the beginning," said Kerry. "I want to understand it all."

" 'In the beginning God created the heavens and the earth!' " quoted McNair solemnly, and somehow the words seemed to bring a new meaning as he spoke them up there under the circle of the heavens.

"You believe the Bible then?" questioned Kerry. "My father thought, that is he sometimes said, that the Bible account of creation might be true only it did not seem to make the world old enough." There was a wistfulness in her tone as she went on. "But how do you explain the strange animals that have been buried ages ago, the deposits of rock that show the world must have been thousands and thousands of years in the making?"

"There is room for all that between the first and second verses of Genesis," said the young man confidently, "Are you familiar with the words?"

"I'm afraid not," said Kerry. "I've never read it much. Of course we read it some in school at morning devotions."

"Then I'll repeat it. The first verse is, 'In the beginning God *created* the heavens and the earth.' The word created has the significance of 'to be made out of nothing.' In the beginning God made the heavens and the earth out of nothing. But we do not know how long ago that was. It may have been ages upon ages ago. It probably was. God has said nothing about the time. But the next verse goes on to say—'And the earth *was* without form and void,' but a more accurate translation of the original Hebrew would be: 'and the earth *became* without form and void.' It became shapeless and empty. A great cataclysm destroyed the first creation. You will find reference to it in Isaiah and Jeremiah, and the New Testament refers to it as a fact of which people are 'willingly ignorant.'"

"How strange!" said Kerry in a tone of deep interest, "I never heard of it before. Do you mean it is a new theory? A new interpretation?"

"Not at all!" said McNair quickly, "no man has a right to a theory about God, or about what He has said. And we are told that no scripture is of 'private interpretation.' It is to be understood only by comparing scripture with scripture. When anything in the Bible is put to that test there is no doubt of its meaning. I could make this clearer to you in the daytime when I could show you the verses in the Bible. Would you like to come up here to-morrow morning sometime and go into it thoroughly?"

"I certainly would," said Kerry eagerly, "it sounds fascinating. My father, of course, knew Hebrew and Greek, but he never had much time to look into things like this, though he used to say that he thought the Bible was the most beautiful book in the world and he wished he had more time to read it. He read it quite a few times the last weeks before he died. He said it rested him. But tell me, what has this to do with what you were talking about last night? You spoke of a silver trumpet, and of Christ coming back to earth again, if I understood you aright. What could that possibly have to do with the creation of the universe ages ago before Christ was ever born? He wasn't there at creation."

"Oh, but there you are mistaken," said the quiet assured voice, "He was there. 'In the beginning God created—' The Hebrew word used for God in that first verse of Genesis is in the plural and means not God a single person, but *the Godhead,* the Triune God, the Father, the Son and Holy Spirit. That brings us face to face with the mystery of the Godhead of course. But over in the book of John, in the first verse we read: 'In the beginning was the Word (Word in the original Greek signifies the Messiah), and the Word was with God, and the Word *was* God. The same was in the beginning with God. All things were made by Him, and without Him was not anything made that was made.'"

"What!" said Kerry, "do you mean that Jesus made the world?"

"He certainly did."

"But He was not born yet."

"Not in His human form. But He always existed, and scripture distinctly says that He was there when the worlds were made and He created them. Jesus is God made human, that He might take man's debt of sin upon himself. Don't you understand?"

"I'm afraid I don't," said Kerry solemnly, "I never heard anything like this before. It does not sound like any creed I ever heard of before."

"It is not a creed. It is simply God's word."

"Go on, please, tell me about His coming again. I know of course in general that he was supposed to have been born on the earth, that He lived a beautiful life, and that He died on the cross presumably for the sins of the world, but I never heard that anybody believed He was coming again. Is it peculiar to a few people? Is it something new?"

"No. The Church throughout the ages has believed it but strangely enough has not given much heed to it for centuries. Yet it is mentioned in the New Testament more often than any other doctrine. Christ Himself promised it before He left the earth. The angels stated it as a fact to comfort his sorrowing disciples while they watched him ascend into heaven. There are many promises of great blessing to those who are watching and waiting for His coming. In fact, He Himself, when He established the Lord's supper, said that His people were to observe it as a memorial to Him 'till He come'!"

"That sounds very strange and wonderful," said Kerry thoughtfully. "It would make life worth living if one could believe a thing like that. Even though everything were very hard, one could stand it, if there were something like that to look forward to. But what makes you think, even if it is true, that it might be soon? It is a great many years since the Bible was written. All those people died and never saw Him come back. Why is He any more likely to come now?"

"Because the things have happened that he said were to be the signs of His coming."

"What things?"

"Events in Palestine; many things concerning the Jews; the talk of world peace; the rise of Rome into prominence once more; the League of Nations; and perhaps more than anything else the falling away of professing Christians from a firm belief in the Bible as the Word of God. Things in the moral, the intellectual, and even the physical world, are all marching along just as prophecy foretold they would do in this age. It is a marvelous story. I would like an opportunity to tell it to you if you are interested, and to bring you into touch with the words in the Book."

"It sounds marvelous," said Kerry, "but it sounds fanciful. It seems too wonderful to be true. It is weird. It is uncanny, like science."

"It is much more true than science," said McNair reverently. "It never changes. This has been truth through the ages, made plain only as the knowledge was needed. God ordered that some of these prophecies should be sealed up until the time of the end, and then the wise should understand, but none of the unbelieving should understand!"

"Oh!" said Kerry softly, "that sounds— Why, I can see how that would be. That is like science too. The wise understand, slowly, bit by bit—take electricity, for instance! But is it really accurate? Can you prove all this you have been telling me? Or have you just accepted some other person's word about it? Excuse me, I do not mean to be rude. I really want to know."

"I understand," said McNair. "Yes, I know it to be true. Yes, I can prove it to you if you will give me opportunity, prove it to you from the Word of God. There is no other place to go. All other sources are shifting sands, one day standing on one theory, another day on another."

Kerry was silent for a full minute, sitting thoughtfully looking at the stars.

"But about that silver trumpet," she said softly, "was that real, too? And you haven't told me why He is coming again and what is going to happen then."

"Well, so this is where you have hidden yourselves away is it?" said a hard nasal voice from the shadows behind them. "Nice night again in spite of all predictions, but I think it'll rain before morning. I saw a cloud off on the horizon. This sort of thing never lasts at this time of year."

McNair started up from his chair.

"Yes, and it is late. Miss Kavanaugh, I shouldn't have kept you here all this time away from your friends."

"It's been wonderful up here," said Kerry beginning to shed her wrappings, and gripping her new bag furtively.

"What have you two found to talk about all this time up here away from everything?" asked Dawson in a tone that seemed to mean geniality, though there was an underlying suspicion in the accents.

"Stars!" said Kerry joyously, "aren't they lovely! I've learned a lot about them, how they were made, and—other things. You ought to talk with Mr. McNair, Professor Dawson. He knows a lot of interesting things. But I'll have to say good night now, I'm not supposed to stay up late on this voyage."

McNair gathered up the wraps and followed her, and Dawson tagged along behind. Again he had succeeded only in dispersing the gathering. But he shut his lips grimly and watched them, a sinister gleam in his black eyes. He had been in his stateroom all the afternoon writing. Time would tell.

The first thing Kerry did when she was safely shut into her room was to unlock her trunk, undo that bundle of pictures, and rip open one of the magazine leaves to see if the notes were still there. They were all there. None of them seemed to have been disturbed.

But her old brief case in which she used to keep her papers and which she thought she had left strapped up and neatly stowed at the side of the locker, was lying unstrapped on her bed. Did she or did she not put it away before she went to dinner?

7

GRAHAM McNair found Kerry on deck quite early the next morning. She was standing by herself, wrapped closely in her coat, her bright wool bag tucked under her arm. He noticed the trailing vivid threads of green silk fringe that had escaped from the top of the bag, the floating vivid wisp of red-gold hair that had escaped from her little brown hat, and the touch of colors pleased him. She looked like a picture with her delicate profile etched against the sea and sky, her bright hair blowing.

But when he came nearer he noticed a shadow in her eyes, something that he was sure had not been there the day before. Even the smile with which she greeted him had an absent-minded air about it.

"You are worrying about something," he stated intimately, after they had exchanged remarks about the morning.

She flashed him a quick comprehending look. "How did you know?"

He met her gaze with a fine understanding one.

"I know," he smiled, "it is just written in your face, that is all. I wonder, if I could help at all?"

"Oh, my face!" said Kerry, "my father used to tell me that he could read me like a book. He tried so hard to train me not to herald all my feelings to the world. And I thought I was succeeding! Just see!"

McNair smiled down at her again.

"Don't worry," he said. "You succeed better than you realize. I haven't been able to read you at all well until this morning when I caught you off your guard. In fact I've tried very hard to find out about one or two things and I am just as much in the dark as when I came on ship board."

Kerry flashed him a glance of wondering interest.

"What could you possibly want to know about me that I've been so secretive about?" she challenged gayly.

"Well, to begin with, I can't quite make out your attitude toward Dawson. I wish I knew just what relation he sustains toward you, what interest he has in you. Please don't think I'm trying to be impertinent. I had a reason for wishing to know."

"*I wish I knew!*" said Kerry fervently, the troubled look coming into her eyes again. "I wonder—would it be wrong to ask advice of a stranger? You have been so kind—and seem so sane! I don't like to burden others with my perplexities but—"

"It certainly would not be wrong!" said McNair eagerly. "I only wish you would let me help you if there is anything I can do. And, please don't count me a stranger. I thought we had got beyond that the last two evenings."

She flashed him a look of friendliness.

"Thank you," she said, "I'll think of you as a friend hereafter."

"And please understand that whatever you say I shall regard in the strictest confidence, and afterward it shall be as if you had not spoken, if that is your wish."

"Thank you, I know I can trust you," she said gravely, "I was only not quite sure whether it was right for me to bother you. Very well, then, Mr. McNair, what would you do if you had lost a very important paper under circumstances that made you think that some one had entered your stateroom and taken it away?"

McNair gave her a quick, keen, startled look before he answered. Then he spoke gravely:

"Generally speaking I should tell the steward of the ship immediately."

"But—would he have any possible way to recover the paper without making a great fuss and letting everybody know about it?"

"Yes," said McNair, still gravely, "I think he would. I have known of instances of such recoveries on other voyages. And I happen to know this man. You can trust him. But—may I know a little more about the circumstances? I don't like to give advice off hand, although perhaps you would rather confide in the steward."

"No!" said Kerry quickly, "I would much rather tell you. I am not sure but I am very silly in imagining anything wrong. I have tried all night to be sensible and think the paper would turn up by daylight, although I had thoroughly searched the room several times, and asked the stewardess. But this morning when I began to search again I found a fountain pen just under the edge of my berth, and inside my *locked trunk* was a strange pencil that did not belong to me. The fountain pen had a blue and white mottled barrel, and the pencil was yellow with a rubber band wound around its middle."

"Ah!" said McNair under his breath.

"But of course there are many yellow pencils and blue pen-holders in the world," argued Kerry.

"What reason has Dawson to want that paper?" asked McNair, "do you know? Or do you suspect? Of course I've seen such a pen and pencil sticking from his vest pocket."

"I'd better tell you everything," said Kerry with troubled brow, looking with unseeing eyes off to sea. "Of course his particular pen and pencil may still be in his vest pocket this morning. I want to be fair."

"I think you had better tell me the whole story," said the young man. "I perhaps can help a lot. And if I can't it won't do you any harm, I'll promise you that."

"Well," began Kerry dropping her voice, "yesterday morning I did not go down to breakfast. I wanted to work. When I opened my door to go out at noon one of the pages I had been copying which had escaped my notice when I gathered the papers up to put them away, blew out of the door and a little way down the corridor. I reached after it, but Professor Dawson who was coming from the other end of the corridor got it first and instead of giving it to me at once as I expected, he held it for what seemed to me like a full minute, while he read it."

"What unspeakable rudeness!"

"When he did give it to me he seemed almost—reluctant— to give it up. I tossed it inside the door and it landed on the bed. I locked the door. I was vexed but I walked with him down the corridor. We did not talk. He seemed rather absent-minded. We went into the dining room together, and later when others had been seated he left the table for a few minutes, professedly to get a joke he wished to read to us. Perhaps you remember that he followed me from the table. You certainly heard him try to make a 'conference' date with me last night, as he called it. So he followed me and demanded that I come out on deck at once as he said he had something very important to say to me."

"Had he ever been associated with your father?" asked McNair suddenly.

"Not that I know of," said Kerry, "he is an utter stranger to me. So I was the more surprised when he began to talk. He said that he wanted to help me, and when I asked him what he meant he said he knew that I was getting my father's book ready for publication and he would be glad to help in any revising or altering that was necessary. He said that he, being a scientist, would be more fitted to do the work than I would. He insinuated a friendship and association with my father which I am sure never existed. I was so angry that I could scarcely answer him, but I managed to control my voice and make him understand that whatever my father had written needed no altering or revising, and that I was not engaged in any such business as he seemed to suppose. I have been my father's typist of course, for some time past, and there were a few remaining pages that needed copying after he died, because of corrections and alterations he had made, but I would as soon attempt to pull one of the stars to pieces and put it together in another way, as to alter anything that my father had written, unless he had given me explicit instructions to do so. Besides, I thought the man impertinent. I do not know how he even knew my father had been writing a book unless some hints had got into the scientific magazines. I was so dreadfully upset about it that I am afraid I was very rude to him. But—when I went back to my room that page of manuscript that I had thrown on my bed was *gone!* I rang for the stewardess, but she said she had not been in the room!"

"Where is the rest of that manuscript now?" demanded McNair in sudden panic.

"Right here in my arms!" laughed Kerry hugging her new woolly bag, with the trailing fringe of vivid green. "I've had it with me ever since."

"Mercy!" said McNair drawing her away from the rail, "what if it should fall overboard! Come away and let's sit down somewhere. Is that the only copy you have?"

"Well, practically. Of course I have the notes. They are carefully hidden. I don't think anyone would find them—"

"You could put it in the safe," suggested McNair, "there is provision on the boat for valuables."

"Yes," said Kerry, "but I was putting the last touches to the manuscript. There were erasures to be made and some diagrams—I wanted to finish it entirely before I landed."

"But you did not tell me about the pen and pencil," reminded McNair when he had her comfortably seated.

"Well, I stepped on the pen when I got out of my berth this morning. I forgot to tell you that last night when I came in I found my brief case which I am positive I filled with newspapers and left strapped and tucked between the dresser and my trunk when I went down to dinner, lying open and empty on the bed. The newspapers were gone! They happened to be just old newspapers however, not of any value. But when I opened my trunk to see if that had been disturbed I found the pencil lying on the top of everything."

"Well, I should say decidedly this is a case for the steward. But one thing first. Do you know, or didn't you remember, that Dawson was in the book shop that morning when you came in to sell those books to Peddington? He overheard all that you said about your father's book."

Kerry turned a startled look upon the young man.

"He *was!*" she said. "Oh, what a fool I was to talk! My father taught me better than that!" And then as comprehension came into her eyes, "Then—*you* were the other one. That is why your eyes looked so familiar!"

Something warm and glowing came into the young man's eyes. "That's nice," he said gently, "then we are friends, aren't we?"

Kerry answered him with a bright glow from her own eyes, and a rare smile lit her worried face.

Then in quite another tone McNair spoke hurriedly:

"Some one is coming down the deck. Suppose we vanish. You go to your stateroom, and I'll send the steward to you. Tell him everything. You can trust him perfectly. By the way, have you had your breakfast?"

"No, but that doesn't matter. I'd much rather get this off my mind."

"Nice morning!" said Dawson in his hard voice, wheeling on them by evident intention as they rose.

"Not so nice as it was earlier," said McNair meaningfully,

"Miss Kavanaugh is going in. How about a little tennis, you and I, Dawson, say in about fifteen minutes? All right. Meet you at the court."

"What are you going to do to him?" grinned Kerry as they walked away out of hearing.

"Keep him where I know he is safe until the steward gets a chance to search his room," said McNair grimly. "You know that paper of yours has got to be found, as well as any copies of it he may have made, or you may have a lot of trouble on your hands."

"Oh, do you think they can find my paper?" asked Kerry eagerly. "I didn't suppose that would be possible. I didn't know what to do. I'm so glad I asked your advice."

"Well, don't worry. We'll keep our eyes on that lad from now on. And be sure you keep your manuscript safe. What's the number of your stateroom? Right. I'll get the steward at once!" He smiled and left her at her own door, and Kerry suddenly felt comforted to know that she did not have to carry the whole responsibility. Oh, if it had been this man who had professed friendship and association with her father how certain she would have been that he was telling the truth!

The steward arrived very soon, and asked keen questions. McNair had evidently made plain the situation.

"Just where did you find the pen? Yes, and what time was it that the paper blew out of your door? Will you show me where you found the pencil? What could he want of the paper? What did the page contain?"

He jotted down her answers in a little note book, and was presently possessed of the whole story. Then he opened the door and called in the stewardess who had evidently been told to wait there for him, and questioned her about the hours of her duties in the different staterooms.

Kerry felt when he left that she had put her troubles into capable hands and that if there was any possibility of her lost property being recovered, he would do it. But she was not prepared to have him return so soon with a sheaf of papers in his hand, her own lost seventy-fifth page on the top. He was smiling grimly.

"I hadn't far to look," he said, "they were all on the top of his writing pad in the dresser drawer. Is this one yours, this seventy-fifth page?"

"Indeed it is!" she exclaimed. "Oh, I am so thankful! I was so worried. And it seemed terrible to charge any man with doing such a thing."

"Well, you needn't worry about that part. More men than you'd think are capable of doing such things, and I'm glad we got this bird with so little trouble. He evidently had no idea you would dare bring your loss to notice. Now, will you just look over these other papers that were with it and see if he has been doing any copying yet? McNair said that would be likely. Of course we can't erase it all from his memory, but the disappearance of all evidence of it may scare him into keeping still about it until your book is out."

Kerry took the pages and ran over them quickly. The first five were a somewhat irrelevant, rather disconnected dissertation of a minor scientific discussion that had been going on in the newspapers for several months. With her training she saw at once and with relief that it was not particularly well done, not very strong, and was quite illogical in places. An article like this could scarcely have much weight anywhere.

But when she came to the sixth page, she found a most scurrilous attack upon her father, and his supposed view of the subject, diabolically clever, supported by quotations from the stolen page. She saw at once that what Dawson lacked in scientific knowledge and cleverness, he made up in cunning. He had taken her father's words out of their context, and had diverted from their original meaning whole sentences that her father had written. It was the cunning of a fox that had done that, not the brain of an honest scientist.

When she had finished reading she explained to the steward, reading him the parts that had to do with her page, and showing him the context of her father's page in the original.

The steward studied the papers for a few minutes, and then said:

"I see, Miss Kavanaugh. He's been quite sly, has he not? Now, I think you would do well to keep the pages that have to do with your own, but I will return these first five pages to his room where I found them. I think that the disappearance of some of his papers will be enough to cause that bird to think a little and watch his step."

"Oh, you have been very kind," said Kerry, "I was terribly worried! But—how do you know *I* am telling the truth? How do you know but I have stolen his papers?"

The steward grinned.

"Well, Miss Kavanaugh, I couldn't be in the business of steward for twenty years on a great Atlantic Liner and not be a pretty good judge of faces, character, if you want to call it that. But if I had needed any backing in what I'm doing it would have been enough that Graham McNair thought you were all right. I've known him since he was a little kid, and he's a rare man, he is. Besides, anyone with half an eye, and a day at sea with him, can see what this other bird is. But now, I hope you won't have any more trouble, Miss Kavanaugh. I'm having a special extra lock put on your door to make you feel comfortable. And any time you want us to put that manuscript in the safe, when you finish working with it, I'll be glad to look after it for you. We'll keep a lookout for this room too. I don't think you'll have any more monkey business this trip. Good morning, Miss Kavanaugh! Don't hesitate to call on me any time you need me. That's what I'm here for."

He was gone, and Kerry standing there with the papers in her hand, was so relieved she found tears of joy coming into her eyes. Of course there was still a possibility that that man would dare to write an article, but even if he did he had nothing to bear him out, no evidence that could stand in court. If it came to real trouble about it, she had it all!

She was still standing there studying the Dawson paper when there came another tap at her door, and there was a tray. Coffee and rolls and grapefruit, a tempting array! Across one corner of the tray lay a dozen lovely deep-hearted yellow roses, and tucked between their stems was a note.

The color flamed into her face as she accepted the tray and smiled at the waiter who had brought it. Roses! The first roses she had ever received! There had often been roses in the family, but always for the beautiful little mother. She bent her head, laid her cheeks against their cool soft petals, and touched them with her lips.

"You lovely, lovely things!" she said softly to them when she was alone. And then sat down to read the note.

> Dear Miss Kavanaugh: it read,
>   Eat your breakfast, and forget your troubles. I'm going to give this bird a battle on the deck this morning and see if I can get him tired out so he won't bother us this afternoon. See you at lunch time.

There was no name signed but Kerry had no difficulty in identifying the writer, and she sat for several minutes cooling her cheeks against the roses, and thinking of what the steward had said about McNair. A great longing suddenly seized her to tell her father about this new friend she had found. Oh, if her father had only lived to know him. But of course, she must remember that the voyage was almost over and she would probably never see him again after they landed. Still it was nice to have known him anyway, and she would always count him a good friend even if she never saw him again. Roses of course did not mean anything under the circumstances. They were just a little token of his sympathy and help, to remind her not to worry. She must not get any "ideas" from them.

Nevertheless she hummed a little tune as she went to put

them in water and afterward she sat down to her tempting breakfast tray and found she was very hungry.

After she had finished she got out the long envelope and opened it. She wanted to get all the hard things done and out of the way. She knew it would be hard to read her dear father's last directions, even though they might and probably would be most commonplace. Just to think he had penned them when his hand trembled and he was so weak he could hardly write would wring her heart.

There was the letter of introduction to the publisher, as she had expected, a beautiful letter, terse and clear, and she read it over slowly. Her father had left it open for her to read she knew, so that she might understand everything fully.

Then there were full directions what to do when she arrived in New York, how to find the publisher, what to say, and what would probably be said to her. She memorized everything carefully, feeling that she wanted to understand every step of the way when she landed, and not have to hunt up a letter to see if she were right.

She had purposely left till the last the small envelope marked "Kerry" in trembling penciled writing, knowing that it contained her father's last word to her about the book itself.

With tears raining down her face she finally opened it.

It was long, and obviously written in separate paragraphs at different times, a paragraph at a time. It was like reading his spiritual will.

Dear Kerry:

The book is done, and I find myself feeling that it is your book. If it had not been for you it would never have been finished. I know definitely now that I have only a few more days left. The doctor told me so this morning. But I am satisfied. I have done the work I had set myself to do. The book will give you a little something to live on, and while I regret that I was unable to give you and your beautiful little mother the luxury I always hoped for, yet I know you two can get along very well on the income you will have. You must guide your mother somewhat in its expenditure, Kerry, for you know her lack of judgment, but she is such a dear, beautiful little mother—!

Here the paragraph broke off suddenly as strength evidently failed, and then took up again on an entirely new theme, probably hours later.

I have been thinking over the book, Kerry! I am glad it is done. Glad I was able to finish it before I went. Glad I could demonstrate a few facts that others have failed to follow through to the finish. But Kerry—I am wondering whether it was worth it all—whether it has been worth while to keep my soul down to this thing. Of course it was great to be able to search out truth, and truth is always wonderful, the more wonderful the more hidden.

But Kerry, I've been wondering, if after all, there wasn't other Truth—bigger Truth I might have digged for—Truth that would have reached and helped more people.

The last few days I've been reading an old Book. You remember the day I told you to hunt me out my Bible? Well, dear, I've been browsing through it every day since then. It has taken possession of my mind to the exclusion of everything else. I have found new truths there, and I have found a great many deep things which I do not understand. It has intrigued me more than any study of science. I have come suddenly face to face with the thought that perhaps, after all, the key to all knowledge, the basis of all science, was here hidden, and I did not understand in time.

I think if I had my life to live over I would begin with this old Book, and never touch science until I had mastered at least its possibilities, searched out its hidden meanings, got a key to its rare language of types and patterns which I have come to feel are hidden here away from common sight as much as ever the secrets of life and creation and power is hidden in Nature—

Here the paragraph trailed off again, the last words almost indecipherable, as though written in extreme weakness. Then another space and the writing began again, clear and plain.

We scientists have studied for years. We have patiently searched out the mysteries of the universe, and have made great discoveries, which from year to year have had to be unmade, changed to fit new discoveries, new, so-called facts. But this old Book has remained unchanged, and as I read it over to-day I can see many things in it that might have explained our problems years ago if we had only thought it worth while to listen. I would like to commend to all my fellow scientists, and to those that shall read my book, and to those that shall come after me, that they make a full study of the Bible; that they unravel the mystery of its imagery; that they dig deep into its peculiar construction and find the hidden meaning before they do anything else. If it is written by God, the God who made Nature, and I believe in my soul that it is, there they may expect to find hidden treasure of truth with every step into its study. It bears, to my thinking, the hall marks of a divine writing. Let some great soul who would know Truth approach it from this angle and he may find that he has at last opened the Source of all mystery and truth for all ages. I know of no one who has tried to study science starting with the Bible viewpoint for a text book. I would like to see it tried.

Again there came a break in the writing and then:

Kerry, dear: Father's little girl, Father's wonderful helper, go over the manuscript and wherever you find a suggestion of the origin of life or of creation as being different from the account given in the Bible, change it. Cut it out. Leave nothing that could discount the Bible words. It is true we may not understand them in their entirety, but I wish nothing in my written words to discount the old Bible. I believe that it knows more about Nature and life and science than any wisdom the world has ever yet known. I wish I could go back and live my life over with the Bible as a start. This is my last word about my book. Let it not stand in any word or syllable as arrayed against the greatest Book of all. You will know what to do, my precious Kerry!—

There was a wider space here and then in words almost indecipherable:

Kerry—I—love you! Precious child! How could I have lived out my last years—without you—"

The line was obviously unfinished, and then below written with evident care and great weakness,

I am trusting *in the old Book!*
                              Shannon Kavanaugh

8

KERRY sat quite still. She heard the booming of the waves outside, she heard the monotonous throb of the engine, she heard the soft splashing of her tears as they dropped on the stiff manila envelope in which the letter had been found, but she seemed to hear above it all her father's voice across the darkness of the valley through which he had passed away from her sight. And his voice in the words she had just read was almost as clear to her ear as the waves beating outside, or as the engine down below, or as her own tears that flowed without her will.

They were arresting words, words that seemed to clear away all earthly trammels, and bring a clearer vision.

That her father, who had all the years been a devotee of science, and had taught her to think it the final authority, should be suddenly shouting at her from his tomb that he had found in his last hour that there was a greater than Science! It was incredible!

Over and over again she read the precious words, thrilling anew at each endearment for herself, wondering at the gracious humbleness of the scholar!

After a little it came to her that she must make a copy of this writing. She must not risk a chance of losing it. Rather that the whole book should be lost than this his precious last words!

She got out her typewriter and made a copy, putting it into the envelope. But the original of the letter itself she folded inside a soft bit of linen handkerchief and pinned carefully inside her dress. She would wear it next to her heart at least until she should be in a place where she could put it away more safely.

She found herself longing to show it to McNair. He would understand. He would be pleased. He loved the old Book too. He believed in it. But she could see the sneer on the face of Dawson if he could read it. He did not believe in the Bible. Only yesterday, at the dinner table she had heard him say to Mrs. Somers whose husband was professor of Biblical Literature in a great American university, that in ten years more there would be no such departments in the thoroughly up to date universities. He said that even now nobody believed in the Bible except as an out of date piece of literature that had occupied a unique position in the world for a most amazing time. He stated in clear caustic tones that the fact that people were getting away from superstitions and dropping off the Bible as a standard of living showed that real education was dawning and the next generation would begin to show a far more highly developed race of beings!

Kerry put her hand over her heart and pressed the soft crackling paper in its sheath of linen, pressed until she could hear her own heart tick with the voice of the paper. It was as if her heart throbs were answering her father's written words, and promising him her loyalty in whatever he had said.

She had not been brought up to believe, nor yet to disbelieve the Bible. It had been a side issue. And now her father seemed to be pointing the way to a light he had found in the darkness just as the shadows of death were closing in about him. It was significant, too, that this his last word should come into her hands just when her own attention had been so startlingly turned to the subject.

Then she remembered that she had still some work to do on the book. She must follow out this his last direction, and take out all such sentences and words as he had referred to. It would be her last precious work for him and the book.

Blinded with tears she got out the manuscript and went to work.

She did not have to read the whole thing over. She knew the subject matter so well that she could easily turn to such portions as would need changing. Somehow since reading her father's last words there was a new thrill in working over the book again. It was as if she had a more vital part in it herself, and as if she were responsible not only to her father but to God for what she was doing.

When lunch time came she wrapped up the manuscript and tucked it safely in her woolly bag, going down early to the table that she might get settled before the others arrived.

Dawson and McNair came in together, and for the first time she saw the gleam of a boyish smile on Dawson's face. The Ph.D. importance was for the time laid aside.

"We're having a big battle," announced McNair, "a tournament on. You ought all to come and see it! Dawson is one game ahead but he's going to lose it this afternoon!"

Kerry looked up in wonder at the chummy tone in which he spoke. He certainly was carrying out his part well. Had he perhaps forgotten all about her little affairs in the interest of the game?

But an instant later he said in a low tone, with a twinkle toward her:

"How's crops?"

"All safely in," said Kerry in a gay little tone.

"Is that right?" he asked without seeming to move his lips or even turn toward her.

"Wonderfully right!" said Kerry jubilantly as if she were talking about the weather.

"Well, don't be surprised if you see me buddying up to the Ph.D.," he said under his breath, "I have a reason."

The rest of the meal was a gay one. Almost the entire table had been down watching the tennis during the morning, and had much to say about the different plays. It was plain to be seen that Dawson was flattered at the attention he was receiving. He talked a good deal and laughed more in his sharp little cackle.

"Is he a fine player?" asked Kerry wondering.

"Well, so-so," said McNair. "Not much on serving, but sly as a fox. You have to watch him! He makes quick little unexpected movements. Tennis is a good way to size up a man I find."

Then McNair turned his attention to the professor's wife who sat at his right. Kerry sat quietly, saying little. She only of the whole table seemed to have no part in the conversation, because she had not been present at the tournament that morning. By and by she caught the little sinister eyes of Dawson watching her; keenly, warily, as if searching her face for reason of her silence. At last he spoke to her.

"You don't play?" he asked and his voice had a sharp little point to it like a gimlet.

"Yes," said Kerry, "I used to play in school, but I'm out of practice."

"Better come out and take a hand in the singles," he challenged, watching her narrowly.

"Thank you," said Kerry coolly. "I'm afraid I'm not interested enough."

After that he said no more to her, but continued to watch her from time to time and did she fancy it or was there a kind of glitter of triumph in those small black eyes?

She wondered if he had been to his room yet, and discovered his own loss? Probably not, for his air was too gay and carefree for that. Well, she must guard her own countenance too and not look too carefree herself. It was just as well to gain all the time possible before he became alarmed on his own account.

So Kerry when the meal was over, went directly to her room again. She saw the rest troop off gayly to meet again at tennis, with a kind of a pang of jealousy. McNair was still talking to the Professor's wife, telling her about some of his experiences in Switzerland, as he walked beside her from the dining room. He did not seem to see Kerry at all. Perhaps this was a part of his plan, but it left a desolate little feeling in her heart that warned her. Still, she excused herself, she had looked forward to telling him about her father's letter. She had felt he would understand.

Then she caught sight of Dawson hurrying around the table toward her and hastened her steps to walk beside an old lady who sat at the head of the table, and so escaped his companionship. She felt that she wanted to keep as far away from Dawson as possible. He was like a snake. That was it! His eyes were reptile eyes. A reptile was even more repulsive, and far more deadly, than a louse!

She plunged into her work again, however, and forgot all save the joy of what she was doing, the delight in fulfilling her father's last request.

By dinner time she had been carefully over the whole manuscript and made the little changes her father had commanded, and she felt everything was ready for the publisher.

She heard footsteps down the corridor that sounded like Dawson's quick, satisfied walk. She knew that his room was the last one on the corridor, for she had heard the steward and stewardess discussing it that morning. She could hear his weird little sibilant whistle, more like a child's than a man's. She wondered if he had discovered that the stolen paper was gone from his drawer, and with it a page or two of his own writing? Probably not. His stride was not that of a worried person. Perhaps he would not think to look after his papers till later in the evening, for it was very close to the dinner hour.

Kerry found herself dreading the moment when she should look at him and know that he had discovered his loss. Well, it was inevitable of course. How glad she would be when this voyage was over, and the anxiety past. But yet—would she?

She wanted to ask McNair a lot of questions. She found a great longing in her heart to have a good long talk with him. The realization brought a sharp reproof from her better self. McNair was nothing to her. He must not be anything to her. She must not let her silly lonely fancy twine itself around an imaginary friendship just because a man had been kind to her. Hers was not to be a life of ease and happiness. She had work to do in the world, and must keep her mind clear and free from daydreams. Moreover she was not one of those silly girls who fall in love with any passing stranger. Love and marriage would probably not be for her. She would never find a man she could admire enough to marry who would even look at her, and she must stop being so pleased and interested in this fine man who had crossed her path for a day or two. He lived in a realm miles above her, and his small kindnesses meant absolutely nothing in his life. She positively must put a stop to this unseemly eagerness for his company.

So she dressed for dinner in her same little quiet dark chiffon, perhaps the only woman in the whole ship's dining room that did not don a different evening garb every night, and went demurely down, her little woolly bag slipped over her arm, and her vivid green shawl trailing brightly over the bag, and redeeming the somber costume.

McNair did not appear at the table at all while she was there. Dawson came late, and looked as if he had made an elaborate toilet. He still eyed her furtively with that glitter of triumph in his gaze, and she decided that he had not investigated his papers yet. He seemed to be enjoying his laurels. By the talk that swirled about her in little gay drifts and eddies, she judged that Dawson had won the tournament but by a very small margin. The ladies were congratulating him, and Dawson was smirking and smiling, and taking it all delightedly, just eating it up. Yes, that was the matter with Dawson, he wanted to be in the limelight. At all odds he meant to be there. And that of course was the secret of his wish to steal her father's writing, and get himself before the world.

She was quiet again at dinner. For in spite of her great relief that the missing page had come back, and that she had in her possession proof of what the enemy had been going to do; in spite of the great elation that had filled her that morning when she read her dear father's letter, and while she had been working over his precious writing; she now found herself filled with a great depression. Probably she was tired. Probably so much excitement was bringing a reaction. She had been working too hard. Her brain was in a whirl! She would not own to herself that part of the depression was due to the absence of McNair. She would not allow such a thing in herself. She must not.

She slipped away from the table while the others were still busy with their dessert, and again she felt the gimlet eyes of Dawson upon her as she left, although she did not turn back to see.

She established herself on deck in her steamer chair, and picked up a little pamphlet that had drifted under it, lodged against the back legs of the chair and wedged itself where the wind could only flutter its leaves.

She looked about for a possible owner, but no one seemed in sight just then, and there was no name on the book. The title attracted her and she opened the pages and almost at once was lost in its message. It was called "THAT BLESSED HOPE" and the very opening sentence revealed its subject as the same that McNair had spoken of, the Lord's return.

Kerry was amazed. She had not known that there were any people anywhere who believed such a doctrine until she met McNair. That she should find this pamphlet at hand this way, right under her own chair, seemed nothing short of miraculous.

She forgot to watch the sea, forgot to draw deep breaths of

the good salt air, forgot even to look up at the sunset that was royal in its colors, spreading purple and gold and scarlet with a lavish hand, and setting the sea on fire as it died into twilight like a burned-out hearth. She read on in this amazing little book, read promises quoted from the Bible. She wished she had a Bible here to look them up. She was glad she had put her father's old Bible in her trunk. She wished she had a pencil to copy down some of these references, for perhaps the owner of the little book would come along pretty soon and she would have to give it up. She read on hurriedly.

After the strange wonderful promises the little book went on to state that the purpose of His coming was three fold. First, to *raise* the *dead in Christ!* What, raise them from the dead? Her heart sprang at the thought. Her father! Would he be that? He was a good man. Who were the dead in Christ? Oh, would that include him? How wonderful, if that were true, to see him coming with God's Son! But could this all be possible? She had never heard such things before. People generally did not believe this surely, not even so-called Christians, or they never would live the way they did. No one could go on living for earth alone with a hope like that in his soul!

She read on eagerly in the dying light.

The second reason of His coming was to catch away all living believers, together with the raised dead! That was what the book said in bright italics. What could that mean? Who were all living believers? McNair must be one of course, for he had spoken as if he were expecting such an event, as if it belonged to him. Did he expect to be caught away? Would she by any chance have a right among that group? Oh, to be caught away to meet a Lord who included her beloved father among His own! There could be no greater heaven than that!

Her eyes filled with tears, so that between the dying light upon the silver sea, and her own tears she could barely make out that the next reason for His coming was to reward His own.

She laid the little book face down upon her lap, brushed the tears away from her eyes, and suddenly saw McNair standing beside her looking down with such a tender protective expression on his face that she almost cried out in her delight at seeing him.

"And so you have found my little lost book," he said dropping into the empty seat beside her. "It blew away yesterday morning while I was talking to some one, blew away from a pile of books and papers I had left lying on my chair, and I searched the deck for it in every direction, but could not find it."

"Oh, I'm so glad it is yours!" said Kerry, "for now you will tell me what it all means."

The young man smiled.

"I'll be glad to," he said, "sorry I couldn't have got around earlier but it was the first chance I've had to talk with the steward since morning, and then I had to snatch a bite to eat, for all day deck tennis surely does make one hungry. What is it you do not understand?"

"Well, first, who are the dead in Christ? The book says that the Lord is coming to raise them to life, that that is the first purpose of His coming. I never heard of any such strange thing. Can really sane people believe that?"

"They do," said McNair solemnly with a glad ring to his voice. "I believe it with all my heart myself and I think I'm fairly sane. There has never been any attempt to put me in an asylum."

Kerry laughed, and there was a glad little ring to her voice too.

"I'm very glad," she said shyly, "I'm glad you believe it, because then I shall feel safe in believing it too. But it seemed too good to believe. Only, perhaps—perhaps it isn't good after all. Who *are* the dead in Christ? What does that mean?"

"It means all those who died believing in Him,—all who have accepted Him as their Saviour."

"Oh!" said Kerry in a puzzled way. "Oh, I—wonder—"

and he thought he saw a sudden droop of her whole little figure as it sat there in the dimness of the first faint moonlight.

"What is the trouble—child—?" he said and his voice was very tender. "Is it—is there—some one—?"

"Yes," said Kerry tensely, "my father! I am wondering—will he be among those dead?"

With a great yearning upon him he sat forward in his chair and leaned nearer to her.

"Tell me about him," he said gently. "Did he—believe? Did he—know the Lord?"

Kerry moved restlessly in her chair and threw up her chin with a gesture almost of despair and pleading.

"Oh, I don't know! I think perhaps—but I know so little about it all. We never talked about these things. But listen! This morning I opened the sealed letter from my father that was to give me the last directions about his book, and I found—a personal letter—from him!"

"How precious that must have been to you," said McNair sympathetically.

"I want you to read it!" said Kerry, brushing away a furtive tear in the darkness, "but it says strange things—things that he never talked about before. He'd asked for his Bible a couple of weeks before he died, an old Bible he kept on a high shelf, and he'd been reading it, kept it under his pillow those last days. In the letter he says that he thinks he began at the wrong end in his research, and that he should have begun with the viewpoint of the Bible. He directs me to go through his whole book and change anything that would not seem to be in accord with Bible statements, and he wishes a paragraph added suggesting that his fellow scientists should study Nature from the viewpoint of the Bible. I've been making those changes all day."

"How wonderful!" murmured McNair.

"But oh!" went on Kerry, "I begin to see that I know so little of the Bible. I'm not sure I've done it right. If I only had some one who knew the Bible, some one I could trust! Oh," she exclaimed, "would you go over the changes I made and check them with the Bible? That will be wonderful, and I'll feel so much better about it. I'll know that what my father really wanted has been done right. His last words were these: 'I am trusting in the old Book,' and he signed his name to that as if it were a statement he wished to make before the world."

"There! There you have your answer, my friend," said McNair in a softly jubilant voice. "I think you can be sure that your father is among the dead in Christ. The old Book gives the plan of salvation and tells of Christ and the coming redemption from cover to cover. You need have no fear. And of course I'll be glad to do all I can. I feel honored that you trust me to do it."

"Oh!" breathed Kerry softly, and he could see that tears were glistening on her cheek.

Then after an instant she spoke again.

"But the little book tells another reason why He is coming again. It says that He is coming for the living believers. What is a living believer. Could I be among those?"

"You certainly could!" said McNair, and now his voice rang with a deep joy.

"What would I have to do?"

"Nothing. It has all been done for you. Your part is but to accept it."

"But—I know nothing about it. How can I accept it? I do not understand."

"You know that Christ Jesus came into the world to save sinners, don't you? You know that He died on the cross to take our sins, yours and mine and everybody's, on Himself. If you are willing to accept that gift and put yourself under its protection you are a believer."

"But how can I believe something that I have never looked into? How can I accept—?" Kerry turned her troubled eyes toward him in the darkness.

"Listen, little girl," he said gently reaching out and laying his hand on her arm. "If I should offer you a cup of tea when you were hungry or thirsty would you have to draw back and say 'How can I drink that? How do I know it is tea? Perhaps it is some deadly poison. I must have it analyzed first!' If you saw others drinking and being refreshed, could you not believe it was good for you also? Or, if you were down there in that dark water below us, sinking, and I should throw you a rope, would you take it, or would you say 'How do I know that is a rope? Perhaps it is only a strand of straw!' Believing is an act of the will whereby you throw yourself upon something, whether you know it is able to bear you or not. Assurance comes when you find it bears you up, but you accept before you have had its strength proved. Do you know any other way to be saved?"

"Why—I have always supposed—I have always believed—that if you lived a good life—?" began Kerry.

"What was your authority for believing that anything you could do would save you?" he asked.

"Authority? Oh, doesn't the Bible tell you you have to be good? Doesn't it say that is the way to be saved?"

"No," said McNair, "just the contrary. It says there is no other way given under heaven whereby we must be saved but to believe on the name of the only begotten Son of God."

"Oh," said Kerry again, dismayed, "I never thought much about it of course. I've read the Bible very little. But do you mean it is as simple as that, as taking hold of a rope when you are drowning?"

"Yes, as simple as that. Here are Jesus' own words: 'Verily, verily, I say unto you, He that believeth on me *hath* everlasting life.'"

Kerry sat still with her hands clasped before her. They were hidden in a sheltered place where few people walked, and there was no one about. It was all very quiet as if they were shut in by the steady throbbing of the boat, and the regular dashing of the waves. Before them was the wide expanse of dark water and leaden sky. There was no moon, and the stars were all put out.

Suddenly she said:

"Then I will believe. I will accept. But—what do I do next? Surely, there is something."

"Nothing. It is all done for you. It is Christ's finished work on Calvary. You take it as a gift, and then rejoice in it just as you would rejoice in a beautiful jewel if some one should give it to you. You can be just as sure of salvation as that. Safe. Forever more! And with the blessed hope that if He does not call you sooner, He will come sometime, soon perhaps, and that you will be among those for whom He comes, and will be caught up together with beloved dead who are His own, to meet the Lord in the air!"

"It is—very wonderful!" said Kerry wistfully.

There fell a sweet silence between them for an instant and then McNair reached over and laid his hand on her hand that was resting now in her lap, and bowed his head near hers:

"Dear Father God," he prayed, "bless this Thy child in her new life. Give her the peace and joy, and the sense of rest in Thee that belongs to those who are trusting in the death of Thy dear Son. We ask it in the name of Jesus."

Kerry was very still as his words died away. She let her hand stay for the instant in the steady warm clasp that held it, and the air about them seemed holy with the new life she was entering.

"Do you mean," she asked shyly, "that I—am counted—a child of God, now?"

"Yes," he said and his voice was vibrant with the triumph of it. "I am so very glad!"

She turned and looked in wonder at him, and her hand trembled in his for an instant more.

"Why—I am glad too. I am sure I would never have found the way—but for you. It is all—so new and strange—!"

Then suddenly into their quiet talk there rolled the menace of thunder, and a lightning flash went round the world in dizzy blinding strokes and was gone, leaving deadly, threatening blackness.

"My dear!" he said springing up and pulling her quickly to her feet as the first great drops of rain began to fall, "there is going to be a storm! We must get under cover at once! Strange! I didn't hear it before, did you? Have you got all your things? Then come! Quick! It is coming fast. Let us run for it."

Still holding her hand he opened his coat and drew it about her as well as he could, and so close together they ran for shelter.

Music and dancing were going on in the heart of the ship. People were laughing and talking, others were playing endless games of cards. Nobody was noticing them. They stood outside of it all for a moment and a great joy was upon them both. They were reluctant to come back to earth again and into the garish light.

"Shall we find a quiet place to sit?" said McNair looking at the lovely flush on Kerry's cheeks, and noting the bright drops sparkling in the red-gold of her hair.

"What time is it?" She looked at her watch. "Oh, no. There are too many people about and we could not talk. I don't want this evening to be spoiled. I'll go to my room now. But—I can never thank you for what you've done for me—!"

He turned and walked with her to the end of her corridor, and as he bade her good night said:

"Wait! Here! I want you to have this. Perhaps you have not one of your own."

He handed her a little soft Testament from his inner pocket.

"I always carry it with me," he smiled.

"But you will miss it," she said as she held it wondering in her hand, and sensed the smoothness of its leather covers, worn with use.

"I shall rejoice to have you have it, and to know you will read it," he said with a smile she knew she never would forget.

9

THERE was no deck tennis the next morning, and many of the passengers remained in their beds. The storm which had burst so suddenly the night before had indeed been preparing for some time. The sun had unfurled her red banner of warning for all who understood the signs, and the purple clouds had gathered quickly and faded. Lowering blue and steel and velvet black the waters were, and rose in frenzy. They lashed the ship as if it were a little toy, and boomed and tore like living maniacs.

Kerry had gone to her room in a strange daze of peace. She wondered at herself. She did not understand what had happened nor why she should feel this way. It was not only that she had had a wonderful evening with a wonderful companion. She tried to be honest with herself. No, it was not entirely the touch of that strong hand holding hers and leading her to God, that had thrilled her so, though that was warm and dear to remember—and—he had called her "My dear" at the end when the storm came. Of course he did not realize what he was saying. Just a pleasant gentle way of being kind. He meant nothing personal by it, and she had not taken it that way. It had been a fellowship far above mere earthly things, that little hour out there on the deck, alone together, and God so near! No, it had not been just one man's presence, dear and beautiful as that was. But there was something else. She had something new in herself. Something untried as yet, but she already felt it to be powerful, something she could lean upon, believe and lean upon.

Then she opened at random the little book he had given her and read these amazing words:

"If we receive the witness of men, the witness of God is greater: for this is the witness of God which He hath testified of His Son. He that believeth on the Son of God, hath the witness in himself."

With this strange message ringing in her heart she lay down to sleep. She put her manuscript under her pillow that night, but the little book she held in her hands, close to her heart. The storm increased all that night, but she slept with a smile on her lips and a new peace in her heart that was not disturbed by booming waves or tossing ship. She had taken Christ on board her little bark, and felt safe.

Kerry had always been a good sailor. She was not alarmed by the rolling of the ship. But looking out of her porthole the next morning at the great wall of water that seethed past as if it would obliterate everything, she wondered at the strange new sense of safety that pervaded her. She sensed that the storm was unusual, but somehow it seemed as if a new assurance had driven out ordinary fears.

It was difficult dressing with the floor taking continually a new slant.

Before she left her stateroom she paused thoughtfully, her hand upon her door. Then she turned back and dropped to her knees beside her bed.

"Oh God," she whispered, "teach me what you want of me, please!" Then after an instant she added, "I ask it in the name of Jesus."

The phrase was to her a new one, but she would never forget its sweetness as McNair had used it out on deck when he prayed for her.

There were not many people about, though it was by no means early. Walking was not easy with such an uncertain floor, but Kerry made her way toward the dining room, and found McNair awaiting her. They were the only ones at their table except an old man who soon finished his breakfast and left them.

Kerry had with her the copy of her father's letter, and she brought it out now and showed it to McNair, keeping careful watch of the door lest Dawson should enter while he was reading it.

But Dawson did not appear on the scene at all that day. In fact even the dining room had very few occupants.

Kerry and McNair had the main cabin mostly to themselves, and spent a happy morning together. They went carefully over the changes Kerry had made in her father's manuscript. It was well that she could recall whole paragraphs from memory, for they dared not take the precious book out of its hiding, Kerry learned wonderful things about the new life she had entered as McNair in making a suggestion here and there opened up new truth to her. She drank it in like a thirsty flower.

But the day was a wild one. The vessel rolled from side to side, and it was difficult to keep a location gracefully. People were constantly falling, and crying out. Frequent crashes of dishes added to the weirdness of the occasion.

As the day wore on it became apparent that something unusual was going on, and McNair went to inquire. He returned gravely, but did not seem disturbed. His face wore a kind of exalted look, as if whatever came his soul had wings. That was the way Kerry thought of it afterward—and there came an afterward, when she went over every little detail of that wonderful time.

But McNair took it all calmly.

Something had gone wrong with the ship, some of its inner workings. He had not been able to pry much information out of the officials. They were working at it, and hoped to right matters.

He did not tell Kerry that the matter was serious, and that he had gathered from listening to asides from the captain and those in charge that the danger was extreme, that there was grave doubt whether the ship could ever weather the storm in her present condition. He merely said:

"We are in our Father's hands. He holds the sea in the hollow of His hand, you know. We are safe even if the ship goes down. It will not hinder us from being present when our Lord returns!"

He gave her a confident smile that warmed her heart as it had never been warmed before, even with her father's beloved smile.

"Oh, I should have been so frightened now," she said smiling bravely back, "if it hadn't been for you—for what you have taught me."

When he went again to inquire he discovered that a seam in the ship had been wrenched apart, and the water was coming in fast, faster than the pumps could take care of it. To make it worse a fire had broken out in the region of the kitchen, for a caldron of oil had escaped from its moorings and upset near an open flame. The fire at present was under control, and the crew were hard at work, but McNair saw that if it went much further there would be something worse than storm to face, the whole ship would be in flames within a few short hours.

He slipped away to his stateroom, cut up an expensive coat of oiled silk, and presently brought two large pieces to Kerry.

"You know, in a storm like this," he said quietly, "there is always a possibility of having to take to the life boats. I was just thinking about your precious manuscript. Couldn't you wrap it carefully in this so that in case anything happened it would not get wet? You might need to have it ready for sudden warning you know. Don't be alarmed, but it does no harm to be ready for emergencies. How about those notes, too, that you told me about? If I were you I would get ready in small compass, anything valuable that could be easily carried. It can do no harm, and may save you a lot of anxiety later."

He said it all so quietly that Kerry could not be unduly alarmed, but Kerry was not a child. She knew there must be grave danger. She made no outcry, showed no sign of fright, but accepted the oilskin gratefully and went to her cabin to do as he suggested. She not only wrapped the manuscript in several thicknesses of oilskin, but got out her notes also, and protected them, and then she planned a way to safely and swiftly bind them beneath her garments in case of sudden alarm, so that there would be no risk of having them snatched from her, or knocked from her grasp if there should be a panic.

All that day and night the storm raged madly. People crept to their berths like rats to their holes. The fearful sounds of straining timbers, the terrible booming of the mountain-like waves as each one crashed and threatened to overwhelm the frail ship which seemed like a toy in the tempest, the cries of people who had been thrown down or catapulted across the cabin, the constant knocking about of furniture that had broken away from its moorings, the crashing of more dishes created pandemonium.

McNair sent Kerry to her stateroom late in the evening, promising to call her if there was any need. He knew the strain was telling upon her and she needed to rest.

Kerry did not undress. She prepared herself for sudden call, for any emergency that might arise, as far as she knew how. She bound the manuscript, her money, and her few small valuables beneath her garments, not forgetting the tiny Testament that McNair had given her. She laid her coat and hat close at hand, and then she lay down.

She had not expected to sleep, but when the morning dawned and she was awakened by a steady tapping at her door, she found that she must have slept all night.

She arose hastily and opened her door.

McNair was standing in the corridor his wan face gray in the dim light. There was a long black smudge down one cheek, his collar was off and his hair was rumpled wildly. He had been fighting fire all night.

For the fire had broken out again in a new place, where the oil had seeped through into some inflammable stuff. It had eaten its way well into the heart of the ship before it was discovered.

He told her very quietly, but his anxious eyes belied his tired voice.

"The Captain thinks there may be a possibility that we must take to the life boats," he said. "A fire has broken out in the hold and if it cannot be controlled pretty soon it will be pleasanter for the passengers in the life boats."

That was a nice way to put it perhaps, but even as he said it Kerry heard the booming of the great waves, and felt the crouching of the ship like a whipped creature under their lashing. As if it could be pleasant out there in that water! That awful water! Could anything be worse than trusting to a little life boat in such a raging sea.

But the young man's steady voice went on:

"The Captain would like us all to gather on the forward deck and be ready to obey orders. He still hopes it may not be necessary, but if the fire should manage to break through the forward hatchway there would have to be swift work to get everybody off in time. Will you bring whatever you must have with you in an emergency, and come as soon as you can to the deck."

"I am quite ready!" said Kerry swinging on her coat with one swift motion and pulling down her little close hat about her face.

"Where are your valuables? Have you forgotten your book?"

"Here!" laughed Kerry bravely, laying her two hands on her breast.

"I fixed them so they cannot get away."

McNair looked down at her, a kind of hunger in his tired worn face.

"You brave, dear little girl!" he said, and suddenly his arm went around her and stooping he touched his lips reverently to her forehead. It was as if a benediction had been given her.

Then suddenly a door far down the corridor snapped open, and a crazy figure burst forth, clad uncertainly in stocking feet and trousers, with a dress shirt flapping its tails wildly above it. It staggered frantically down the corridor, bringing up against first one side, then the other, but bumping on, and crying madly in a hoarse maudlin scream:

"Fire! Fire! FIRE! This ship is on FIRE!!!"

Kerry saw to her horror that it was Dawson gone fairly mad with fear.

From every door on either side there burst forth other figures now, all in strange array, and began to rush along after him, falling, screaming, climbing over one another, in deadly blind panic, coming on like a stampede of wild cattle.

McNair pushed Kerry behind him into her doorway, and shielded her by stepping in front of Dawson and extending his arms as he tried to plunge past.

"Get out of my way!" screamed Dawson, kicking blindly at McNair. But McNair put out his foot and neatly tripped up Dawson, sending him sprawling on the floor. Then holding up his hands to stop the rest he spoke in a clear commanding voice:

"Stop! Right where you are ! Don't go another step!"

Strangely enough they obeyed him. The motley crowd in nightgowns and pajamas, with hair in curl papers, and one with no hair at all, stopped short and looked at him.

He seized the instant's quiet and attention at once:

"Friends, there's no such cause for hurry! It may be several hours before a crisis will arise. The warning was only sent out that you all might be prepared for a possible emergency which we hope will not come. The crew are working hard to make everything safe for us, but the Captain thought it best to ask you to get ready if there should be need to take to the life boats. He would like you to come on deck within the next ten minutes if possible. Bring any small valuables, and put on warm clothes. You may have to stand in the wind for some time. Go back and prepare yourselves. Go back, I tell you! Look at yourselves! You don't want to go on deck looking like that!"

As rapidly as they had come out they all scuttled back, all but Dawson who was crawling frantically away on hands and knees, casting a green furtive glance back at his late assailant. A more abject ghastly face Kerry thought she had never seen. He disappeared around the corner, and McNair turned to Kerry, reaching out his hand for hers.

"Come!" he said, "let's get on deck before the mob returns. There's time enough. Don't get excited—*dear!*"

Kerry's heart beat wildly, but she grasped his hand as if she had been a little child, and let him lead her to the companion-way and help her up.

Just ahead was Dawson, struggling up, lunging full length on the deck, picking himself up frantically, and backing against the wall of the outer cabins, his hands outspread, his black hair blowing straight up, his eyes distended, his shirt tails flapping in the wind. And straight before him as the ship lurched suddenly there rose a mighty sheet of water, towering mountains high, and curved as if it would engulf them all.

Almost lying upon his back against the cabins as the ship heeled over, Dawson sprawled, and uttered another of those unearthly yells, beyond all reason, or thought of sense, just clean frightened out of his wits, a fox caught in a snare:

"Fire, WATER, FIRE!"

McNair steadied Kerry against a doorway and seizing Dawson shook him!

"Look here, man, haven't you any sense? Shut up! You'll create a panic. If you say that once more I'll gag you so you can't talk!"

Dawson, too sick to resist, hung there in the grasp of the

taller man, and dropped his jaw open, gave a frightened assent, and dropped down on the deck with his back against the wall and closed his eyes. If he had not been such a pathetic sight it would have been funny. Kerry found her Irish giggle coming in her throat, and curving about her lips even in such a time as this. To think a man could become so abject. His shirt tails flapped about him, and he seemed to have no thought but fear as he lay back and clutched for hold against the ship.

And now the others were appearing, in frightened groups, in strange array, but sober, grave, quiet for the most part. A woman fainted when she saw the wall of water as the next wave reared its head above the ship. But for the most part they gathered sanely, quiet enough, some trembling, some crying softly, a man here and there swearing.

Kerry stood within a sheltered nook where McNair had put her and waited. She felt as if her inner self were hidden yet further in a secret place, where God was guarding. She looked about on those piteous huddled figures in the gray dawn of the morning, their faces wan with terror, some too weak and sick to stand up, and found herself longing to tell them of the refuge that she had found. How many of them were ready to go? How many of them were believers? If a few moments or another hour saw them all laid in watery graves would they be "believing dead"? Oh, if she just knew how to go to them and tell them to get ready, to accept the finished work of Calvary before it was too late.

She slipped down presently beside a little girl huddled on the deck with her mother who was too ill to know or care what was going on. Putting her arm around the child Kerry tried to comfort her, and tell her that she need not be afraid, tried to tell of Jesus, and the peace she had found in believing. It was all so new and her tongue so unused to explaining the things of the spirit, but the little girl looked up and smiled, and drew close to her.

"Will He hear me if I pray?" she whispered, and Kerry

bowed her head as the child whispered. "Oh God, make this ship stop rocking and make my mother well, and save us all please, and don't let there be a fire!"

The little girl crept away to the side of her mother and lay down, and Kerry looked around. Was there another she could tell? She knew that McNair had gone back to bring others to the deck. She knew that it might be only minutes before it would be forever too late and her heart burned within her.

Close beside her on the other side lay an old woman, wrapped in costly furs, her gray hair straggling around her drawn and frightened face. Kerry crept over to her and leaning down whispered, "Do you know Jesus?" The woman stared at her wildly for a moment and then answered with a moan.

"Oh, I used to! But I've been forgetting Him for years. Thank you for reminding me. I'll try to pray!" The haggard eyes closed and Kerry could see the pale lips were moving feebly.

Looking up, Kerry saw a weird grotesque figure with flapping shirt tails, furtively stealing along toward a life boat. No one else seemed to be watching him, and with almost uncanny strength he finally succeeded in swinging himself up and dropping into the life boat. Poor self-centered soul! All those helpless women and children about and he thought only of himself! Kerry found herself wondering if anyone had ever told him of Jesus, the Savior from Self.

Four hours they huddled there upon the deck, momently expecting death; while down in the hold the brave crew were working with blistered hands, blinded eyes, and singed faces, risking their lives to save the ship. And Graham McNair worked with the rest.

From time to time as he could be spared, the captain sent him up to the deck with messages, and at last there came a blessed relief when the captain himself, smoky and disheveled, came up to say the worst danger was over. The fire had been definitely quelled, and all precautions taken that it should not break out again. The leak also had been mended, at least temporarily, and all hands were now working to repair other damages that the storm had wrought.

He thanked them for their coöperation, and the quiet way in which most of them had obeyed orders, and he had a word of praise for McNair and a few others of the passengers who had come down and worked shoulder to shoulder with the ship's crew.

While he talked Kerry happened to be looking toward the life boat, and she saw Dawson's white face lifted above the edge looking down and listening. While the captain still lingered, smiling wearily about upon his big family of passengers, Kerry saw Dawson drop stealthily down from the life boat, linger behind the rigging for a moment stuffing in his shirt tails, and then come boldly down deck in his stocking feet toward the captain.

"Captain," he said in a voice quite unlike the one in which he had been screaming a few hours before, "what I'd like to ask is, When do we have something to eat? I've been across the Atlantic a good many times and I never had such treatment as this! We've all paid good money for our passage and service on the way, and we haven't had a bite to eat since last night at dinner. It's nearly time for dinner again. *When do we eat?*"

The captain faced Dawson with a grin, for in spite of having tucked in his shirt tails, Dawson still presented a grotesque appearance and seemed utterly unaware of it.

"Well, brother, suppose you go down in the kitchen and help the cook get up a meal? How about it? We've been fighting fire in the kitchen for the last ten hours, and the cook and all the helpers have had to help fight. Would you rather burn alive, man, or get good and hungry? However, I believe there's plenty of bread down there. Suppose you run down, and get an armful of buns and pass 'em around. How about it?"

A roar went around the deck which grew and rippled away

into mirth. The strain was broken. The tensity of hours was relaxed. The tired frightened people laughed. They laughed and laughed, and suddenly Dawson realized that they were laughing at him, and with a ghastly look of hate he turned and hurried away.

The laugh had done more than all words to reassure the frightened people, and little by little they began to get back to normal life again, and to notice their own appearance. They crept away to their rooms, and in an unexpectedly short time hot soup and bread and coffee were served to everybody, and all took courage.

10

SOMETIME in the night the wind changed, and the terrible waves grew calmer. When morning broke the clouds were lifting, and those who ventured out reported that the storm was over.

Kerry and McNair were among the first to go on deck.

They stood in a sheltered spot watching the majesty of the waves with their backs against a wall, and Kerry's hand firmly tucked under the young man's arm. Years of friendship seemed to be knit up between them, as they marveled over their great escape.

One by one as the sea grew calmer, the passengers crept out on deck and back to their steamer chairs. By noon most of the chairs were filled. The sun had come out, and people were sitting in the sunshine and beginning to smile again. It was rumored that if all went well they would reach New York the next day. Word had come by radio of disaster and storm all over that part of the sea. They realized that theirs had been a real escape.

The last to crawl out on deck, immaculate as to attire, sour as to expression, belligerent as to attitude, and peagreen as to color, especially around his mouth, was Henry Dawson, Ph.D.

There was no gratitude there. He had a personal grudge against the captain for the storm, for all the physical and mental pangs he had suffered, and the indignities he had endured. He was neither a good sailor nor a good sport. He argued that a ship ought to be prepared for emergencies, and there was no excuse whatever for a ship getting as far out of its course as this ship was, even in a storm. Such delay was inexcusable.

Kerry kept out of his way as much as possible, but whenever she lifted her eyes in his direction she seemed to feel his baleful glance upon her. There was something sinister about it that gave her an inward shudder. It was as if whenever he looked at her he was plotting something against her. That was silly of course. She must stop thinking about it. But how glad she would be when she was safely landed in New York and had that manuscript in the hands of the publisher!

That evening, that last evening on board, Dawson suddenly changed his tactics. He fairly haunted the steps of Kerry and McNair. He smirked and smiled, and made himself as affable to both of them as was in his naturally grumpy power to do.

Several times they shook him off on one pretext or another, only to find him appearing at another point as soon as they came on deck. He brought magazines to show them, he appeared on the scene with confectionery for Kerry, he even went so far as to attempt to carry her wooly bag for her, but she gripped it fiercely and declined his offer.

Finally he brought a steamer chair and settled down beside them, next to Kerry, much to her dismay. Whenever McNair talked to her he would cut in.

"Where are you going to be in New York, Miss Kavanaugh," he asked. "I'd like to take you out occasionally while I'm there. See a good show or dine at a roof garden, take in a few night clubs and that sort of thing, you know."

"Thank you," said Kerry, "I expect to be very busy while I'm there. I shall not have time to go out at all I'm afraid. My stay is a little uncertain, and I shall have every minute full."

"Oh, well, you have to eat, you know, and we can plan to take dinner wherever it will be convenient for you. All work and no play makes the proverbial Jack a dull boy, you know."

"Well, I'm afraid it will have to be dullness for me this time," said Kerry firmly but cheerfully.

"Well, where are you going to be located?" he asked point blank. "We surely can make some sort of a date after you find out what your engagements are to be."

"I'm not at all sure," evaded Kerry. "It depends on a number of things."

"Well, here," exulted Dawson eagerly, taking out a pencil and a card from his pocket, "let me suggest then. I know a wonderful stopping place, very reasonable in price and convenient to down town. I've stopped there sometimes myself, and the food is excellent. They have a very nice little orchestra—"

"Thank you," said Kerry coldly and let the card lie on her lap where he had dropped it.

"Let's take a turn on the deck, Miss Kavanaugh," said McNair suddenly, "I'm chilly, aren't you?"

Kerry arose with relief, and the address dropped to the floor, but Dawson hurried to restore it to her.

She took the paper with reluctant hand, and when they had walked near the railing she lifted her hand as if to drop it over the side in the darkness.

"Don't be so rash with that!" said McNair holding back her arm, "Dawson is coming on behind again, and besides, I'm not so sure but it might be as well to keep tabs on that bird. If he thinks you are going there he might turn up and have a rendezvous himself, and we might need to trace him. Suppose you let me keep that paper."

Kerry obediently handed it over to him.

"I'm sure the only use I could possibly have for it would be to keep as far away from that quarter as possible," laughed Kerry.

"Come this way, quick," said McNair, "I believe that fox is following us again. We'll double cross him this time, anyway."

And then when they succeeded in losing Dawson again he said:

"By the way, if I should ask that same impertinent question that our friend the Ph.D. asked would you freeze me too?"

"Oh, no," said Kerry laughing, feeling a choking sensation of tears behind her laughter, for she realized all too keenly that this was the last night of the voyage. "Oh, no! I would tell you the truth. I haven't the slightest idea where I'm going. I don't know any place to go. I haven't been in New York since I was seven years old. There was an old friend of father's, a lawyer, in New York, and I have his old address, but I haven't an idea if he is even still living. Then of course there is the publisher— I could ask him where was a respectable place."

His hand tightened a little on her arm as it rested in his.

"Who is your publisher?"

Kerry told him.

"Well, wouldn't it be better for your business to have an address you could give them when you first arrived?"

"I suppose it would," said Kerry humbly. "I really hadn't thought much about it. It seemed so unimportant until I got the manuscript safely placed and out of my hands."

"Of course," said McNair. "But you see it is important to me. I hope to be in town for a couple of weeks before I move on to other appointments. Not that I would suggest shows or night clubs as a recreation, but I would like to take you to hear one or two good concerts, and perhaps to a meeting or two if any of the great speakers I know are in town just now. But perhaps you wouldn't have time for such things either."

Kerry's eyes shone.

"I'm afraid," she said demurely, "I'm afraid I would have time for almost anything of that sort, even if I *hadn't* the time."

"Well, then, might I humbly suggest a place where I am sure you would find comfort?"

"That would be most kind," said Kerry, "but,—I'll have to tell you the truth. It would have to be a very cheap place indeed. I haven't got much money, and I can't take time to look for a job until I get this manuscript safely out of my hands. I may have to do a little more work on it. My father suggested certain things to the publisher and if they want any changes there might be a few more days' work before I would be free."

"I see," said McNair. "Well, the place I would suggest would be about as cheap as anything decent you could get in the city I think. It is a little old-fashioned house, in a very un-fashionable street, and the little old lady who lives there stays because she loves her old house, though the neighborhood has changed and is mostly commercial all about her. It would not however be far out of the region of your publisher."

"Oh, that would be wonderful!" said Kerry with a great relief. "I am so sick of hotels. And to be somewhere that I could trust people would be next to heaven for me. I am frightened at the idea of a new city, although I ought not to be for I have knocked around the world a great deal in my short life."

"Well, you can trust old Martha Scott. She used to be a servant for my mother before she was married, one of the real gentlewoman type of old-fashioned servants. She came over from Scotland in her youth, and went out to service, and when she came to my mother she had been having hard experiences. But she adored Mother, and seemed to think she had found the nearest spot to heaven that could be had. She will gladly do anything in the world for you when she knows I sent you there. She makes a kind of little idol out of our family, the reflected glory from my mother I fancy."

Kerry looked wistfully up at the tall form beside her in the darkness.

"That would be wonderful for me," she said. Then more hesitantly, "your mother, is she—?"

"My mother is with the Lord!" The young man said it joyously. "If she were here I would take you to her as fast as ever I could get you there, She would love you, I know, and mother you. But she will be among those who will come to meet us when we are caught up to meet the Lord in the air!"

The wonder of his words, the tone in which he spoke, and the intimate way in which he spoke of herself, all combined to thrill Kerry as she never had been thrilled before. There seemed no words wherewith to answer but at last she spoke:

"You make me feel that life is a very different thing from what I thought it. You bring the other world quite close and you take the hardness out of the hard things here. I shall never cease to be thankful for what you have taught me."

"There are a great many stars out to-night!" announced Dawson's flat voice as he suddenly appeared in the offing.

McNair's finger tightened on the hand he was holding.

"Yes," he said rising, "the stars are out, and we were just going in. Going to be a strenuous day tomorrow, you know. Had a strenuous day yesterday too. Good night!" and McNair and Kerry drifted away together.

"Oh, say!" said Dawson quickening his steps behind them, "I came up to say that I made a mistake about that number. It was forty-three fifteen, not forty-two. Let me have the card, Miss Kavanaugh, and I'll correct it."

"Oh, that's all right, Mr. Dawson," said Kerry sweetly. "I can remember that. Forty-three fifteen you say. All right. Thank you. Good night!" and Kerry vanished down the companionway.

"The poor fish!" said McNair as he escorted her down her own corridor, "does he really think you're going there, do you suppose, or is he just inventing excuses to annoy us?"

"I think he takes you for another scientist," laughed Kerry.

"Well, I suppose we can't steal out on him again tonight, can we? Then suppose we come out early and have a little time together before he is up. How early will you be out?"

Kerry made all her simple preparations for landing, that night, and was ready at the hour appointed.

McNair led her to a lofty place, and in the rose and pearl of a new day they looked upon a sea as sparkling and blue as a quiet mountain lake. One would never dream that so short a time ago it had risen like a giant monster high above the ship threatening to swallow it. It seemed incredible that it should lie before them now sparkling like a summer morning.

All too swiftly the brief moments fled. Breakfast was a thing to be considered, too. And they were coming into traffic now, the traffic of the seas. A fine excitement pervaded the whole ship. People passed them and smiled, called joyously to one another, as their boat limped into harbor.

After breakfast they climbed once more high above the deck where most of the other passengers were gathering and watched the sky line of New York grow out of the sparkle of the morning.

Kerry had packed the few things she would need at once in the old bag in which she had taken her precious books to the book shop. Her trunk had been carried away, and she had only the bag and her brief case for baggage. She had, of course, taken the manuscript out of its oilskin wrappings, and it was neatly wrapped in paper, ready to be presented to the publishers, for she hoped to have it safely in their hands before another night should pass.

Kerry and McNair were among the last to leave the ship, for they lingered aloft till the last minute, loth to bring their happy morning to a close.

"I wonder where friend Dawson is," said McNair, looking back toward the cabin. "We seem to have been altogether successful in escaping him this morning."

Just then he caught a glimpse of his sinister face, peering out of a doorway. He vanished at once.

"Wait here a second," said McNair, "I'd like to see what that bird's up to."

He was back in little more than the promised second grinning. "You didn't leave any valuable papers in your stateroom did you?"

"Not a scrap," said Kerry confidently.

"Well, he's going to make sure anyway. He's just sneaked in there, and is poking among some trash the stewardess has left outside. I still have a feeling that he has something up his sleeve somewhere. I wish I knew his idea. But perhaps he is still looking for the lost article, and is afraid to ask the steward."

It did not take much time to pass the customs, for McNair had courtesy of the port, and rushed the business through, and it was obvious at once that Kerry was not smuggling anything in her little shabby trunk with its still shabbier contents. As they had waited until toward the last, the way would have been comparatively free, had it not been that a record-making ship arrived at that very hour on the other side of their dock, and a great crowd swarmed out to meet it.

McNair's nice calculations to wait until the crowd were gone were quite in vain. The people were packed closely and it was almost impossible to move.

McNair insisted on taking Kerry's bag, added to his own bags, leaving her nothing but her brief case to carry. He kept her protected as much as possible from the crowd as they made slow progress toward the outside world. Once McNair looked back and saw Dawson stretching his neck, and finally jumping upon a box and looking over the heads of the crowd as if he were searching for some one. He turned away quickly not to catch his eye, and he and Kerry edged slowly along.

Kerry's brief case was hugged closely under her arm, her hand slipped through the leather handle. As the crowd pressed close, suddenly from the side away from McNair she felt a pull and the strap gave way in her hand.

Clutching wildly as a group of people came between herself and her companion, she felt the brief case wrenched away from her, but when she turned and cried out she saw only an indifferent crowd of hurrying people who resented her blocking their way.

An instant more and McNair was by her side again, staring above the surging crowed, his face intent, angry!

"Take these!" he said and dropped the bags at her feet. Before she could speak he was gone.

She saw him take his two hands and part the crowd to right and left and dive in. Then the mob closed in and she could see nothing more. The bags lay at her feet and people were stumbling over them.

She realized that she could do nothing but stay right in that spot. The terrible realization that her precious manuscript was gone surged over her like one of those great waves that had covered the ship. For an instant it seemed that she must just sink down right there where she was and give up. What was there left to live for if she had lost her father's book? True, she had the notes safely hidden away in her trunk, but who knew but that the same diabolical brain that had planned to slash the handle of her brief case and snatch it away from her in the crowd had also somehow gained access to her trunk after it left her stateroom!

There she stood with the bags at her feet, on her face utter despair, knocked about at the mercy of the crowd like a leaf in a storm, and feeling as if the very foundations of the earth were rocking under her feet. Lost, lost, lost! To think she had carried the manuscript all the way across the ocean, and protected it so carefully, only to lose it at the last minute, as she was almost at her destination! How could she ever forgive herself and go on living? She felt as if she had failed her father in the great trust he had laid upon her!

And now if the book ever came out for the world to see, it would come under another's name, and her father would be forgotten! Or, worse still, the book itself might be mutilated, changed, made to bring a false message instead of the one her father had labored his whole life to finish!

These thoughts like bright swords rushed through her

heart backwards and forwards without mercy. They surged into her brain with sharp bright pains. They cut through her eyes when she tried to strain her vision to see what had become of McNair, and they choked in her throat and seemed to smother her. For a minute or two it seemed to her she was going to crumple right down on the dock and let the wild horde of sight seers trample over her. For this disaster that had befallen her seemed the culmination of all her troubles. Death, her mother's disloyalty, poverty, nothing had daunted her. But now she had surely reached the limit. This was dishonor, to have failed her father in the trust he had left her!

As the crowd knocked her this way and that in their mad scramble to get nearer the great record-making ship, she began to wonder how long she could stand the buffeting. Her feet were very tired; strange they had not felt so when she stood so long on deck watching the harbor entrance. Her back was aching too. Oh, it was nerves of course! Even now the tears, silly tears, were stinging in her eyes. She could not let them ride down her face. What would the crowd think of her standing there and crying like a baby!

She tried to gather the bags into smaller compass, tried even to stand on her own to see if she could catch a glimpse of McNair somewhere. Oh, why had he left her like that? Of course he must have seen some one snatch that brief case, but how futile to run after a thief in a crowd like that! If he had only said some little word—! But of course he did not have time.

Then she began to torment herself with questions. He had not told her to stand still. Perhaps he expected her to follow. But a glance at the bags told her that was foolish. He would know she could not carry them all, and there was not a sign of a porter about. All porters and service of every kind was centered over there by that new arrival.

She glanced back at the ship she had just left, but already it had an alien air. There were no familiar faces on the decks.

Even if there had been she could not get to them. Besides she must stay right here in this spot.

But suppose McNair never came back. Suppose after she had waited hours he did not come. Suppose he had been run over, and nobody knew him, and he should be killed—!

And now she could feel the tears really coming in such a choking flood that she knew she must do something to stop them or she would be a sight to gaze upon indeed.

It was just when the tears almost got the better of her that she suddenly remembered that she had a new Source of strength and why should she despair? Why had she not drawn upon it in her trouble? She had a Father who was Lord of all the earth. Even now He knew what had become of her suit case. He was able to take care of it much better than she had done. He was able to care for McNair also. If she could trust her heavenly Father with herself, her life, her beloved dead, could she not trust Him now with a few earthly possessions?

She drew a deep breath and closed her eyes, and her breath was a prayer. "Heavenly Father, help me to trust you now. Do what you will with me and mine."

She opened her eyes.

The crowd still jostled her. Her feet were still weary and her back still ached. The brief case was still gone, and McNair was gone, but her horrible burden was gone too. She was God's and right here was her chance to show that she trusted Him.

A little old lady crushed against her, pushed by two rough looking men who were trying to get nearer the ship. She stumbled over Kerry's bag, and fell down. She would have hit her head against a post had not Kerry caught her, and lifted her.

The old woman was crying. She put up withered hands and wiped the tears away with a coarse cotton handkerchief. Kerry could feel her tremble as she held her.

"Did you get hurt?" asked the girl kindly.

"Naw, Miss, not hurt exactly, but I'm all of a crumple. You see I ben terrable wore out, worryin' about my boy. He's one o' the crew on that there ship, an' the radios on the streets ben sayin' the boat was lost, and now she's come I had ta come and see my boy, and they won't even let me get near."

"Oh," said Kerry sympathetically, "that's hard, but I'm sure if you wait the crowd will go away sometime. Stay here by me for a little till there is a way through."

"You're very kind," said the old woman wiping her eyes nervously, "did you come down to see the ship come in too?"

"No, I came in on the other boat, the one on this side," said Kerry trying to speak cheerfully.

"And was you out in the storm?" asked the woman.

"Yes, we had a terrible time," she answered, "but—we got through it. And there—see! The crowd is moving away. I think if you would go through there now, you might get near. I'd go with you but I have to stay here by the baggage till my friend comes."

"Oh, you've got a friend," said the old woman wistfully, "that's nice! A pretty little buddy like you ought to have a friend. Well, good-by. You ben a good friend ta me. Ef you hadn'ta caught me I'd a ben tramped to death. There! There's an opening, I'll be going."

She slipped away like a little black wraith and Kerry turned back to her own anxiety again.

The crowd was indeed thinning at last but there was no sign of McNair anywhere. Kerry looked at her watch and saw that it was a full half hour since he had left her. Oh, what had become of him, and where was her precious manuscript?

II

WHEN McNair saw that hand with an open knife steal around behind Kerry and cut the leather strap that went around her wrist he had both hands full, two bags of his own, a suit case and Kerry's bag. He tried to shout but everybody else was shouting and the sound was snatched from his throat and ended in a weird croak.

It was impossible to identify the hand that snatched the bag in that dense crowd, but McNair instantly dropped the bags at Kerry's side, and dashed in the direction he had last seen the brief case, frenzied for the girl whose fortune had been stolen from her, right before his eyes. It seemed incredible with all the care they had taken, and all they had come through, that it was really gone. Yet he hesitated not an instant, hopeless as his mission seemed to be.

Of course the hand that took that brief case might have belonged to any common thief, but McNair was looking for a sleek black head, wearing a steamer cap of tweed, and a dark gray overcoat with a London cut.

He was conscious of being thankful that the dock had a limited width, and there were no spaces at the side where thieves might disappear. He was also glad that he was tall and could look well over the heads of the crowd.

As he lunged on keeping a sharp lookout to right and left, he wondered whether Kerry had heard him. Would she have understood? Had she realized the loss of her brief case yet herself? Would she stand still and look after that baggage as he had told her in his haste, or would she walk on and leave it behind, not realizing that it was there? Well, it could not be helped. The manuscript was the main thing. It must be saved if everything else was lost.

And perhaps the thief would double on his tracks and return to the ship, or hide somewhere! McNair's heart was pounding hard with the intensity of his excitement, and his breath was coming fast.

Then he sighted Dawson stalking ahead of him, not even running, carrying a brown brief case under his arm nonchalantly just as if he had carried it all the days of his life.

He was a full rod ahead and not looking back, but he was making good time. McNair wondered if he dared just walk up to Dawson and charge him with stealing a brief case. What was he going to say when he overtook Dawson, provided Dawson did not manage some uncanny get-away before he reached him?

McNair was almost within hailing distance of Dawson when a couple of large trucks drove out to the wharf. The crowd parted to let them pass, and McNair barely got out of their way in time, but Dawson slipped out of sight behind them, and seemed to be nowhere when they were passed. However, McNair strode on. He must cover the distance to the street as fast as possible. Once there he could call a policeman.

But he went on till he reached the station and ticket offices before he got another glimpse of Dawson swinging through the revolving door. McNair was after him instantly, and nearly caught him as he went through the opposite door to the street, but a crowd of incoming travelers got between them again, and Dawson was out in the street hailing a taxi-cab before McNair had a chance to get through the door himself.

The cab had arrived and Dawson was just about to enter it when turning he caught sight of McNair and wheeling to the right ducked behind a big oil tank truck and was off again, the brief case still tucked firmly under his arm.

How long McNair continued that race, how far they went, how many corners they turned he was never quite sure, but he was nearly winded and Dawson in spite of his shorter legs was a half a block ahead when at last a fire engine crossed Dawson's path, with a hook and ladder truck, and an ambulance close behind, and for the instant he was penned in. He turned this way, and ducked that, and almost got killed trying to get between two cars, but just as he thought he had lost him, McNair still running and panting, his arms waving wildly, ran full into the arms of a burly policeman.

"Catch!" he yelled. "Catch that man quick! He's stolen—that brief case!"

The policeman waited not to hear more, he was off like a flash, and the next instant, Dawson Ph.D. found himself confronted with the law, stalwart and grim.

Dawson stepped back in well-feigned amazement.

"I beg your pardon, sir, what is all this about?" he demanded as the policeman laid a detaining hand on his well groomed shoulder.

And then McNair arrived.

"He has taken a lady's brief case," stated McNair between gasps as he tried to steady his voice.

Dawson looked up at him amusedly, though he was white as a sheet and his little black eyes had a frightened look.

"Brief case?" he said, "Oh, brief case? My brief case?" and he laughed his hard little cackle. "Why, bless my soul! It's McNair! Why, hello, old man! Glad to see you!"

Then to the policeman:

"I beg your pardon, sir, this gentleman knows me. We have

just come off the same ship together. He knows who I am. This is my own brief case, an old one, that I have carried with me on my travels abroad. I presume he has followed the wrong man, not recognizing me. How's that, McNair? Good joke? What's the matter? Somebody lost a brief case? Can I help in the search?"

But McNair did not smile. His eye was on the brief case, and a glint of triumph was in it.

"Do you know this gentleman?" asked the policeman, eyeing the two men cannily.

"I know who he says he is," said McNair, his voice now back almost to its natural tone, "but if that is your brief case, Dawson, how does it come to have its handle slashed through with a fresh cut of a knife?"

The policeman scanned the leather handle.

"Oh!" laughed Dawson easily, "that happened in Algeria. I was—"

"Just wait a minute, Dawson," said McNair authoritatively, "if that is your brief case how comes it that Miss Kavanaugh's green silk shawl is inside of it?"

And at that same instant the policeman's wary eye caught the gleam of a long green silk strand of fringe hanging out through the tongue of the brief case.

Dawson's eyes went fearfully down to the condemning thread.

"Why, the idea!" he stuttered, "that's only a bit of a thread—off of somebody's clothes,"—and he tried to brush it away. But the thread did not yield. Instead a second thread came greenly out to testify against him.

"Why, my dear fellow!" said Dawson Ph.D. "I really don't understand this. How could I possibly have picked up another brief case instead of mine? I was sure I had my own. Now, what do you think of that! I must have left my own on the ship. I'll have to hurry right back—" and he turned and made as if to slip away in the opposite direction. But the heavy hand of the law was upon him, and upon the brief case which he carried.

"No, you don't!" said the policeman, "I'll just take a little hand in this myself. Suppose this other gent here tells what he knows about it all. He was the guy that was follerin' you!"

"But my dear sir—!" began Dawson.

"That'll be about all from you at present!" said the representative of the law. "How come it, Mister?" to McNair.

"I was walking with the owner of the brief case when it happened. She had the case under her arm. We were coming off the ship that just docked, pier 12. A hand came out of the crowd and cut that handle which was round her wrist, and another hand jerked the case from under her arm, and the thief ducked behind the crowd and disappeared. I dropped my baggage and followed, and that man has crossed and recrossed streets, and ducked under trucks and cabs and cars and turned corners and double crossed himself all the way up here. He knew perfectly well I was after him. He's been trying to get hold of the contents of that brief case all the way across the Atlantic. If you don't believe me come back to the dock with me and ask the steward of the ship, and ask the lady that owns the brief case. She's waiting for me down there now, right where it happened."

"Come on with me!" said the man of the law, grasping the sleeve of the would-be scientist.

"Why, certainly!" said Dawson Ph.D. affably. "Of course I'll go with you. I certainly am sorry to have caused Miss Kavanaugh all this trouble. You see I must have picked up that brief case on deck when it was laid down, instead of my own and Miss Kavanaugh probably has mine. I shall be glad indeed if it was mine that was stolen instead of hers, for mine had very unimportant matters in it, a few photographs and some notes of articles I meant to write, nothing but what I could easily duplicate."

The policeman said nothing but hailed a cab, and put Dawson in it, motioned McNair to follow, and gave an order to the driver. On the way down he hailed a fellow officer and added him to the party.

Dawson, after the first block, managed a superior smile, and attempted a feeble conversation with McNair, but the police interrupted:

"Got a knife in yer cloes?"

"Knife?" said Dawson innocently.

"Never mind, don't bother, I'll find it," and a burly hand went investigating in Dawson's pockets.

"Oh, yes, knife. Why of course, I always carry a knife."

The knife came to light. A wicked blade, delicately sharp. The policeman snapped it open and played a tough finger over its edge. He lifted a knowing eye and winked toward McNair who was watching him. Then he snapped the blade shut and stowed it away in his judicial pockets.

Dawson settled back with a pleased smile as though he were enjoying the ride.

"Where did you leave Miss Kavanaugh, McNair?" he asked after another two blocks.

McNair affected not to hear him. He was wondering whether Kerry would be where he had left her, or whether after all this time she might not have somehow managed to park the baggage and start after him herself. Women did queer things sometimes, when they were frantic, and Kerry had reason to be frantic. It must be a full hour since he had left her. And would the steward still be on the boat, or gone out into the city on leave?

Five minutes later the taxi had threaded its way through the congested traffic and left its party at the wharf.

McNair hastened ahead, and so it happened that as Kerry searched the wharf where now the crowds were beginning to thin out she caught sight at last of McNair, with Dawson coming on behind escorted by two burly policemen, walking with measured tread one on each side of him.

As soon as he caught sight of her McNair lifted the brief case like a banner and waved it above his head, and she got the effect of his smile even while he was some paces off.

Kerry was standing where he had left her in a little oasis from which the crowd was cleared, her bags at her feet, and when she saw McNair she waved her hand. Oh, it was good to see him again after the long wait, to know that he had not been run down in the New York traffic, to know he was coming back again. Whatever came, whether the lost were found or not, it was good to see him.

And could it be that he had really found it, the precious book, or was it only the empty brief case from which the contents had been taken?

Then she saw Dawson and began to hope. If they had Dawson, he hadn't been able to get away with the papers yet. Still, he was cunning. There was no telling but he had thrown it away somewhere. And perhaps McNair didn't know she had the manuscript there. He might have thought she had packed it in her trunk.

As soon as Dawson saw her he made a show of haste, donned an apologetic air, and came smiling up.

"I have a great apology to make," he smirked, rubbing his hands in a way that reminded Kerry of Uriah Heep. "I must—have—somehow—in the confusion on deck at the last minute picked up your brief case instead of my own. It was most careless of me, but they are exactly alike, and I don't wonder at my mistake."

Kerry looked at him levelly. Was it possible this man expected her to believe that?

"That couldn't have been possible, Mr. Dawson," said Kerry going straight to the point. "I haven't had my brief case out of my hands since I left my stateroom this morning until it was snatched from me a little over an hour ago right here in this spot."

"Well then, my dear lady," began Dawson eagerly, "they

must have got exchanged last night somehow. It must have been my brief case that you had and they snatched it from you. But it's of no importance, I'm glad to tell you, only photographs and notes of my trip. I'd be glad to have them back of course, but nothing that really mattered."

"Mr. Dawson, that is not possible," said Kerry again looking him straight in his frightened eyes. "I arranged my things in my brief case this very morning before I left my stateroom. I know exactly what is in there. A package of manuscript wrapped in white paper and fastened with rubber bands, two manila envelopes containing other papers, a map of New York that I got on ship board, and my green silk shawl."

Dawson's shifty eyes looked furtively toward the policeman, but his smile grew even more fixed.

"Well, there's some mistake somewhere of course," he said, rubbing his hands anxiously, "perhaps my own case is still on ship board. I'll just run back and see, if you'll excuse me."

He turned and would have left them, but a big hand clamped down upon his shoulder.

"Just a minute, sir, till the lady sees if all her property is in the case. Then if youse wants to go back on the boat we'll go with you. Will you open the case, Miss?"

Kerry, with hands that trembled from sudden new anxiety unstrapped her brief case and examined it, pulling out the green silk shawl and slinging it over her shoulder, where it blew about her gallantly and showed in contrast the delicate features, and the red-gold hair.

"You're looking awfully well this morning, Miss Kavanaugh," observed Dawson in a wild attempt to keep up his rôle of intimacy. The rest of the party stood like stone images watching Kerry as she took out one by one the things she had named and began to count the pages of the manuscript.

"I don't imagine he had any time to disturb the pages yet," said McNair quietly; "he had all he could do to get away with it."

When she was sure it was all there Kerry looked up and smiled brightly at McNair.

"Oh, I can't be thankful enough to you," she said, ignoring the rest, and speaking just to him, "it—was—so terrible, when I thought it was gone!"

The policemen stood stolidly, pretending to look away, but they did not miss a glint of the sun on her bright gold hair, nor a turn of an eyelash. They could have pictured to a fraction the light in McNair's eyes as he smiled back at her.

"Well, now I certainly am glad!" said Dawson rubbing his hands the harder, "I certainly should have felt bad if anything of yours had been lost through my carelessness!"

"Do you wish this man detained?" asked the officer grimly.

"Oh, no!" said Kerry eagerly, as if the quicker he got away the better she would like it.

"Well, then I'll just run back to the ship and see if my brief case is still where I know I had it this morning," agreed Dawson cheerfully. "It isn't of much consequence of course, but I might as well get it while I'm down here. Good morning. I'll look you up again!" and he tipped his hat as airily as if he had just rescued her from trouble and was glad to be able to do it.

"Can you beat it?" said McNair looking after the dapper little scientist. "If you could see the chase he led me, scuttling around corners exactly like a rat, you would scarcely believe he was the same person!"

"Oh, but to think you caught him! How did you know it was he? Did you see him take it?"

"Well, not exactly, but I knew about what to look for, and when I caught up with him your shawl did the rest of the trick, hanging out some fringe for identification. But come. Let's get out of here before the poor little rat comes back and tries to track us elsewhere. What luck! Here comes a porter. I thought they were all dead! Now, may I have the honor of carrying that brief case the rest of the way, or have you reached the point that you can't trust any human being except yourself?"

"I can't trust myself, certainly," said Kerry. "I wouldn't have believed that anyone could get that case out of my grasp. It seems incredible even now."

He put her into a taxi and got in beside her.

"Now, where to?" he asked her. "Hadn't we better park these bags at the Pennsylvania station and get you right to the publisher's before the place closes for the afternoon?"

"Oh, yes, if that's possible. But I must not detain you any longer. I have given you trouble enough already."

"You don't mean to say you are going to try to shake me now after all this. No, lady, no, I'm bound to see this manuscript safe in the hands of the publisher, and you with a properly signed receipt for it before I leave you again."

"You are very good to me, and you must be awfully tired," sighed Kerry leaning back and drawing a long sigh of relief.

"Well, I guess you are pretty tired yourself," he smiled, "but you can't be any gladder than I am that this incident has ended so well."

While they waited at the publisher's for Kerry's letter of introduction to be sent up to the great man with whom Shannon Kavanaugh had corresponded, Kerry told him about her own feelings when she had been left alone with the knowledge that the manuscript was gone; and how it suddenly came to her in her despair that her heavenly Father was looking after her, and she need not worry.

"And He did!" she said with a gleam of exultation in her eyes.

"He always does," said McNair gravely. "I have a friend over in London who sent me a little card last Christmas bearing these verses: 'Cast all your care upon Him for He careth for you.' 'And the Peace of God which passeth all understanding shall keep your hearts and minds through Christ Jesus.' And underneath he has put it this way: 'Put your care into His heart and He will put His peace into yours.'"

Then McNair told her of his race.

"If I were you," he said, "I would tell your publisher all about it, let him know that some one else is trying to get a line on the book and use it. You can't tell what that little rat may do even yet. He seems quite determined to get something out of this for himself. I wouldn't put it past him even now to write that article. You had better leave the stolen pages and Dawson's paraphrase of them with the publisher. It will be safer than with you."

"I will," said Kerry, "thank you." Just then the boy came to say that the publisher awaited her, and Kerry took her precious manuscript and went to audience at last, thinking on the way how wonderful it was that she had found him in and could see him right away. It was going to be so good to get that manuscript out of her keeping. Was this, too, a part of God's keeping? But of course it was. She felt like shouting her gratitude.

12

RIPLEY Holbrook received Kerry most cordially. He showed at once his deep respect for Shannon Kavanaugh, and he looked at Kerry as kindly as if she had been his own daughter.

He was an oldish man with gray hair and keen eyes. He received the manuscript as something long awaited and much desired. Kerry found herself warmed and comforted by his manner. She had perhaps entertained just the least little bit of doubt whether after all the publishers would be so eager for the book now that her father was gone. But there was no doubt about that any more. The book was greatly welcomed.

After Mr. Holbrook had asked in detail of her father's last days, and expressed his sympathy in her loneliness, he went over carefully every item mentioned in Shannon Kavanaugh's letter that Kerry had brought, agreeing gladly to it all, as in substance he had agreed by letter six months ago.

He called his secretary and gave her directions for typing a special contract.

"Are you in a hurry to go, Miss Kavanaugh, or could you wait and attend to the signing now? Of course it will do to-morrow as well, or any time in the near future that is convenient, but I like to get these preliminaries over."

"I would rather wait, Mr. Holbrook," said Kerry, "I've had a good deal of trouble getting this manuscript safely into your hands, and I would like to feel that the responsibility is entirely over."

"Trouble?" asked Holbrook, turning over the pages and glancing interestedly at a diagram that caught his eye.

Then Kerry told him of her experiences with Dawson, both on sea and land.

He listened, watching her keenly as she talked, drawing his brows in a frown as the story proceeded, studying carefully the stolen page, and Dawson's caricature of it which she handed him, making occasional notes on a pad that lay on his desk.

"Dawson? Dawson? Henry Dawson did you say was his name? Seems to me I remember that name!" he said when Kerry's story drew to a close with the incident on the dock that morning.

Then turning to his secretary he said: "Miss Reeves, look up my file on Henry Dawson. Ph.D. did you say, Miss Kavanaugh?"

The secretary ran through her filing case and brought out papers.

"There was a Henry Dawson connected with that trouble we had on the Graves-Ransom copyright," said the secretary after a moment's perusal of the papers.

"Ah! Yes, I thought that name was familiar! That was a very peculiar case. We never were quite sure—Well, I'm glad you mentioned it. We'll look out for the current scientific publications. These papers will be helpful in case there is any trouble. But of course, now we know it we can easily forestall any such trouble as we had before. I'll get in touch with the lawyer in our office and get more data on this man. Be assured we will protect your rights fully. Miss Reeves, see that Miss Kavanaugh has a duly signed receipt for this manuscript, and have it put in our safe at once!" he ordered.

"And now, Miss Kavanaugh, where are you stopping?" he asked.

"Well, I'm not quite sure yet. I came straight here to get that manuscript out of my hands at once," said Kerry with a long breath of relief. "I did not know what might happen next."

"You certainly deserve great credit for guarding it so faithfully. We are greatly in your debt, and I expect shall be more so before we are done. I notice your father delegates you to correct all proof, and advise with us regarding any matter relating to the book. I hope you are not going to be far away. We want to rush this book right through. It is to both your and our advantage to get it on the market with all possible speed while your father's work and personality are still in the minds of the people."

"I am hoping to secure a room not far away," said Kerry, "a friend on the ship knows of a convenient place. I shall let you know my address as soon as I am sure I can be accommodated."

"That is very good!" said Holbrook, "and shall you be at leisure to come and help us as soon as we are ready?"

"Why, yes," hesitated Kerry, "I'm going to look for some kind of a job at once. I—really—must. But I thought perhaps I could do whatever you need done in the evenings. Would that be possible?"

"A job?" said Holbrook. "Well, why not, perhaps in our office? Your father recommends you so highly that I am sure you would be an asset in any office. I'll speak to our manager and see if there is any chance of a vacancy. It really would be good to have you right at hand if this work is to be rushed through. At least I am sure we could give you something temporary until we are through with the book, and then perhaps find you something better if there isn't anything fitted for you here."

"Oh, that would be wonderful!" said Kerry, hardly able to believe that her way was to be so smooth after the trouble through which she had come. It filled her with the greater joy because she knew it was being done for her great father's sake. It thrilled her to be with those who respected him so much and did not try to minimize his talents as her mother had always done.

McNair, in the outer office where she had left him, watched Kerry come out at last, her eyes shining, her cheeks glowing, her bright hair curling about her face, and thought what a pearl of a girl she was.

He watched her as she came slowly down the long room between the rows of desks and busy workers, talking as she came to the grave keen business man who walked beside her and was obviously pleased with her. He rejoiced that she had found sympathy with her publisher. He knew the hard world so well that he had feared perhaps she was too hopeful.

Kerry looked up as she came to the bench where McNair waited. How easily she seemed to know just what to do. How well she comported herself in spite of her shyness. What a rare father she must have had—or a mother. He suddenly realized that she had not mentioned her mother. Was she dead perhaps?

Then Kerry reached his side and said:

"Mr. Holbrook, I want you to know Mr. McNair, the friend who so kindly recovered the manuscript for me this morning."

Then indeed McNair got a keen glance from Holbrook's eyes. He shook hands heartily, looking deep into the younger man's eyes as he spoke, as if sifting him to see if he were worthy.

"We certainly are deeply indebted to you also, Mr. McNair," said the publisher. "If Shannon Kavanaugh's last book had been lost to our house we would never have ceased to regret it. I am glad to meet you."

When they were out in the taxicab again they beamed like two children.

"Well, he seems to be the real thing in publishers as far as I can judge," said McNair heartily.

"Why, he was just wonderful!" said Kerry, shining-eyed like a child telling her joys. McNair wanted to kiss her again, but somehow he didn't dare. This was not a lonely corridor on the ship, the terrible storm was over, and death was no longer imminent. This was a different Kerry, this shining-eyed, successful daughter of a great man who had just signed her father's contract.

"He made the royalty five cents larger than they had promised father, and he is going to send me a check for advance royalty as soon as they have read the manuscript," went on Kerry eagerly. "I have the contract here. Read it and see what it says."

McNair glanced through it and saw that it was altogether fair, as he had expected it to be, coming from that company whose name stood high among the world's best publishers.

"And, oh, I forgot! I've got a job!" laughed Kerry childishly. "They're going to give me work right there in the office for a while, at least till the book is done, and if I make good I think from what he said I can stay."

"Well, I should say your fortune was made," answered McNair happily. "I'm glad of that. I hated to see you running around New York day after day, week after week, hunting a job, the way many a girl has to do. I meant to look up something for you myself among some of my friends, but now I see my offices are not needed."

"Well, you certainly have done enough," said Kerry, "I never can thank you for all you have done."

"Don't try, please," said McNair with one of his rare smiles that said more than words. And then as the taxi drew up in front of a dignified building he added:

"Now, we're going to have dinner. I wonder if you are as hungry as I am. This place is a favorite haunt of mine. They usually have pretty good stuff here."

"Hungry?" said Kerry. "Of course I am, but—you shouldn't have brought me to a place like this."

"This is my treat!" said McNair. "We've vanquished the enemy and now we have a right to celebrate," and he led her into a great beautiful quiet dining room where obsequious waiters hastened to make them at home.

"Here, at last," said McNair as he took the card the waiter handed him, and prepared to be at ease, "I think we are free from Dawson for a little while."

Such a happy time as they had, eating and talking and laughing together. McNair told her a little of his own life. His business had called for a good deal of traveling, but he hoped within another four or five months to be able to settle down and have a real home again which he had not had for the past three years. He had business in New York that would keep him for a few days and then he was due for a trip to California that might hold him for weeks. It had to do with large contracts, and the opening of a new office in the West with a new Manager, whom he must install and oversee until the work was running right. But meantime, he meant to make the best of his time in New York and help her to get acquainted with the city, if she would let him.

Kerry's delight said plainly that she was all too willing to let him. Kerry felt that she had never been so happy. She wondered if it was right to be as happy as she was.

They talked too, of sweet and holy things, and Kerry said she had a lot of questions she wanted to ask him when she had them thought out clearly in her mind.

"By the way," said McNair as they reluctantly tore themselves away from the quiet room, "I took the liberty of telephoning my Mrs. Scott while you were talking to your publisher. She said she had the second story front room that was just vacated yesterday and she would be delighted to have you for as long as you wanted to stay. Would you like to go there and rest for a little while, and then would you care to go out and see the town a bit, perhaps go to some good music if I can find any? Or are you too tired? Perhaps you would rather wait until another day."

"Oh," said Kerry ecstatically, "I'm really not tired. I'm so relieved and happy! But indeed, I couldn't let you do anything more for me. You've done already far too much."

"Then you do something for me," he smiled, "make me have a pleasant evening. I'll be just out and out lonely if you don't take mercy on me."

"Well, then I will," laughed Kerry.

So they stopped at the station and got their bags, and he took her to the old-fashioned house in the busy business district, tucked down town in quite an unfashionable place, but fine and clean and comfortable, in spite of the faded old furniture. Mrs. Scott proved to be a motherly soul, and welcomed Kerry as though she had been longing for her all her life. She tried to make McNair come in and stay but he said he had mail waiting for him at the hotel and must go and see what new developments there were. So he went away, promising to have Kerry's trunk sent at once, and to return himself before eight o'clock.

Kerry lay down without any idea of sleeping. She was too excited to even close her eyes, she thought. But when the trunk arrived a little before six o'clock it waked her out of a sound sleep, and she jumped up not knowing where she was.

When Kerry unlocked her trunk and hung her small shabby wardrobe in the closet she felt at home. From the big windows of the old brown stone building she looked down to the busy street in the early evening and was interested in all the hurrying people going to their homes. New York seemed a dear friendly place. Graham McNair was coming pretty soon to take her out. It would be the first time in her young life that a young man had ever taken her out in the evening. How strange, how wonderful it was going to be!

She put on her little evening frock. It was the only "dress-up" she had, and she brushed her little black hat and coat, and polished her shabby shoes. Then she hunted out the string of pearl beads, her only ornaments. She looked at herself a trifle wistfully in the glass. It would have been nice to have something new to wear this first time going out with a young man. But there! She must not be dissatisfied, with such wonderful things happening all day long!

With a sudden wonder coming into her face she dropped upon her knees beside the bed.

"Oh, dear Father—God, I thank thee!" she said.

McNair arrived at half past seven, and sent up a bunch of cool purple violets. In delight Kerry pinned them to her coat. He reported that there were no musical concerts that evening but he had tickets for the next night at Carnegie Hall. The symphony orchestra would present a fine program with a wonderful Russian violinist as soloist.

"However," he said, "I ran across an old friend from Scotland. I did not know he was on this side of the water. I find he is speaking this evening. He is rare. I know you will like him. And you'll be especially interested because he is talking on the Lord's Coming and the signs of the times."

So Kerry went to a wonderful meeting, almost the first religious meeting she had ever attended, because the Kavanaugh family as a rule did not frequent churches or meetings of any kind, except to drop in now and then for the music. Isobel Kavanaugh was apt to have a headache when church was proposed of a Sunday. It rather bored her unless she had a new hat. And Shannon Kavanaugh had lived his life so within himself that he had got into the habit of staying at home unless somebody pried him out. So little Kerry had grown up without the habit of church-going.

It was all new to her. The company of earnest people came because they loved it, and all brought their Bibles. The two or three gospel songs that were sung while they gathered thrilled her with their words. She delighted in the hearty genuine way in which the audience sang. The prayer was a revelation, just as if the petitioner were standing face to face with God. And then the address from the man with the sweet rugged face, and the burr on his tongue! It was not a sermon, just an unfolding of scripture compared with scripture, till the whole made an amazing story of something that was shortly to be!

Kerry was deeply stirred, more deeply than she had ever been before. And then, quite suddenly at the end, the speaker said:

"I see my dear friend, brother Graham McNair, in the audience. Will he lead us in a closing prayer?"

If the wall behind the pulpit had suddenly opened and disclosed God's throne, perhaps this new child of God would not have been more thrilled than to have the man beside her arise and begin to talk to God in that wonderful way, just talking about them all, and bringing them to the notice of the Father in the name of Jesus. She felt as if he had made special mention of her own name when he spoke of all their needs, so perfectly did his words fit the longings of her inmost soul.

They stopped at a restaurant afterwards, another quiet exclusive place with a good string quartette playing somewhere at a distance.

"For you know, we haven't really had but two meals today," McNair explained with a smile.

He told her while they were eating that he had found some disturbing mail at the hotel. There was trouble and misunderstanding out at the new western office, and he might have to go out sooner than he expected. He had sent out several telegrams that might straighten things out, but it was a little uncertain yet. However, they would fill the time with sightseeing and interesting things as long as he was there, that is, as much time as she could spare.

They arranged to meet early in the morning and do certain parts of the city so that she might learn her way quickly about. Then they began to talk about the meeting. Kerry was full of questions about the wonderful signs of the times of which she had never heard before until McNair himself had told her on the ship.

She hurried upstairs after he had left her to look out of the window before she turned on her light, and see if she could see him. Yes, there he was standing under the arc light at the corner just across from her window. How tall and straight he was! She watched till he hailed a taxi and stepping in was whirled away out of her sight. Even then she stood staring at the empty spot which he had just left, conjuring her vision of him.

A figure stepped down out of the shadow of a doorway across the street and came and stood in the light, looking after the departing cab. Then he turned and looked back toward Kerry's lodgings, and up toward the windows, and walked slowly up the street opposite the house. Something in the swing of the shoulders, the turn of the head, reminded her of Dawson, but of course it could not be. She watched the man a moment then pulled down her shade and turned on the light, humming a measure of the hymn they had sung in meeting that evening. How glad and thankful she was to be on land and in a quiet safe house with a good woman, and to have such a friend as McNair to show her the way about the city. Gladder than all to be free from the bondage and care of that awful, precious manuscript and to know it was safe in the hands of the publisher and he was now responsible.

Then she remembered that she had meant to ask Mrs. Scott for a drinking glass for her room, and decided to go down at once and get one before the woman had retired for the night.

But when she opened her door she felt a draught as if the front door was open, and listening she heard voices—a man's voice and Mrs. Scott. The man was asking if she had any vacant rooms, and she was offering to show him a room on the third floor. She could hear the front door closing and their footsteps coming up the stairs. Just in time she retreated, and pulled her door to, but not too soon to hear Dawson's familiar flat voice ask:

"And who is on the second floor front? I should like the second floor room if possible."

And Mrs. Scott replied:

"No, that's filled. A very nice young lady from England just took that room today."

They passed on up the stairs and Kerry could hear no more, but presently Mrs. Scott came down alone, and apparently the new lodger had taken the room and remained for the night.

Kerry thought no more of getting her drinking glass. She sank down in despair on the edge of her bed with her hands over her face. What should she do now? If that was really Dawson then he meant to dog her steps. For it could not be just a happening that he had found the same house. He must have traced them somehow.

And now, what should she do? Get out again and get away somewhere? She could scarcely do that. She had paid a week's rent in advance, and could not afford to lose even the small price that had been charged. Besides, if she went somewhere else he might find her again. She could not keep up the game of hide and seek continually. She almost wished that she had had the man arrested that morning. Perhaps that would have frightened him away. But what could be his possible object now? Unless indeed he thought she still had the manuscript and there was a chance of getting possession of it again.

When this idea came into her head Kerry got up and went to work as quietly as possible moving furniture around. She put her trunk across the door firmly, then made a further barricade of the bureau, a table, the bed and two chairs, straight across the room, wedging a pillow securely between the last chair and the bed so that even if the door were unlocked it would be impossible to budge it an inch. Until it was removed no one could get either in or out. She wondered grimly what would happen in case of fire, but decided it would not take long to push her barricade away if it became necessary. Anyway, she was free from burglers to-night, and to-morrow she would ask McNair's advice. Then she went to bed and slept soundly.

She was awakened by a tapping on her door early in the morning. Instantly alert she sprang from her bed wondering if Dawson would dare knock. She removed both the chairs in a twinkling. She threw her kimono about her shoulders, and began to shove her trunk away when she was reassured by the voice of the landlady.

"It's just a telegram for you, Miss Kavanaugh," she called, "I signed for it. I'll shove it under the door."

Kerry thanked her and was quickly in possession of the telegram.

A telegram! Now who would telegraph her? Her mother? Sam Morgan, perhaps? But how would they have her address so soon? Even detectives could hardly have managed that yet. The publishers? But she had not yet told them where she was located.

A vague premonition of trouble pervaded her as she tore open the envelope and read:

> Found telegram at hotel calling me West immediately. Am leaving on midnight train. So sorry to miss day together. Will return soon as possible. Meantime use caution. Advise with publisher or landlady in any perplexity. Am writing. Anxious about you.
>
> Graham McNair

Kerry found her knees growing weak under her, and sank into a chair, the yellow paper trembling in her hand. He was gone! Then she was all alone! And Dawson now in the same house with her! What should she do?

13

IT seemed to Kerry that the very foundations of the earth were shaking under her again. And when she came out of the first dissappointment and began to look her soul in the eye honestly she had to own up that it was not the thought of Dawson in the house that had appalled her. It was only that her new friend was going far away and no knowing how soon he would return, if ever.

She knew that this was a wrong state of mind. She had no reason whatever to think that McNair had anything but a friendly interest in her, and she had no right to any deeper interest in him. True, he had been kind to her, had done much for her for which she could never thank him enough, not only in rescuing her lost manuscript, but also in giving her a new anchor for her soul. Yet none of those things should make her feel that sick longing after him that now threatened to over-whelm her.

She let her hands fall into her lap over the telegram and stared off across the room at the dingy wall paper of scraggy red roses on an indefinite ground and tried to arraign herself. What had she been doing? Falling in love with an entire stranger? A worthy man she had no doubt, but one about whose life she knew almost nothing. He might be already engaged to some one far more his equal in every way than she was. He might have entirely other ideas. He might be even very rich. She had no idea at all. Thinking back he had said nothing that gave her any chance to judge his financial standing in the world. But she could judge by his clothes and all his little belongings which were of the best quality that he was not poor. And she was. What presumption on her part to allow her heart to attach itself to him in this way!

Kerry had lived abroad enough to have acquired a very strong class feeling in these things. Poor girls abroad, unless they belonged to royalty, did not expect to have attention from rich young men. It was only in Cinderella story-books that such things happened.

Moreover, she had started out in the world to earn her own living, and it was a poor handicap to lose her heart in this way to the first good kind man whom she met. She would not have it. She would not allow herself to even admit that she had been so silly and childish! She shut her lips firmly and got up. She went to the stationary washstand and washed her face in good cold water, rubbing her cheeks vigorously to take away their white look. She dashed water over her eyes again and dried them, and found the tears still came unbidden. Then she went and dropped down on her knees beside the bed and tried to pray.

"Oh, Father—God, you see what a little fool I am! I can't seem to do anything about it, either! I'm just all crumpled in a heap, and I feel so alone and miserable! Won't you help me?

"I know it's ungrateful of me to even think of feeling bad about the loss of a stranger-friend, when you've been so wonderful to me, bringing back the manuscript and making the publisher so nice, and giving me a real job with such nice people, but I just can't seem to help feeling very sad and sorrowful. Could you please do something about it for me. Take any wrong feeling I have about this away. Don't let me be what my father used to call unmaidenly. Don't let me want something I shouldn't have. Make me content with the wonderful things you have already given me, and then give me strength to smile. I ask it in Jesus' name."

Kerry remained upon her knees for some minutes after she had finished praying, and it seemed to her that her trouble was lifted from her heart in some wonderful way, and a peacefulness came in its place.

When she got up she read her telegram again, and got a thrill out of almost every word. He was anxious about her. Well, that was wonderful! Only friendly anxiety, of course, she must remember that, but it was nice to have even an absent friend, a mere friend, care a little. How kind of him to suggest advisers in his place! Of course he didn't know that Dawson was rooming in the same house. That probably would have disturbed him. Still, why, after all? The manuscript was safe and she had nothing else that he could steal. She would ask the publisher that very day to suggest a bank, and in it she would put her small hoard of money for safe keeping, and would also rent a safety deposit box and put those notes of the book safely away in it where they would be safer than anywhere else she could hide them. Then let Dawson do what he pleased. He could not hurt her. Besides, she had God, and the publisher and Mrs. Scott. They would all help her.

So she washed her face again with the cold, cold water, and felt refreshed, and then she set about making plans for the day.

It was early. It was only half past seven. She would dress at once and get out of the house before Dawson was awake. She knew his habits at sea had been late. He would hardly expect her to be about so early.

She took the book notes with her, stowed flatly in a manila envelope and carefully pinned inside her coat. When she went out of the house a half hour later, moving quietly, cautiously down the stairs, she did not appear to have anything with her but her small hand bag containing her purse.

When she let herself out of the house she kept close to the buildings so that anyone looking out of the upper windows could not see her unless they leaned far out.

She walked rapidly and got herself out of the region of Mrs. Scott's house as soon as possible, not knowing, nor caring much where she was going. She had taken the precaution to bring with her a little folder containing a map of New York, and a list of streets and notable buildings. When she got far enough away she meant to stop somewhere and peruse it. She remembered there was a great Central Park in New York. She had walked in it once with her father when she was a child. There were squirrels and a lake, and benches here and there. She would find this, and study her map.

There were only working people on the streets at this hour. They were hurrying to their daily tasks. The shops were still closed, and the houses had an air of being asleep.

But there were little restaurants open here and there, wafting appetizing smells of coffee and frying ham. She decided, however, not to be lured into eating yet. She was too near to Dawson's vicinity. And besides, if she waited until a little later in the morning she could make two meals out of one and save money. She must be careful of every cent now.

The morning was clear and brisk. It was almost spring, but there was a tang in the air that was heartening. Kerry tried to forget that McNair was already many miles away and hastening West as fast as his train could carry him. She tried also not to exult in his promise that he would write. That would be one more reason why she could not leave her present lodging in spite of Dawson's invasion, for she would want to wait and get her letter, else she would lose track entirely of McNair. Perhaps that was what she really ought to do, she argued with her anxious young soul, just go away and lose herself and never see him again, but it seemed so ungracious when he had been so kind; also, it showed up her weakness which she was not going to own even to herself.

But there was enough to take her attention in this new city, without arguing about fine ethical points.

McNair had marked the map he had given her, showing several points that would be outstanding waymarks, and giving the location of her new home so she would run no risk of losing herself. Now she took careful account of which way she had turned and felt sure she could find her way back.

She felt a little timorous venturing thus alone, but then, it could be no worse than London, and she knew her way about London and Paris. She would soon learn New York. If only the city did not also hold that uncanny Dawson she would feel quite at her ease.

Presently she found herself on Fifth Avenue, and enjoyed every step of the way. There were no crowds at this hour and she might walk at her leisure and admire the shop windows which were all interesting, and the great churches. There was the Public Library. She was glad to have located that. She would spend many hours there reading. In fact, that might be a very good place to hide herself away from Dawson after working hours.

In the vicinity of the better shops she lingered studying the display, wondering how prices compared with London, wishing she had been able to buy some new clothes before she came. There were one or two things she needed badly. The most imperative was a new pair of shoes. She must get them right away. It would not do to take her new job looking shabby. Of course her one new black dress would do for office work, and for anything else she must wait until she knew what her salary was to be. It probably would be very small at first.

At half past ten she presented herself at the pubisher's office. She found a still more cordial greeting than yesterday, for they had been reading a little of the manuscript and were even more impressed with it than they had expected.

Mr. Holbrook told Kerry that they had found a spot for her, and her duties would begin on Monday. The salary named was not great, but it was quite a little more than Kerry had dared to hope. She could easily live on it, she felt, and have a little something left over for new clothes unless clothes in America were vastly more expensive than in London and Paris.

Kerry asked advice about a bank and Holbrook named a bank, gave her a letter of introduction, offered several suggestions, and finally ended by inviting her to spend the week-end with his family at their suburban home.

Kerry shrank from accepting any invitation among strange people. Moreover she felt herself unprepared for social life. She would need new clothes to spend a week-end, and she had hoped not to have to spend money just now. But she recognized the intended kindness, and the fact that her invitation was a tribute to her noted father, and she knew that it was good policy to accept. Moreover, there was Dawson. It would be good to get away from him. Perhaps if she could keep pretty well away from the house to-day, and avoid him to-night, and then be away over Sunday she might be able to discourage his further annoyance.

So she smiled and thanked the busy publisher and took herself away promising him to meet him at the Grand Central Station at one o'clock on Saturday.

Kerry found a plain little restaurant on a side street and had a combination meal of breakfast and lunch, a bowl of soup with bread and butter. She was determined to live within her means.

While she ate her lunch she turned her wardrobe over in her mind. Of course they might be plain people, the Holbrooks, still they were city people, and she had noticed that even many of the shop girls in New York were smartly dressed. It certainly would not be a credit to her father to appear old-fashioned. It might tell against her in the business world which she was about to enter. Still, she must not take much from her small hoard.

When she had finished there was still twenty minutes before bank closing time, and she wanted to get those awful notes in a safe place before another night, and also to put away as much of her money as she could spare from everyday expenses.

She felt as if a great burden had rolled from her shoulders when those notes were in a safety deposit box, and she was out on the street again. She had saved out some of her money with a view to a possible new coat or hat or both, and so she turned her footsteps toward the stores.

She began her search in the great Fifth Avenue shops, scanning the wonderful garments of the wealthy first, just to judge of relative prices in America and abroad.

She looked the garments over, but the supercilious women who presided over the stately halls of commerce where the elite sought their garments, looked Kerry over and found her shabby in the extreme. They let her see by every glance they gave her, by the very inflection of their voices as they answered her shy questions about price and size, that they did not consider her a possible purchaser, and Kerry soon drifted away to the elevator again and back to the street.

She did several imposing exclusive shops in this way, and finally with dejected attitude found herself idly wandering down a side street, to get out of the noise and crowds. She decided that it was foolish to get new things just for a visit over Sunday. Eventually she would have to have some new clothes, but that could wait till she had more money saved up. She began to wish that she had put all her money in the bank—except enough for food and lodging and car fares. It was much better to have nearer four hundred than three hundred in the bank. Besides, it would be years before she could afford clothes from the Fifth Avenue shops.

She walked aimlessly for two long, long blocks, realizing that she was very tired and did not know what to do next, nor care; wishing she could creep away somewhere and cry and never crawl out again. Suddenly she saw to her right a lovely coat.

Now a new coat was something she had long desired, and very much needed. The coat she wore was an old one of her mother's, too large, and worn threadbare in places. The fur, though often carefully combed, was stubby and dejected looking, and the lines were all wrong for the present season. She had been conscious of its shabbiness all the way over the water, but never so much as since she had passed the ordeal of those cold-eyed sales women on Fifth Avenue. Yes, she certainly needed a new coat. The coats of the people who passed her fairly cried out to shame hers. In London she had not minded so much. She was used to going about London looking shabby.

But this coat as it hung in the window lured her joyously. It was all that a coat should be, which she could not say even for the expensive Fifth Avenue garments she had been examining. Not one of those had tempted her. They were all too sumptuous, too extreme.

Kerry had not lived in London and Paris without knowing good lines in a garment when she saw them, even though she seldom possessed one. And now as she paused before the window and gazed, critically, she knew that the garment before her was unusual; by cut and style and character it bore the hall marks of a master artist.

Its material was a soft supple wool that hung like doe skin. It was Lincoln green, a real Robin Hood color, trimmed luxuriously with lovely beaver fur. Kerry knew instantly that it was made to sell at a high price. Yet there was a card in the window announcing in large letters "All Coats Reduced to $39.50." It seemed incredible. There was, of course, some catch about it. This one would be an exception, put there just to draw trade. But she would go and see how much it was.

She lingered at the window studying it a moment. She dreaded to encounter more cold-eyed saleswomen. Yet—

there was no harm in inquiring the price. If this was beyond her purse then she would stop trying, and decide she ought not to buy a coat.

But she did need one. And this was so lovely, just the color that suited her hair. Her father always loved her in green. He even thought the old green chiffon made her look beautiful. And this coat was the same shade of green, only it had depth, and velvety softness about it that made it most charming. And the fur was exquisite, such a lovely silvery sheen. The brown and green went wonderfully together. Oh, she would love to have that coat! It would go well with the green chiffon. If she could borrow an iron of Mrs. Scott and iron out the chiffon, perhaps it would not look so forlorn. She might get some lace or a flower and freshen it up a bit. She went into the shop and asked breathlessly to see the coat in the window. Yes, it was thirty-nine fifty.

"A wonderful bargain," the salesgirl said. She was a pleasant eager girl herself, with none of the Fifth Avenue airs. "It's a Worth coat, you know, one of our exclusive models. You won't find another like it in the city," she poured forth as Kerry allowed herself to be buttoned into it.

Kerry stood in front of a long glass and saw herself in wonder. The green of the coat, and the soft silvery depths of the brown fur brought out all the tints in her clear skin, and made the red-gold in her hair flame.

"Oh," thought Kerry suddenly, "I'd like Graham McNair to see me in this!" and then her cheeks flamed amd made her yet more lovely. She turned sharply away from the mirror and dropping her shamed eyelashes she began to study the texture of the material, and the quality of the fur on the sleeve.

"It's really the greatest bargain we have in the store to-day," said the girl in a confidential tone, "a real model, you know. And you're fortunate to be small enough to wear it. That's why it is put down so low, because it's a small size, and getting toward spring, and we never hold over our exclusive models. We always let them go at a bargain."

Kerry turned back to the mirror, and the miracle of its hang and cut, the trick of its lapel and pocket and fastening held her again. Well, it might be, perhaps, a real imported model, straight from Mr. Worth's great establishment, but if so, why at that price? Why wasn't it up on Fifth Avenue selling for a hundred and fifty or two hundred dollars? It was prettier than anything she had seen up there this afternoon, and just as good quality. More likely, it was a copy of some model, perhaps a stolen copy at that, of the great dressmaker's choice achievement. But what matter? And who was she with her paltry little hundred dollars in her shabby purse, to demand real imported models? If the coat had warmth and beauty and "lines" combined with low price, what more could she desire?

"I'll take it!" she said at last with a sigh of satisfaction, thinking with a little frightened gasp that now she would have to bring the whole of her wardrobe up to that lovely coat.

Kerry carried the coat away from the shop with her and felt like a child with a new doll. A sudden sharp pang of longing came to her to run away and tell her father about it. He would have loved so to have her have something pretty. He used to worry about her never having pretty clothes, and was always promising to get them for her when his book was done. Well, now she had it, and she could feel that he had bought it for her, for it was the price of the precious books that he had cherished all these years that had made it possible.

Kerry went on down Thirty-fourth Street, walking on air, with no idea whatever of where she was going, till she came to a shop window where dresses were displayed. She stopped and studied them, for one had caught her eye. It was made almost exactly like her green chiffon, except that it had some bows of velvet ribbon with long ends. That was an idea! Why couldn't she get some velvet ribbon? Bows were easy to tie! She could make a new thing out of that poor little old chiffon dress. It wouldn't know itself.

Her eyes wandered over the rest of the things in the window. There was one dress at the back that had a wide soft

collar of lace like a cape. With a collar like that she could make
her black dress quite different!

She went into the store and found no collars for sale, nothing but dresses, but they directed her where to find a depart-
ment store not far away, and Kerry went happily on her way.

She got several yards of velvet ribbon, green to match the
coat, for she was sure it would match her dress. She found a
lovely lace cape collar like the one she saw in the window, not
real lace, of course, but none of those in the windows seemed
to be real. And if one were neatly and becomingly dressed
what difference did it make after all?

She found a store where all the felt hats were reduced. A
whole window of lovely little felts for two ninety-eight
apiece! There was a dear little green one just the right color!

Kerry was growing excited now. Here she was getting a
whole outfit and not spending half the price of one of those
impossible Fifth Avenue coats!

She found her shoes at a bargain sale on Seventh Avenue,
amazingly pretty and cheap. And then, suddenly, she realized
she was tired and wondered what she should do next. It was
still only half past four and quite daylight. She did not want to
get back to her lodging till dusk, so that if Dawson should be
lingering about she need not encounter him. It would be easi-
er to linger, and reconnoiter when it was dark. So making
inquiry of a policeman she took the elevated train to the park.

It was wonderful to sit down there in the comparative quiet
and rest. She piled her bundles on a bench beside her, and
went happily over her purchases in her mind, arguing with
herself about each one as a woman will when she has spent
herself and her money, and distrusts her own judgment after
it is too late.

Kerry had almost forgotten her keen disappointment in
McNair's sudden disappearance, and her anxiety concerning
Dawson's appearance on the scene. But now it all came back
and sat upon her. The happy evening she spent with McNair
last night seemed now a dream, as far away almost as her fa-

ther's death, and much more improbable. It was just as lovely, just as treasured in her heart as it had been last night when
she lay down to sleep, but it seemed ages ago. A whole day of
experiences in a new city is a great leveler. She felt as if she had
been utterly on her own in New York for several months.

Yet she dwelt upon the past dream wistfully, tenderly. She
thought of the things she had heard in the meeting, of the
great truths McNair had taught her, and sent up a swift prayer
that they might not seem unreal also.

There were children playing about the park, with nurses
gossiping in groups and wheeling baby carriages. Kerry
watched them awhile, now and then glancing down at the big
white suit box that held her new coat, and the little packages
in her lap, pleased that she was to have some new things. She
wondered if she could mend the handle of her brief case with
needle and coarse thread so it would do for an overnight bag?
For she had spent all the money she meant to spend no matter
what she had forgotten.

She glanced at her watch. It was only five o'clock. The approaching spring made dusk slow in coming. But in an hour
or so she would go and find a cheap restaurant and get some
supper, though she was almost too tired to eat.

She was planning how she would make her green velvet
bows for the chiffon dress when she heard footsteps approaching. She did not look up. She was watching a little
child in the next path feeding peanuts to a little gray squirrel, a
cunning little fellow who put his gray hand over his white
heart and begged for more.

"Good evening!" said a flat thin voice. "I thought I'd find
you somewhere around here! People always go to Central
Park sooner or later when they first come to New York!"

Kerry looked up with a start, growing dismay in her face, a
kind of consternation upon her that stunned her for the moment.

Dawson stooped over and picked up the coat box, moving
as if to sit down beside her.

Kerry caught at the cord of the box, and drew it toward her, standing it on edge on the bench, like a barricade between them.

"That's all right, I can hold it," persisted Dawson, still holding the box.

"I prefer to have it here," said Kerry out of a throat that had suddenly gone dry as a reed.

"Oh, then, all right. Suit yourself!" laughed Dawson disagreeably. "I suppose you don't trust me. Well, that's what I came about. I want to explain."

"It's really not necessary to explain. Mr. Dawson," said Kerry suddenly, gathering up her packages and looking obviously at her watch. "I was just going—I was just waiting till it was time—"

Dawson looked at her warily.

"You don't think you're waiting for McNair, do you? Because I can tell you he's gone. Took the midnight train last night. You knew that, didn't you? You see we were at the same hotel, and I happened to be down in the office when his telegram came calling him West. I used to be an operator on Western Union, several years ago when I was getting ready for college, and of course I couldn't help reading the code as it came in."

Something cold and powerful seemed to be gripping Kerry's throat like a vise. Cold chills started running up and down her spine. She felt all at once very little and helpless.

"Oh, God, my new Father—God!" she cried in her soul, "help me quick!"

This man was uncanny! There was no getting away from him!

She did not know just what it was she was afraid of, but she knew it was time to run to cover, so she cried to the only help she knew.

Lifting her eyes with a wild desperation in them, she saw in the near distance, a great green and white double decker bus come rumbling along gayly toward the curb at the end of the little path that led to her bench. Gripping her coat box, and her little packages she sprang to her feet.

"Oh, I must get that bus," she cried and fled away down the dusky path barely reaching the curb in time before the bus started on again. She did not look back. She dared not. She climbed in and sat down in a far corner, glad only that she had got away, having a strange feeling that she was protected by an unseen power.

She did not know which way she was going, nor whether her enemy had followed in some passing taxi, or whether she might not be going in an entirely wrong direction. She only knew she was going. By and by when she was far away from this spot she would ask some questions of the sphinx-like conductor. She would go so far that if she was out of her way she would have to stay in this same bus and come back with it.

So Kerry rode to the end of the line and back again into the region she knew. By that time she was half ashamed of herself for her foolishness. After all what could the man do? He was just annoying, that was all. She had no more papers that he could steal. He would gain nothing by doing harm to herself. She must be sane and simply freeze him out if he turned up again.

She stopped at a little restaurant and got her supper, and in the early dusk went back to her lodging house, feeling that she had shaken off her foolish fear of Dawson.

As she stepped into the gloom of the poorly lighted hallway a figure appeared in the door of the stuffy little parlor on the left, and a flat voice broke upon her startled ear:

"I was just about to say, when you broke away and ran for that bus, that I have tickets for a good play to-night, and I'd be glad if you would go with me!"

14

KERRY stood nonplussed. She felt almost too angry to speak. It was almost like an insult that a man who had twice stolen from her and evidently even now must have some ulterior motive in his constant following of her, should presume to pay her attention of this sort. Still there was nothing gained in letting him see her annoyance, so she summoned her patience and replied coolly:

"Thank you, Mr. Dawson. I am very busy this evening. It would be impossible for me to go out anywhere."

"Well, then we'll make it to-morrow evening," he said calmly in his flat businesslike tone.

"I shall be away over the week-end," said Kerry and then was sorry she had admitted even so much.

"All right, we'll say Monday night," said the unbaffled little fox, "I'm sure there'll be some good play Monday night."

Kerry drew herself up to her full height and looked him in the eye.

"You'll have to excuse me," she said curtly, "I don't care to make engagements to go out. As I told you, I am very busy all the time."

Kerry tried to pass on to the stairs, but Dawson planted himself in her pathway.

"Look here!" he said determinedly, "you can't always keep on running away from me. You've got to hear me out. I was attempting to proceed in the usual way, but your abrupt manner makes it impossible so I'll come to the point at once. I intend to marry you!"

"Oh, mercy!" said Kerry taken off her guard, and ending her exclamation suddenly with a clear hysterical laugh. Then sobering as quickly she said in a freezing tone:

"That is quite impossible, Mr. Dawson! I have no intention of ever marrying you! Will you let me pass, please?"

She swept past him and up the stairs, her head up, the very set of her slender shoulders expressing haughtiness.

Dawson stood below watching her, a kind of conceited doggedness clothing him like a garment. As she swept out of sight on the floor above and paused to unlock her door his voice came flat and distinct, like a heavy bundle falling on the floor beside her:

"That has nothing to do with the case, Miss Kavanaugh. I still intend to."

Kerry got herself inside her room and locked the door. Dropping into a chair with her bundles beside her she dropped her face into her hands and shook with ill suppressed laughter, but when she lifted her face again she found it was wet with tears also, that had drenched her hands.

She got up presently and went and washed her face, but every now and then the hysterical giggles would break out anew. She just could not stop laughing and crying. And yet it was not funny that she should be pestered with this horrid little man. It was most annoying. It was a desperate situation. His last words echoed up to her door made it quite plain that she had not squelched him in the least. How long could a thing like this last? How long could one stand it and not go mad?

She threw herself across her bed and buried her face in the pillow.

"Dear Father–God, won't you please help me!" she cried again and again. By and by she grew calmer and was able to think the thing through. There was a reason of course for this sudden development, and she began to see what it probably might be. Failing in his first purpose of gaining notoriety from stolen bits from her father's new book, he had conceived the idea of gaining his point in a wider and more definite way by accepting the position of son-in-law to a great man. He would thus assure himself of at least reflected glory, and climb to fame over her dead father's name, using his wonderful book as a stepping-stone.

A surge of indignation went over her leaving her weak and furious at the thought, and making her loathe the little man beyond his worth.

"I must stop this!" she said aloud to herself, and sat up, smoothing back her hair. "I am God's and He will take care of me. Besides, He has made a way for me to get away from it all over Sunday and when I come back I shall have my new work."

So she got up and went to making green velvet bows for her dress. Later she took her chiffon dress down to Mrs. Scott's neat kitchen and pressed it. When the bows were added it looked quite as if it just came out of the store. Mrs. Scott came up to see how it looked with the bows in place, and Kerry put it on. They had a nice little homelike chat together over the dress, and when Mrs. Scott went downstairs Kerry felt cheered and comforted. Perhaps most of all because Mrs. Scott had told a little incident or two of her life in the McNair family, how kind and thoughtful Graham McNair had always been, and what a wonderful mother he had had. Kerry, as she locked her door and lay down to rest, felt happy in the thought that she might call him her friend. How different he was from Dawson! Oh, if he could only have stayed a little while perhaps Dawson would not have dared tag her around this way! Still, now he had declared his purpose it would really be less sinister, because she could surely avoid him most of the time and perhaps he would get discouraged after a while.

Kerry slipped across the road to a shoemakers early in the morning and got the handle of her brief case mended. It would have to do for an overnight bag, for the only bag she had was far too large, and shabby.

Several times during the morning Kerry thought she heard the door at the head of the third story stairs open for a moment then close again, as if some one were listening at the head of the stairs, but at at last about noon she heard Dawson come down and go out the front door. Then she hastened her preparations and soon was out and away, hoping perhaps she had escaped his vigilance. Yet she half expected to see him lurking about the train gate as she went out with Mr. Holbrook.

If he was there she did not see him, and was greatly relieved to be seated at last in the train and on her way to a suburb along the Hudson.

The trip, which lasted a little over a half hour was a pleasant one. Holbrook talked much about her father and the reverence in which he was held in the world of scholars. Kerry found herself wishing again that her mother could hear all that he was saying. Oh, if her mother had only realized what the world thought of the man she had so quickly forgotten for a little ease and luxury! Kerry knew Isobel well enough to know that she would almost have been willing to starve rather than lose the prestige of being the wife of a man whom the world held in high honor. But her mother never had believed that Shannon Kavanaugh was anything but an idle dreamer. A shabby idle dreamer. Dear, of course, in a homely way and good to use as a mirror in which to reflect her own lovely useless little self, but a nonentity as far as the world was concerned.

The home at which she presently arrived in a shining limousine from the station, seemed palatial to Kerry who was used to cheap hotels in back streets in the crowded portion of European cities. It was built of stone with many arches, and wide porches, and fascinating gables, roofed in heavy slate that gave the effect of thatching. English ivy climbed lavishly everywhere, and the grounds were lovely and well kept. Even this early in the spring the lawn had an air of freshness and tidiness as if there had been no winter. There were daffodils bursting out in riotous bloom along the hedges and borders, and a great bed of pink and white and blue hyacinths filled the air with wonderful fragrance.

Even before she got out of the car Kerry could see the river shining like a great band of silver in the distance, and boats plying up and down. She exclaimed in delight at the view as they stood for a moment on the porch before going in.

"Why! It must be almost like heaven to live in a place like this!" said Kerry.

The tired business man looked down indulgently on the sweet girl face, framed in that halo of red-gold hair, and wondered what it was about this girl that was so refreshing. He wished—

He did not know what it was he wished, for the door opened at that instant and another girl about Kerry's age stood there with a reproach upon her lips, and sharpness in her eyes.

She might have been a pretty girl but there was too much paint and lip stick to even pretend to be natural, and the black hair was too severely arranged showing the whole of the pretty ears, giving her a touch of boldness.

"For cat's sake, Dad! Why this unearthly hour? I told you to come on the twelve train. You knew we were due at the country club at two. Now we'll have to simply rush through luncheon and no time to change!"

"Have a care, Natalie, child, don't be rude!" protested her father indulgently. "This is Miss Kavanaugh. You can surely take time to speak to her. As for the twelve train, I told you that was out of the question. Saturday is the busiest day of the week. I was lucky to get off on the one train."

Natalie surveyed her guest with cool appraisement.

"Awfully glad to see you," she announced coolly. "Where is your bag?" She glanced disapprovingly at the brief case whose mending stitches seemed suddenly to Kerry to shout to her hostess for recognition—and *get* it, too. "Now, Dad! Didn't you tell Miss Kavanaugh to bring her golf and evening things? I told you the very last thing last night you know!"

"Look here, Nattie, can't you let us come in? I had no opportunity to tell Miss Kavanaugh anything, child. We met at the train gate five minutes before one. You wouldn't have had her wait and go back to pack, would you? Certainly you must have things enough to lend her if she hasn't brought hers with her."

Here Kerry arose to the occasion with a bit of her own lofty manner acquired somewhere in Europe and used only on rare occasions.

"Oh, don't mind me," she said with a queenly lift of her chin, and a smile that could be daunted by nothing, "if I haven't the right things for the occasion I'll just sit here on the porch and watch the view. It's grand enough to fill several whole days and nights too I should think."

Natalie stared at her and gave a queer little laugh of contempt.

"Oh, if you feel that way!" she said. "That's the way Dad talks. That's why we're stranded out in this dead dump instead of being in our town house. Well, I'm sure I'm glad if you enjoy it!"

The luncheon was indeed a somewhat rushed affair, for Natalie occupied the center of the stage, and kept things in a tumult.

Mrs. Holbrook proved to be a slender nervous woman, smartly dressed, and rouged, an older edition of Natalie. She was wearing her hat all ready to go out. Between them they nagged the husband and father most unmercifully about everything that was mentioned, yet he seemed fond of them. The mother was scarcely warmer in her greeting than the daughter had been, yet there was about the home an atmosphere of informality, as if every member of the family brought home whom they pleased quite freely, and Kerry felt almost at once set down as a visitor on account of the office, to whom they had to be polite for business reasons.

When the meal was half done two young men came in, one dark and slim and lithe, Natalie's twin brother, Harrington Holbrook, the other a big Celtic-looking athlete who immediately absorbed Natalie to the exclusion of all others. Kerry would have been quite willing to sit in the background and listen, but Harrington Holbrook was seated beside her and he at once began to talk to her with far more friendliness in his voice than either his mother or sister, who after their first greeting, had left her practically to herself. Mr. Holbrook's whole attention was taken up in lazily and amusedly defending himself, which he did in much the same manner as he might have brushed off a litter of puppies or kittens who were swarming over him. There was a stroke and a pat in his voice each time he put them off.

When Natalie had finished the pastry with which the meal ended, she arose abruptly.

"Come on, folks. It's time we were in motion."

She paused reflectively, studying Kerry's neat black frock.

"You'll have to have some togs!" she said, pointing her finger at Kerry rudely. "Get a hustle on. Can you dress in three minutes?"

"Oh, couldn't you just please leave me out?" pleaded Kerry shrinking back. "I would just love to sit here and read."

"Indeed no," said Harrington with firmness, "you're my partner you know. Fix her up, Nat, and make it snappy! We're going to do eighteen holes anyway this afternoon."

"But I really don't play golf!" exclaimed Kerry in agitation.

"You know I never was on a golf links but twice or three times in my life, and then I just knocked the balls around a little."

"Well, if you don't play it's time you learned," said the youth cheerfully.

Kerry looked about to protest to the father but he had vanished upstairs, and there was nothing to do but follow the abrupt Natalie and be clothed to suit the family.

Natalie produced a little French knitted dress of orange and brown that fitted Kerry very well and made her look more like a vivid little flame than ever. For a hat she deftly knotted a broad band of brown velvet ribbon about Kerry's head, remarking as she did so in a most casual tone:

"You've got stunning hair, you know!"

But there was no admiration in the tone, no hint that she meant it for a compliment. Kerry had a feeling that she was merely taking account of stock socially for her own afternoon. She wanted her guest to make a good impression for her own social prestige.

She rooted out a pair of golf shoes that fitted Kerry fairly well, and Kerry, much against her will, went down where the car and the young men were waiting.

Young Holbrook took her in with new approval.

"Good work, Nat!" he said, and then to Kerry, "I say, you're some looker, do you know it?"

Kerry found herself getting red with annoyance. She was not used to such frank personalities and they embarrassed her. But she managed to summon a laugh.

"It's the borrowed plumage," she said, "fine feathers make fine birds. Oh, what a wonderful view!"

The young man followed her glance.

"Yes. Nice river, isn't it? But rather too much commercialized now for beauty. Too many dirty boats going up and down you know!"

The young man had placed Kerry by his side in the front seat, evidently intending to do the driving himself. Natalie and the other young man were already in the back seat, Natalie in a flaming scarlet frock and cap.

"What are we waiting for, oh, my heart?" asked the big Celt, casting his blue eyes up toward the house, and then at Natalie.

"Oh, Dad and Mother! The other car has a flat tire and something wrong with the carburetor and has to go to the garage and be fixed. Isn't it tiresome?"

"In that case I'll have to rustle out of this comfortable seat I suppose," complained the youth.

Both young people got out when the elder Holbrooks appeared, and took the middle seats, but they kept up a constant run of talk about it. Kerry wondered if she were getting old maidish. These young people seemed so openly rude to their elders. Or was this merely American, and had she become Europeanized.

The afternoon was surprisingly pleasant, although Kerry had not anticipated pleasure in it. She shrank from exposing her ignorance of the game, she shrank from appearing among strangers in borrowed garments, and she shrank most of all from the attentions of the Holbrook youth who continued to flatter her at every opportunity. It amused Kerry to think that from being almost a recluse she had blossomed out in one short week into receiving attentions from three different men! Even a proposal of marriage from one of them! She could barely suppress a sudden grin of amusement as she remembered the occurrence of the evening before, and a sudden gratitude came over her that she was out here in this beautiful open and not cooped up in her room hiding from Dawson.

"Pep her up, Harry!" had been the final greeting of Natalie to her twin as she sailed off with her own escort, and soon Kerry and Harrington Holbrook were left far behind while Kerry was being taught "strokes" and the various details necessary to the game.

The young man was good company. He accepted her as a comrade, and did not make her feel uncomfortable. There were certain things about him that made her think of his father, kind, and amusing and not self-centered. Yet now and then when he spoke of his "work" which she presently discovered was with a great architect, she glimpsed that keen look that the elder Holbrook had worn in the office the first day she had seen him.

Mrs. Holbrook left them at the club house. There was bridge and a tea later. They did not see her again until the eight o'clock dinner.

Mr. Holbrook in knickers, and plain stockings and a gray sweater looked like a big nice boy. He passed her once on another fairway and smiled.

"Having a good time, little girl?" he said, and Kerry felt her heart warm within her. He was her boss, her father's publisher! How good God had been to her!

The evening was much worse than the afternoon.

Kerry came down in her green chiffon looking sweet and lovely. The velvet bows had made her frock another thing and were most becoming. A string of pearl beads and her lovely hair were all the adornments she ever needed, though she did not know that. But the eyes of Natalie scorched over her dissatisfiedly.

"I'll have to get to work on you again!" she announced rudely looking her over. "You can't go to the club house tonight in that thing!"

"Natalie, really!" protested her father, "your jokes are carried a little too far for courtesy I think."

"I'm not joking, Dad," said Natalie, "I'm dead in earnest. Ask mother if I'm not."

Mrs. Holbrook turned her sharp attention and a lorgnette on Kerry's quiet little garb.

"Why don't you let her wear that little green tulle?" she said turning to her daughter. "She seems to look well in green. It brings out her hair."

"I thank you," Kerry said quietly. "If you will just kindly leave me out of your plans this evening I shall be so much obliged. I had no idea of going out anywhere or I should not have felt free to come. You will really make me more comfortable if you will just go and let me stay quietly here reading. I couldn't think of letting you dress me up again. It is most kind of you of course, but really, you know, I don't belong."

"Now, Natalie, you see you have really been rude," said her father trying to look severe and failing.

"Not at all!" said the mother sharply. "Natalie is perfectly right. Miss Kavanaugh came out here not knowing what we were expecting to do, and didn't bring along the right things. It's Natalie's place to lend her something. Besides, when we entertain a guest we usually take her with us wherever we go. I have arranged for her to be there of course."

"Say, look here!" spoke up the young son of the house, "I've got something to say about this. Miss Kavanaugh is going with me this evening and I like the dress she has on. It looks like the woods at twilight, and her hair makes you think of the sunset left over."

"Don't get poetic, Harry," scoffed his mother. "Miss Kavanaugh's dress is not in the least suitable. It is too somber. She would feel uncomfortable in it."

"Well, it strikes me you all are rather dumb," persisted the young man. "Didn't Dad say Miss Kavanaugh's father had recently died? Perhaps she doesn't feel like wearing all the doohickies the rest of you do."

"Oh!" said Mrs. Holbrook casting a sudden accusative look at Kerry, as much as to say, "What are you doing here then?"

"Oh!" said Natalie as if an affront had just been offered her.

Then Kerry lifted clear eyes and spoke steadily:

"Mr. Holbrook, you are very kind. You are all very kind. But that is not the reason. I should not have come if I had been going to put my recent sorrow upon other people, and anyway my father did not approve of mourning, or anything like that. The truth is I am wearing the only dress I happen to have at present. I'm sorry that it does not seem to suit the occasion, but you see I'm not suitable myself I am afraid. I've always lived a very quiet life and I've had no occasion to have dresses for dances. You see I don't dance either. It hasn't been in my line."

Then up spoke the father of the family, gravely with open admiration in his eyes and voice:

"Well, I think Shannon Kavanaugh has reason to be proud of his daughter!" he said. "If my daughter had come up as fine and sweet as this girl has, without all the folderols the world thinks necessary to-day, I certainly would be delighted."

Natalie gave a toss of her head at this and made a wry face.

"Oh, Dad! You're so old-fashioned!" she laughed contemptuously.

"I'm sure it's very commendable in Miss Kavanaugh to be content with what she has," observed Mrs. Holbrook coolly.

"It is!" said the elder Holbrook. "It's most commendable in her to take an interest in the real things of life instead of giving herself entirely to play as most of the women and girls I know are doing. But there's one thing I want distinctly understood. Miss Kavanaugh is our guest, and she is to do exactly as she pleases. If she doesn't want to go to dances she doesn't have to. Understand? And she's not to be made uncomfortable about it either."

"Oh, of course!" said Mrs. Holbrook coldly, eyeing Kerry disapprovingly, "but you must remember, Ripley, it was you who suggested taking Miss Kavanaugh to the club house and introducing her."

"Yes, Dad," put in Natalie impudently, "and it was you who told us to invite all our crowd. You gave me all the dope to tell them about Miss Kavanaugh, how she was the daughter of a distinguished scientist and all that, and now I've got them perfectly crazy to meet her, and what am I going to say?"

Kerry listened to the family conference in dismay. The mother and daughter talked on about her exactly as if she were not present. But presently Kerry interrupted:

"Really, Mrs. Holbrook, I couldn't think of causing you embarrassment. Of course I will do whatever you wish me to do. If going over there will relieve the situation I'm perfectly willing to go, and would be delighted to meet your friends. And, although I am much embarrassed to put you to the trouble, I am willing, of course, to wear what you wish—if you have something simple that you won't mind my wearing. You must remember, I don't dance. Perhaps that will be an embarrassment to you also."

"I'll make it my business to see that objection is out of the way by the next dance," put in Holbrook Junior. "I'll be delighted to teach you."

"Thank you," said Kerry smiling bravely, though she felt on the very verge of tears, "you are all very kind I'm sure, but there won't be any next dance for me, and if you please I would rather not learn. I shall not have time for such things, and—well, it isn't in my line you know."

But Mrs. Holbrook had taken command and taken Kerry at her word.

"How about that little black frock you thought you might return, Natalie? Perhaps she might look well in that. Black would be stunning with that hair of course. What was the matter with it that you did not like it? I forget."

"Oh, it had those funny little new style puffs around the armhole. I can't abide even tiny sleeves, on an evening gown, and the back wasn't low enough cut for the present style. It looked frumpy."

"That sounds more like me," smiled Kerry. "Did you say you were returning it? Then if it fits why couldn't I buy it? I would like that much better than having to borrow, and maybe having something happen to the dress while I had it on. Could I afford it? Was it very expensive?"

"I should say not!" said Natalie with contempt. "It was only twenty-five dollars! They were having a bargain sale, and I thought when I saw it in the window it was darling, but when I got it on I looked like one of the pilgrim fathers."

Kerry winced inwardly at the idea of paying out twenty-five more of her precious dollars, but still, she would have one more dress, if it was at all wearable, and it seemed a case of necessity. This was her publisher's house, and she must do him honor. She must be decently dressed.

The ladies adjourned upstairs, and the dress was brought out. Kerry found it quite wearable although she did not care especially for the style, a tightly fitted waist of transparent velvet with many tiers of black malines ruffles floating out like feathery spray down to her very feet. But the round neck was becoming and not too low, and there were tiny puffs of sleeves at the very top of the shoulder. Kerry had to admit to herself that she did look rather nice in it in spite of these objections. And then, the only alternative was a jade green taffeta of Natalie's which boasted a very low corsage, clasped over the shoulders with straps of rhinestones and no back at all, as far as the waist line.

"I'll take this," said Kerry quietly, "that is, if you are sure you do not want to keep it. It will probably be quite useful to me." And she produced the money at once.

Somehow her action seemed to inspire more interest in Miss Natalie. She offered some showy shoe buckles and a rhinestone necklace, but Kerry thanked her and declined.

When she was ready a few minutes later, with her new coat on her arm, she had the little green silk shawl from China slung across her shoulders like a scarf, and the effect was rather startling.

"Oh, I say!" ejaculated the younger Holbrook as she came down the stairs, "I didn't think you could look any prettier, but you certainly are some peach now!"

"Don't be rude, Harry!" condemned his mother cuttingly as she sailed down in purple tulle and amethysts, and took a quick furtive survey of Kerry. It annoyed her that this girl who was evidently not of their world, could yet take a discarded gown that had made her daughter look like a frump, and make it serve her beauty so regally. That hair of course was most unusual.

There was something in reflected glory. Since her husband had willed that this girl must be entertained, it was just as well to get any possible advantage from it that there might be. So Mrs. Holbrook surveyed her young guest critically, with reluctant approval and as Kerry was about to put on her new green coat she swept it aside and substituted for it a long evening wrap of her own black velvet with an ermine collar.

"That's a very lovely garment of course, my dear," she said condescendingly, "but it will crush your skirt terribly. Take this instead."

So Kerry went to the dance looking like a young princess, and wondered at herself. On the way over to the club house sitting beside Harrington Holbrook she thought of Graham McNair and the wonderful Saturday night one week before out on the ocean in the moonlight. How she wished she were going with him somewhere to hear him talk of the things of another world, rather than with these people who were not of her kind.

15

A dance meant nothing at all to Kerry. She had never actually attended one although of course she had seen dancing at hotels and other places in her travels. At school the girls had danced but it never interested her so she had taken no part in it. It had not occurred to her that there might be anything in the gathering to which she was invited, that would be incongruous with the new life of the spirit into which she had recently entered. She was simply being polite.

But when they arrived at the club house, and the introductions began, she felt more and more out of her element, both physically and spiritually. She did not like the way the women were dressed, voluptuously, with much painted faces. Perhaps her father's prejudice against such things made her dislike them more than she otherwise would have done. She did not like the way the women talked. Not all, but many of them, especially the young girls were openly, carelessly profane, and used expressions that she had been taught to feel were coarse. Some of the older women in the dressing room were gathered together having a royal gossip about a poor young thing who evidently used to be of their number, and now was in some kind of disgrace. Kerry couldn't help wondering, as she stood before the mirror fastening back a recalcitrant wave of hair, whether these same unholy, self-righteous women had not prepared the way for the girl to walk into disgrace. Surely an atmosphere like this was not one in which to grow in righteousness.

Back in the great club room again with the Holbrooks, being introduced right and left, to girls and young men, and women and old men, Kerry suddenly perceived herself a celebrity. So this was why she had had to be better dressed. She was the daughter of one of the world's great men. Well, perhaps she would consider this a part of business, and swallow it down as such. She was taking her father's honors. How he had disliked having a fuss made over him. Yet she found herself glad that he was honored by the world, and that she might know that people cared.

But there came cocktails.

That was another thing that Kerry had not considered would affect her. Of course she knew people in social life drank such things but her father had taught her to hate it. It was just another separating custom, that was all.

Quite simply she declined them, but met so much remonstrance that she discovered at once it was a sore point. People raised their eyebrows questioningly at her. One large dowager asked her if her father had been a prohibitionist, and jokes flew around about the eighteenth amendment. Kerry had no idea what it was all about. She knew nothing of American politics, and little of American customs, having been away so long.

But she noticed that when she declined the second cocktail young Holbrook declined also, and in spite of the jeers and loud protests of his friends he continued to shake his head.

She turned to him with a bright smile.

"What's the idea?" she asked, "aren't we allowed to eat and drink as we please?"

He grinned.

"Come on let's get out of this," he said in a low tone. "I'll take you for a ride in the moonlight."

"Lovely!" said Kerry, "only we must do our duty here first you know."

So Kerry stood smilingly and talking to people, told them bits about her father, and her travels, and the foreign lands she had seen, just a dash of color here and there and they were satisfied. They did not really care to hear any connected conversation. They struck her as being filled with a fine frenzy of excitement, doing and saying things that were expected of them, interested in nothing save to whoop it up and keep the mad whirl going.

The orchestra struck up, and the dancing began. Jazz! Kerry's ears were attuned to the fine old masters. Her father had seen to it that what music she heard was of the best. This sounded to her like the noise of a city filled with hand organs and bag pipes. The wail of lost souls, and the protest of over-burdened bodies. Involuntarily she winced as the first notes crashed in.

Young Holbrook was watching her.

"You don't enjoy all this, do you?" he asked, a note of surprise in his eager young voice.

Kerry smiled.

"Why, it's—different!" she said without enthusiasm, "I've not been used to a life like this, you know."

"But that's the queer part about it," he said in a puzzled tone, "just for that very reason I'd expect you to be crazy about it. Weren't you awfully bored, never seeing life? Weren't you always wanting to do what other people did? Weren't you terribly dissatisfied?"

"Yes," said Kerry, "I was often unhappy, very, and always wondering why I had to live. And I think in those days, perhaps until quite recently, I would have welcomed all this. I would have reached out eagerly for it. But—not now. It—somehow—does not seem real to me. It is—well—just passing the time away and trying to forget one is alive!"

"Gosh!" said the young fellow, casting his eyes avidly over the bright assembly that was now most of it moving excitedly about in couples in time to the music. "Why, that's what it is of course, just passing the time away! What else could you do? You don't live but once, and you're a long time dead!"

"Only once," said Kerry with an exultant smile, "but it lasts forever! And it means, oh, a great deal! And then—you may not have to die at all, but—whether we live or whether we die—it's—oh wonderful—! And I've just found that out!"

"You mean you've found something better than all this?" he said with a sweeping gesture toward the ball room.

"Yes," said Kerry, turning bright wistful eyes upon him. She found herself wishing this nice boy might understand too. "Why, you see, I've just found out we were not put here on this earth just to have a good time. This is a sort of preparation time, a college course, a testing through which we have to pass, to get ready for the life that is to last forever, and is to be so wonderful that we cannot even understand how great it is!"

"Oh, gosh! You don't mean religious stuff, do you?" asked the boy with a disappointed tone, "I thought for a minute you were talking about something real! You looked so interested!"

"Oh, but I am interested," said Kerry with a radiant look, "and I've only just found out what a marvelous thing it is. No, I don't think you'd call it religious stuff," she said thoughtfully. "It's not what I've always called religion. Religion is a kind of system, isn't it? Something men have thought out for themselves. For instance Confucianism and Buddhism and things like that. This is different. It's God's own word."

He looked at her a moment in amazement, noted with admiration the eager light in her dark eyes, the lovely flush on her young cheek, the whole flaming beauty of her charming face, and his own look softened with appreciation.

"Tell me about it," he said softly. "Let's get out of here, shall we?"

But at that instant a group of young men rushed up eagerly and surrounded Kerry.

"Why aren't you dancing?" they demanded in a breath. "May I have this next dance?"

"No, I was here first, Forsythe!"

"No, I was the one that started first—" put in a third.

They clamored about her, and for one brief instant Kerry tasted the honey of popularity. Was it the new queer dress with its dusky ruffles to her toes? She wondered. She never realized at all her own lovely face set in its frame of red-gold hair, above the new frock, with the dashing green of her shawl trailing over one shoulder. She did not know she made a picture as she stood at the far end of the great dancing floor, a distinguished little figure, the beautiful daughter of a beautiful mother and a great father! She was only annoyed that the conversation had been broken in upon.

"But I don't dance," she said brightly and brought dismay upon all three.

"Well, can't you learn?" they asked eagerly. "We'll take turns teaching you."

"She doesn't care to learn," said Holbrook coolly, "and we were just going to ride. Miss Kavanaugh wants to see the Hudson by moonlight."

"What's the little old idea, Harry, hogging the guest of honor, I'd like to know?" asked the young man they called Forsythe.

"Oh, we'll be back after a while," said Harrington Holbrook withering him with a glance and leading Kerry away.

"Will it be all right for us to run away a little while?" asked Kerry wistfully as she followed him with a worried glance back. "I wouldn't like to annoy your mother and sister."

"Oh, sure! They won't know where you are from now on. They'll think you're sitting it out somewhere. All the girls run away for drives. We'll drop in again during the night. Anyhow the mater is deep in a game in the card room. She wouldn't know you now if you were introduced."

Kerry was glad to get out into the fresh spring air, and the enchantment of the moonlight. She settled down in pure delight, exclaiming over the beauty of a group of cherry trees just coming into exquisite bloom.

The boy shot the car out into the highway, and stepped on the gas. Kerry caught her breath with joy. Why, this was like flying. Her experience in automobiles hitherto had been mostly confined to city taxi cabs.

"Oh, this is wonderful!" she said as they flew along the white ribbon of the highway past sweet smelling trees in bloom, and fresh earth upturned in gardens. She drew long breaths of delight and her eyes shone starry. The boy looked at her with keen appreciation. "Some girl!" he said to himself enthusiastically.

By and by he turned from the highway into a still sweet lane where there were high borders of hedges, and a silver gleaming of moonlit water ahead.

He parked the car near the edge of a great bluff overlooking the river, and sat back happily.

"Now," he said joyously, "this is something like!" and he slid his young eager arm around Kerry with astonishing swiftness and possessiveness, and drew her close to him, at the same time gathering her two hands that lay in her lap.

Kerry sat up with suddenness, and drew her hands away, gently but firmly.

"Oh, please don't, Mr. Holbrook," she said earnestly, "I—want to respect you—and myself too!"

"Whaddaya mean, respect?" asked the boy in a hurt tone, "I didn't mean any disrespect to you. I'll say I didn't! Why, I respect you more than any girl I ever saw, and that's a fact!"

"Then—please don't!" said Kerry again firmly.

"But *why?*" he persisted, "I was just being—friendly—and

cozy! Everybody does it nowadays. Do you mean they don't do it over in Europe?"

"I don't do it," said Kerry, and then remembered with a sudden quick flash of condemnation that McNair had held her hand once on shipboard. But that was different! Or was it different? What was there different about it? Why had she felt no condemnation? She must put that away and think about it. Maybe it wasn't different. Maybe she should have done something about that too. McNair of course was a stranger too, and nothing to her—at least— Her thoughts were ashipboard now, and not in an automobile at all. But the boy by her side was persistent.

"Do you mean you don't believe in petting? Why not?"

Kerry hesitated, still wondering why this case was so different from the one on shipboard, arguing it out with herself.

"I think," she said gravely deliberate, still thinking it out, feeling her way as she spoke, "I think, because it is playing with serious things, real things, that usually—only—come once!"

And then her heart leaped up with a secret she did not dare to face just now, and put away hastily in the innermost secrets of her thoughts.

The boy sat looking thoughtfully out across the silver water to the opposite shore where lights gleamed out from windows, and showed here and there a little settlement.

"Well, perhaps you're right," said the boy, "anyhow I think it's nice you feel that way. I guess you like a girl better if every fellow hasn't mauled her. But say, I didn't mean that the way you thought. I was serious all right. I like you better than any girl I ever knew. That's right, I do! I knew it the minute I came into the dining room this noon! You certainly are a winner!"

Kerry laughed.

"Why, you hardly know me," she said gayly, "but it's nice to have you friendly. Of course I like to be liked. But come, let's talk about something else. What are all those lights down the river there? Why, they seem to be moving."

"That's a Hudson River steamer. It goes up to Albany you know. It will go right past us here."

They watched the boat as it came nearer, moving like a thing of spirit, its many lights gleaming out and separating till it looked like a moving palace.

"What was that dope you were giving back at the club house?" asked Holbrook at last. "It sounded interesting. If it isn't religion, what is it? Ethical Culture or some of those new fangled cults? I'd like to find out what makes you different."

"Well," laughed Kerry, "I don't know that it has had time to make me different yet; I'm quite new to it. And yet, when I come to think of it, it has made everything different for me. I seem to be another person. It's as if I was born again into a new world. I look at everything in a different way. I never knew before that God was real, and could be realized in everyday life. I never knew that He made us because He wanted our companionship and help, and that we by sinning had made ourselves unfit for such companionship. I didn't realize either that I was an utter sinner, and that God loved me so much that He sent His only Son and let Him take my place dying that there might be a way for me to be saved."

"Whaddaya mean, 'saved'? Whaddaya mean, 'sinner'? I'll bet a hat you never committed a sin. I don't see all this talk about sin. I understand nobody believes in it any more anyway. It's what you think is right, that's the dope. Why, I've never done anything very bad. Why should I say I'm a sinner? I've lived a pretty decent life. Of course I've done some petting and you think that's all wrong, but I didn't mean any harm by it. And I don't tell rotten stories the way most of the fellas I know do. Of course I got into a lot of scrapes at college, but every fella does that. I don't call that a sin, do you?"

"I have recently come to know," said Kerry gravely, "that sin is something we are born with, that is a tendency to sin, and that the great sin, the sin of all sins, is unbelief in Jesus Christ the Savior of the world. Unbelief and indifference. Probably all the other things grow out of that."

"Belief? Whaddaya mean belief? I didn't know anybody believed in that dope any more, only perhaps a few old ladies and missionaries."

"Oh, yes, they do!" said Kerry earnestly, "and, really, you know, it is the most wonderful thing to believe in. You just accept it, and it makes you all over. It cures your soul, and makes things different. You are 'born again.' That's what the Bible calls it."

"The Bible!" said the young collegiate, "but that's all out of date."

"No, it isn't really!" said Kerry. "I've tried it. It works, just as it says, and it's the most wonderful up-to-date book I ever read. Why, it not only tells you all about yourself and fits right into your own experiences, but it tells things that are happening right along every day now, things in politics and history, and the way nations are doing things—!"

"Say! What are you giving me! Trying to string me? My psychology professor in college said—!"

"Yes, I know," said Kerry, "they do, but he didn't know. He'd never heard of these wonderful things that are being discovered to-day. But you see I'm very new at this myself. I can't begin to tell you about it all. I'm just learning myself. But if you are interested there is a man holding meetings at a little church I went to the other night. He is going to be there another week. He is telling the most wonderful things about the Bible! I know it doesn't sound much when I try to tell it, but it's great. And there is just one thing, I know that Jesus Christ has forgiven me, and that I'm a child of God, and it makes all the difference in the world in my life and how I feel about things!"

They sat there a long time talking, while Kerry unfolded to him the simplicity of the gospel of Christ. He marveled at her words, objecting now and then as modern youth is taught to do, yet unable to answer her simple faith in the simplicity of salvation.

Suddenly Kerry looked at her watch.

"Mercy!" she exclaimed, "do you know what time it is? Five minutes of two! What will they think of us? It is Sunday morning and they will all have gone long ago and will wonder where we are. What will your mother think of me?"

"Oh, no they won't have left the club house yet. They never do Saturday nights till nearly three. But we'll get right back now. Gosh, you're a funny girl. It's been interesting. I don't know another girl I would have sat with all this time and listened to her talk religion—excuse me, what was it you called it? Christianity! That's it. But say, it's good dope. If it was true it would be some fairy tale to live, wouldn't it? Of course I'm not saying it is, but that dope about the Jews and the nations of Europe, and the chemicals in the Dead Sea are mighty interesting even if they aren't true. They certainly are coincidences anyway. What did you say the man's name was that told all these things? I wouldn't mind hearing him myself some time. What do you say we drive down there tomorrow if we can find out when he speaks. The paper might tell. Know what church it was?"

"Why, no," said Kerry. "I haven't an idea, but I could find it if I was in town."

"Well, if you're on deck in time to-morrow morning we'll drive down to the city and hunt it up. It'll be O.K. with me unless you prefer another nine holes of golf in the morning."

"Why, I'd love to go to the church if you think your mother and sister won't mind."

"Oh, they won't mind! They have a standing date in bed Sunday morning. They don't expect anybody around before lunch time."

Kerry was much relieved to find that the club house was still in full blast when they returned, and the elder Holbrooks had not missed her.

"You look as fresh as a rose," said Holbrook senior as he helped her into the car a half hour later. "You too, Harry. You usually have too many cocktails aboard Saturday night for your own good and others' comfort."

"I hope you haven't had a dull time, not dancing," said Mrs. Holbrook apologetically, realizing that she had paid very little heed to her young guest.

"I've had a wonderful time!" said Kerry happily. "I've seen the Hudson by moonlight!"

"Oh, yes," said the woman of the world sleepily, "I suppose it is rather a sight when one sees it for the first time. I hope Harry hasn't been a dull escort."

"Gosh, Mud, you couldn't be dull with her! She's got a mind! She's no end interesting! She's not like these poor little saps at the club house!"

"Well, Son, I'm glad you can still appreciate a good mind when you meet one," said the father indulgently. Then turning to Kerry: "You must sleep late to-morrow morning. They all do here. Of course I'm off for a little golf early, but you won't be disturbed."

But Harry broke in.

"Oh, gosh, Dad, we've already got a date for morning. We're going for a drive. We'll be home round lunch time, but don't mind if we are late. We'll get some hot dogs or a milk shake on the way if we are hungry."

"For mercy sake, Harry! Don't go to dragging Miss Kavanaugh around your favorite haunts," said his mother stifling a yawn, "she'll be bored to death. Let her sleep in the morning."

"Don't you worry, Mud. We've got an understanding all right. Give you my word I shan't bore her this time."

As Kerry, in her luxurious bed, half an hour later, sank away to sleep she found herself thinking about the young son of the house. He was a nice kind boy. Was he really interested in what they had talked about, or just trying to be good company?

Kerry found him waiting for her in the breakfast room next morning at the hour they had agreed upon. Five minutes later his father walked in clad in golf attire.

His face lit up with pleasure when he saw them.

"Well, this is a delightful surprise," he said. "I expected to have to eat breakfast alone. Are you doing eighteen holes this morning too?"

It was the son who answered, virtuously and crisply as if he wished to call attention to the fact:

"No, Dad, we're going to church."

"Church!" said the father laughing, "*you* going to church?" He gave a gay laugh and took it as a joke, but the son's face was altogether serious.

"Sure, Dad. I mean it."

Mr. Holbrook's eyes sought Kerry's face for an explanation, but Kerry was taking it all quite as a matter of course, and the father sobered instantly.

"Well, I'm sure that's commendable, especially a nice morning like this. Where are you going? Better choose some place where they have good music. Remember Miss Kavanaugh has come from Europe where they have the best."

"We're going to a church Miss Kavanaugh chose," said the son importantly, "somebody from Scotland is speaking there."

"Ah! I see. Where is it? Fifth Avenue, I suppose."

"Why, I don't just know," said Kerry shyly, "but I am sure I can find it. I went there one night and it's not far from where I am staying."

"I see," said the host smiling pleasantly, "well, sorry you're not to be on the links this morning. We might get Lawson or Rambo and try a foursome. But it's a nice morning for a drive. Better take the new car, Harry, if you're going to drive yourself. Mother won't be wanting it till afternoon."

So with great joy Kerry rode away into the brilliant spring morning, to find her church again. It seemed almost as if she might be going to find McNair too, so happy she was.

They had to drive down past her lodging house before Kerry knew which way to direct Holbrook. As they passed, the door opened and Dawson hurried out with a suit case, looking this way and that before he plunged across the street and round the corner. But for once his uncanny vigilance was at fault. He did not see Kerry, as she shrank back startled. He was not expecting to find her in a seven thousand dollar car.

In the end they located the church, after a little skirmishing, and succeeded in getting good seats in the gallery in spite of a big crowd that was already gathering.

"This is a pleasant room," said Holbrook looking around interestedly. "Not stuffy like most churches, with dull windows, and no sunshine. I declare it looks really cheerful. Though I must confess I haven't seen the inside of many churches since I was a kid, except for weddings. I wouldn't expect to find anything as nice as this so far down town. And what an audience! Gosh! Look at 'em standing up around the walls and sitting on the pulpit steps. Why, it's like a first night show. Who did you say this guy was? People must know about him."

Kerry repeated what McNair had told her of the speaker, and he watched him when he came to the platform with real interest.

"I like his mug," said Holbrook after he had studied him a minute or two, "he looks like a real he man. Gosh! He's homely, isn't he? But I like him."

The first burst of the gospel singing seemed to startle the young man, but after a verse or two somebody handed them a book, and she heard his clear baritone joining in with the rest. Somehow it made her very glad to have him take hold and be interested this way. She wondered if there were a possibility that he, too, might learn to know and love the Lord Jesus. She felt that she had found so much in the new life already that she longed to pass it on to some one else. It seemed the only way she could show her gratitude for having found the truth herself. It thrilled her to think that this nice boy had not sneered at her, nor turned down the church service.

Young Holbrook listened intently to the prayer and Bible reading, much as if it were all new to him, but when the speaker with the quaint burr on his tongue began to talk, his eyes were fixed upon him in utter absorption. He sat as if fascinated.

Kerry, watching, was glad, and prayed in her heart while she listened:

"Oh, Father-God, speak to him through this preacher. Help him to find Jesus Christ!"

When the service was over the young man lingered looking wistfully toward the platform where many were thronging the preacher, shaking hands, stopping to talk with him.

"Gosh! I never heard a preacher like that!" said the young man. "He's human, he is. Gosh if I could hear preaching like that I'd go every Sunday, I swear I would!"

"He's to be here for another week, I think," ventured Kerry.

They drove back by the silver river in the bright noon sunshine talking together quite naturally as other young people might have talked over a movie or the possibility of rain or another war. They were talking of the possibility of the return to earth of One called Jesus.

"Gosh! If that was true it would make some change in things here, wouldn't it? Gosh! I'd like to be around when that happened. That is, if I had a drag with God some way, so I knew where I'd be."

"Why," said Kerry with assurance, "that's entirely possible. A friend who knows Him well has been telling me that is what the Bible promises, that all who believe on the name of the only begotten Son of God have exactly that through Jesus Christ. He's up there now before God to plead for us—all of us who are willing to be His—He will 'present us faultless.'"

"Oh, gosh! But you don't know me!" said the young man gravely. "I wouldn't come in His class at all."

"But I thought you told me yesterday that you weren't a sinner."

"Well, not exactly a sinner, of course!" admitted the boy. "But when you come to face God, why of course that's different—if there is a God at all—I wouldn't stand a chance at all with God."

"Well, I don't really know much about these things myself, for I'm a very new child of God, but I've been told, and shown that the Bible says, that 'God so loved *the world* that He gave his only begotten Son, that whosoever believeth on Him *hath* everlasting life.' The man this morning said that Christ puts His own righteousness over us and God doesn't take account of us and our lives at all, because they've been bought and covered over with Christ."

Mile and mile they talked, and Kerry found herself recalling word by word the way in which McNair had led her, and as she talked she seemed to be nearer to him, and was exhilarated with the thought that now she was really passing on what she had found.

All too soon they arrived at the Holbrook home, and found everybody out on the porch waiting for them. Natalie in a ravishing pink taffeta was lounging in the hammock swing with her Celt beside her, and began at once to jeer at her brother for going to church. Kerry hated it for him, and wished they wouldn't. It seemed to her that all the beauty of the morning was being dispelled.

But the young man received their taunts with a baffling seriousness.

"Say, you all don't know what you've missed. Some great speaker from Scotland. Say, you ought to go and hear him. He's great! Dad, did you ever know what a lot of things are going on to-day that were foretold in detail in the Bible hundreds of years ago."

"Oh, listen to him!" laughed his sister, "he must have been to a spiritualistic seance, or an evangelistic tent or something."

"Sounds a bit leery, I admit," smiled the father.

"Extremely fanciful, I should say," said the young man's mother loftily. "Shall we go out to the dining room now?"

The afternoon was filled with gayety. People came by twos and threes, dropped in to talk and laugh, and a few to have a quiet game of cards. There was music occasionally, and much laughter and banter and tossing of frivolous conversation back and forth. There did not seem to be any chance to escape. There was a girl named Amelie Rivers who absorbed young Holbrook to the exclusion of everybody else. Once he looked across the room at Kerry and sent her a swift smile which cheered the loneliness a bit, but instantly his mother, who seemed to be keeping close watch on him, sent him on an errand and Amelie with him.

Kerry was glad when tea was served and the afternoon was drawing to a close. She felt relief at the thought of getting back to her own little lodging room. The noise of the afternoon was getting on her nerves. The radio kept up a continual clatter above the voices of the guests, and Kerry wondered how they stood the confusion. But nobody else seemed to mind. When the radio soloed in a high soprano or bellowed in a howling bass, they only raised their voices louder and kept on their even course of conversation. Kerry, stranded in a big chair in the great arched window looking toward the river felt like one caught on a little island in the midst of a noisy eddying sea.

Evening came and with it no relief, till finally, when the young people began to dance, the older ones to play cards, the men went down to the pool room in the basement, and the Amelie girl continued to demand young Holbrook's entire attention, Kerry quietly excused herself on the plea of having to work on the morrow, and went to bed. She was glad that her week end was over, and that she might go back to real living on the morrow. Her last thought at night was that perhaps when she went back to her room there would be a letter awaiting her from McNair.

16

KERRY went to town the next morning on the train with the elder Holbrook.

Young Harrington had offered to take her in the car, in fact had been most assiduous in pressing the drive upon her, but his mother had succeeded in sidetracking him. Most apologetically, when she heard what was going on, she interrupted.

"I'm so sorry, Harrington, but I promised Amelie you would drive us over to the Thornton's this morning, and I'm afraid you could not possibly get back in time."

Young Holbrook frowned and was quite rude to his mother about it, but she remained firm.

On the whole Kerry was glad to make her adieus and get away. Fervently she thanked Mrs. Holbrook for her kindness, and for further vague invitations which she somewhat reluctantly added to her husband's statement that of course she would come out often. Kerry did not intend to come again if she could help it, and she knew that Mrs. Holbrook did not intend to issue further definite invitations if she could help it.

Mr. Holbrook was absorbed in his morning paper most of

the way to town, but Kerry was glad to have a little quiet to herself before she entered upon her new duties. She felt as if her spirit were ruffled up with the last hour at the breakfast table. Yet she could not help feeling glad that she had had opportunity to introduce Harrington Holbrook to the things of the spirit. At least he might think of them sometime again, and find the way of salvation. And she suddenly realized that she cared very much to have others get what had brought such peace to her own troubled soul.

Kerry found her new work most interesting.

She was given a desk all her own in a large pleasant room with many other desks. There was a typewriter that swung back out of the way when not in use, and behind her chair a great letter file which was her special charge. Her work was also to include some proof reading and that appealed to her.

At the first glance she saw that her fellow laborers were educated people who would be congenial associates, and she was on her mettle at once to do her best work. She felt before the day was over that she had the friendliness of the whole office. Every one had been kind in showing her about and giving her little hints that helped her quickly to fall into line and get her work done as it should be. Even Ted, the fifteen-year-old office boy who brought copy up from the printing shop, and ran all the errands, was thoughtful, bringing her a glass of water when he brought some to a neighboring desk. At noon Ted took her to the corner to show her a neat little tea room tucked away in a side street where he said they had the best apple pie and crullers in the whole city, and soup good enough to eat itself.

Kerry accepted his friendship joyfully and gave him one of her rare smiles that somehow seemed to catch its brightness from the glory of her red-gold hair. When she came back from her lunch she brought him three round sugary doughnuts in a paper bag.

"They were so good," she said with another smile, "I thought you'd like to taste them to-day."

His eyes danced with pleasure.

"Oh, gee!" he said gratefully, "that's nice of you. I bring my lunches and I didn't have much to-day. My mother was sick and I had to put it up myself. Only brought some bread and an apple."

Late that afternoon when Kerry left the building Ted was standing at the curb beside his motor cycle. He waved a comradely hand:

"So long!" he said cheerily. "They weren't hard to eat, were they! Well, see you sub-se!" and he swung his leg over the saddle and steered away with a great sound of chugging and back-fire.

Well, he was only a boy, but it was nice to have some one who was friendly, and informal. It took away the great loneliness that possessed her in this new land.

It was nearly a mile from the office to her lodging, but Kerry felt the exercise was good for her and besides, it saved money and she must conserve every cent. Her weekend party had taught her that there were many little changes that must be speedily made in her wardrobe now that she was a working woman. Not that she meant to lay in a stock of evening and sports clothes, far from it. But there were a number of articles that she should have, and they must be bought as fast as she could afford them.

As she started on her walk a hope sprang into her heart that gave light to her eyes, brought a flush of pleasure to her cheek, and quickened her footsteps. Perhaps there would be a letter awaiting her from McNair.

It was dusk in the hall when she unlocked the door and went in, but it was light enough to see that there was no letter lying on the hall table where she had seen other letters on Saturday, presumably for other occupants of the house. Disappointment dropped down upon her, but unwilling to give up the possibility she tapped on Mrs. Scott's door and inquired, thinking perhaps it had been put away for safe keeping till her return. But there was nothing.

Rather heavy-hearted, with a sudden weariness and unaccountable loneliness upon her she went up to her room.

She had not realized how cheap and sordid everything would look after the luxury in which she had been. Yet it seemed a quiet haven to her, and she was glad to get there.

She dropped down upon her bed, and laid her tired face in the pillow. After a few minutes' rest she got up and turned on the light, smoothed her hair, rubbed her cheeks till they were pink, and smiled at herself in the little crooked mirror. She must not give way like this. She was here in New York for a purpose. She must not let things by the way distract her and upset her, and deter her from the work that was hers. If she had not let herself get notions about McNair she never would have felt so downcast when he did not write. Of course he was busy and she could not expect him to take the first minute to keep his promise; and anyway, what had he to say to her, a mere stranger, except pleasantries and an apology for having had to leave before he had fulfilled his promise of taking her around the city. It would be only a letter of courtesy anyway. Why did she mourn for it? She simply must stop thinking about him! God had used him to show her the way to find Him, and now had taken him away before she allowed herself to become too interested in him. She would take hard hold of the things he had taught her, and remember him only as a good kind friend who had gone his way back into his own world.

She got out her little Testament and read a few verses and found comfort for her desolate young heart. Then she decided to go out and eat supper and hunt up her church again. A meeting had been announced. Of course, that was what she would do. And she would take pencil and note book along and take down all the wonderful preacher said, so that she would have references to look up afterward. For she had noticed on Sunday how often he mentioned chapter and verse of something he quoted.

So she got her supper and went to meeting. Listening again

to the great preacher she forgot her loneliness, and yet, in spite of herself she could not forget McNair.

His friendship lingered with her and she found herself thinking that she would tell him this or that, or she would ask him some question about a certain point that was brought up.

The interval since she had seen Dawson had dimmed her dread of him, and as several days passed without her meeting him on the stairs or in the street, she began to hope that he had given up his annoyances, and was perhaps going about his own business. She knew that he was still in the house because she heard him going upstairs late every night, but she had formed the habit of throwing a small rug across the crack of her door so that even her light would not give him notice of her presence there, and so felt secure in her own premises.

The work at the office grew daily more absorbing and interesting. As the week went by Kerry liked more and more the people with whom she worked, and she found them being friendly to her, not only for her own sake, but for her father's sake. For little by little it had leaked out among the offices, who she was, and several people high in authority had come and introduced themselves. Some even said they had known her father years ago, or had had the privilege of hearing him speak in his younger days before he went abroad. So she was very happy in her work, and before the end of the week had lost some of her feeling of being an alien everywhere.

Sometimes Ripley Holbrook would pass through the room where she was busy, and would stop at her desk to ask her how it was going, and say that he hoped she would come out to see them again soon. That made it nice, too, for all the others showed her that they felt she was high in favor.

Ted brought her a daffodil one morning that had fallen from a florist's car, and another time a little pink geranium in a pot from the shop where the florist's car belonged. He had done the man a favor and begged for the plant. Kerry carried it home and kept it on her window sill, watering it daily. It bloomed sweetly in the city gloom, and seemed like a silent companion full of good will.

Harrington Holbrook breezed into the office Friday morning just when she was busiest and insisted that she should promise to take a horseback ride with him in the park on Saturday afternoon, but she sweetly declined.

"In the first place I can't ride, in the second place I have nothing suitable to wear riding, and in the third place I couldn't anyway, I am a working woman, you know."

The boy went away at last when she had convinced him that she wouldn't go, with a kind of hunger and dissatisfaction in his eyes. But Kerry did not sigh. She kept on working, eager for the afternoon to come when she might go back to her room and see if there was any mail for her.

Yes, it would keep cropping up, that eagerness for McNair's letter! In spite of everything she kept looking for it.

"If it would only just come and settle me!" she told herself. "Of course just a little formal note in excuse, but I hate to think he has entirely forgotten when he was so kind and interested."

But the week went by and still no letter.

Sunday morning she went to church again, and took a seat near the back. Just before the sermon began Harrington Holbrook came in and sat beside her.

"I just thought you'd be here!" he whispered grimly, and then settled down to listen. And he really seemed interested! Kerry couldn't help being glad to have him there, and so friendly, but she kept worrying a little underneath it all. If the Holbrooks knew that he was seeking her they would not like it. At least his mother would not, she was sure of that. And it might put her in a bad light before her employer. It would look like a secret understanding between them. Yet it was good to see the look of interest in his face again as the sermon went on. He really was listening. Perhaps he would get something that would be lasting for his whole life.

He wanted her to go with him somewhere to dinner, but

she declined. She was glad that she had promised Mrs. Scott to share her solitary dinner, and she knew there was to be chicken in her honor.

Harrington lingered, keeping her much longer than she desired, carrying her fifteen minutes out of her way, for he had his car of course, and insisted on taking her home. But he asked her several questions about the meetings, and expressed satisfaction that the minister had held his own through a second hearing. He said he had never heard any other preacher who wasn't disappointing the second time. He went away at last, declaring that she simply must come up for the next week-end and they would have a day at golf together again. As she went up the steps she laughed to herself. Here was another who would stick to her in the face of all discouragements!

And then, even as she smiled over it she looked up and saw Dawson coming!

The days went by, one by one, pleasant enough, but lonely, and with a dull ache because no word had come from McNair, and Kerry had about given up expecting any.

For five weeks she managed to sidestep Dawson. Perhaps he did not think of looking for her at church, or else he had some purpose in holding aloof. She began to wonder uneasily why he stayed in her vicinity at all. At times his threat that he was going to marry her came up suddenly like a hidden pin to prick her sharply with an unreasoning anxiety, but for the most part she was glad to forget him, and to rest in the hope that he had got over his foolishness.

Kerry came home one night more than usually tired, determined to curl up on her bed and read for a while and go early to sleep. But when she unlocked her door and turned on her light she looked about her in dismay.

All the bureau drawers were pulled out, and everything that had been neatly arranged within was spread around on chairs and bed. The desk where she had put away her few papers was open, and the papers were lying in a heap upon the floor as if they had been taken out and examined one by one. The closet door stood open and her garments were tumbled around, some on chairs, some on the floor, some hanging with their pockets turned inside out.

Her locked trunk which had stood against the wall had been broken open, everything tossed about, and the trays turned out upon the carpet. At one side lay a pile of printed pages which upon examination proved to be the leaves of the magazine which she had used on shipboard as a hiding place for a few days for the notes of her father's book. She was sure she had removed all of them most carefully, yet evidently her purpose had been suspected and every page torn apart. Some of the edges were still adhering where they had been pasted. How thankful she was that she had been so careful in taking the notes to her safety deposit in the bank. Could any little scrap have been overlooked that could give her enemy anything on which to hang trouble for her?

She suddenly sat down weakly in a chair, shaken, nervous, ready to cry, and looked about upon the devastation. There was not a cranny in the room that had not been ransacked! Why, even the edges of the carpet in some places had been ripped up and turned back! What could it all mean? Was the man crazy or did he think that she had something by which he could profit if he could get possession of it? A great fear took possession of her! If she only had some one, some good counselor! Some sane adviser! And of course she thought of McNair at once.

Then as suddenly came his words so hastily written in that last message. "Advise with publisher or landlady in any perplexity."

She had not had that telegram out for a long time, it had been too unsettling, especially that last sentence, "Am anxious about you." It came to her now with a dull thud on her heart. Oh, if he were only here to help her! Well, she would take his advice, anyway. To-morrow she would ask for an audience with Mr. Holbrook and find out if there was any possible reason why that uncanny Dawson should have to haunt her this way, and what possible reason he could have for going through her possessions. And to-night, right now, she would tell Mrs. Scott what had happened. But first she would ask God.

She dropped upon her knees and breathed a quick petition for guidance and help, and then hurried down to the landlady.

Mrs. Scott was always pleased to see her. She told her her hair looked like the morning sunshine, and she smiled now as Kerry entered the kitchen where she was preparing her bit of supper.

"Mrs. Scott," began Kerry trying to keep the excitement out of her voice. "Have you been up to my room to-day? You know you spoke something about taking the curtains down."

"Why, no, darlin'," beamed Mrs. Scott, "I didn't get up. The man came to fix the furnace, and then Mrs. Brown from up in the Bronx dropped in just before noon and I kept her for lunch, and when she was gone it was that late I thought I'd leave it till the morrow."

"Well, won't you please come upstairs just a minute? Somebody has been into my room. I want you to see it before I disturb anything."

"Been into your room, darlin'? Why, how could that possibly be? I've bided right here all the day. The furnace man was never up the stair at all. He came in by the back way, and he couldn't ha got up and me not see him. There's been nobody here at all outside of Mrs. Brown. Of course the gentleman in the third floor might have gone up, I didn't notice, he's that quiet, but I always hear him when he's about and I think he's been out mostly all day. He's out now, I'm sure, for I went up half an hour ago to put in clean towels, he likes plenty, and he wasn't about. I noticed his hat was gone. You don't suppose a burglar could have got in, now, darlin'? See, the night latch is on."

Mrs. Scott had wiped her hands on the clean roller towel, turned down the gas under her cooking and hurried after Kerry, talking as she went and stopping in the front hall to examine the front door latch.

But when Kerry unlocked her door and the good woman beheld the disorder she lifted her hands in horror.

"Oh, my darlin' dear!" she exclaimed. "Now who could ha done the like of this? Such a mess! And you left it all put by?"

"Everything was in order when I went away this morning. The door of the closet was shut, the clothes all hung up, the bureau drawers all in order and closed, the desk shut."

"But who do you 'spose it might be?"

Kerry hesitated. Should she cast suspicion on Dawson?

"Mrs. Scott, did Mr. McNair tell you anything about me when he brought me here? Did he happen to mention my father?"

"He certainly did, darlin', he said your father was a great man who wrote science books, and you were here gettin' his last book printed to sell."

"Well, then, Mrs. Scott, I'm going to tell you what happened on shipboard. Sit down a minute, please. Here, I'll clear a chair for you."

"But wait, darlin', hadn't we better send for the police before we disturb things? I'm thinkin' that should be the way."

"Why, I'm not sure," said Kerry looking troubled. "I think perhaps you ought first to know what has happened before this."

So Kerry told the story as briefly as possible, and Mrs. Scott sat down in the little rocker with the patchwork cushion and wrapped her hands in her neat kitchen apron, and listened.

"The spalpeen!" she said. "The spalpeen! Now would you ever! And me thinkin' he was so quiet like and genteel! But it takes them quiet ones! And to think of me takin' in your enemy just like that! You poor little darlin'! I'll never forgive myself! And Mister Graham'll never forgive me!"

"You mustn't feel that way, Mrs. Scott. It certainly is not

your fault. Perhaps I should have told you about him before, only I hated so to bother you with it, and I didn't see anything else he could do!"

"The spalpeen!" ejaculated the good woman getting up suddenly. "I'll tell you what we'll do. A friend of mine has a son that's a policeman on this beat, and he'll tell us what to do. He won't do anything about it unless you say, but we better ask him. I'd feel better about it myself if somebody kind of professional knew about this business. Mister Graham put you in my charge, he did, and if anything should come to his young lady he'd never forgive me."

Kerry's cheeks suddenly flamed.

"Oh, Mrs. Scott, you must'n't feel that way!" she said again. "I'm not Mr. McNair's young lady at all, just a friend he met on shipboard. He was kind to me, but you haven't a bit of obligation in this."

"Obligation or no obligation, I'm bound to be held to account by my young gentleman. And you may not know you're his young lady, but I do. I could read it in his eyes. I've knowed those eyes for years, an' they never lied to me, and they said to me as plain as eyes could speak that the young lady he put into my charge was to be looked after very particular, because you was something very precious to him, and I'm goin' to keep my promise. Now, don't you worry one mite. I'm goin' to get that police boy in. He comes home to his supper about this time. I'll call up his mother on the telephone, and get him over. It can't do no harm at all."

"But I'm not sure we ought to put it into the hands of the police," said Kerry with worry in her eyes. "I thought I would ask the publisher to-morrow. He will know if there is any possible harm the man can do to Father's book. I'm sure he couldn't hurt me, only annoy me of course."

Kerry had not said a word about Dawson's threatened intention of marrying her. That seemed too awful to tell, too embarrassing.

"We're goin' to have perfessional advice!" asserted Mrs. Scott, her hand on the door, and vanished, then suddenly put her head back to say:

"Don't you touch a thing till I get back. I want he should see it just as it is."

Ten minutes later Mrs. Scott returned triumphant, a burly young policeman following her, stamping up the stairs, curiosity on his face. She had evidently given him a hasty sketch of the whole affair.

He stomped into the room, shut the door and looked around him, listened to all that was said, took hasty and approving cognizance of Kerry, and asked a few slow questions.

"Anything gone?" was the first question.

Kerry began to look around.

"Why, I hadn't thought to look," she said. "There wasn't anything I thought he would want—if it was he who did this. Every scrap of my father's writing is safe, one copy in the bank, the other with the publisher. I wasn't anxious about anything else."

"Better look around."

Kerry began to investigate. She gathered up things rapidly, capably, putting them in piles, invoiced her clothing, her few treasures, her pictures—Ah! Her father's photographs—the snap shots! Where were they? She had kept them in the little drawer of the desk!

Yes, they were gone!

Not very valuable in a sense, except to herself, and yet— what would that fiendish man want of them? Perhaps to use in some article he was writing?

She looked further, and found three little books missing, books that bore Shannon Kavanaugh's name written by his own hand on the flyleaf, with a few notes on the margins here and there. They were not valuable books in themselves, only small treatises on some scientific themes which her father had used as reference. It never occurred to her that they might help the enemy. She had kept them only because they were dear with memories of the vanished hand that had held them, and commented on the different paragraphs. Ah! Well, they were gone, too!

Further investigation could discover nothing else missing.

"Let's see this guy's room, M's Scott," demanded the policeman. "Looked up there yet to see if he's got 'em?"

"Why, no," said the landlady looking a little scared. "Now ain't I dumb? But you see we hadn't noticed they was gone."

They mounted the stairs, Kerry's heart beating wildly, in time to the sturdy tramp of the policeman's big assured feet.

Mrs Scott half nervously, half triumphantly unlocked Dawson's room door after timidly tapping to make sure he was not already inside, and they all stepped in.

A neat drab suit of clothes and an overcoat hung innocently in the closet, all with empty pockets. A steamer cap of well remembered snuff color lay upon the closet shelf. A hair brush and three or four handkerchiefs occupied the upper bureau drawer. A traveling bag contained pajamas and a clean pair of socks, with a few other garments. Not a scrap of paper, not a book, nor a picture. Not a sign of a snap shot anywhere. Absolute innocence!

"Don't look like this guy expected to stay long!" commented the policeman. "Say, you leave them things be a few minutes down in that room on the next floor. I'll bring the chief. We'll mebbe get some finger prints."

"Oh, is it necessary to do that?" asked Kerry distressed. "I don't know whether I'm justified in going so far—"

"Can't do no harm, Miss. But it looks ta me like this guy might be a real one mebbe. Anyhow, I'll bring the chief and see what he says. Might be some old hand. Anyhow we'll find out if it is the same man that has this room."

So the policeman walked away and presently returned with another one, and they two inspected both rooms again and hunted for finger prints in each. They said little and Kerry did not know whether or not they got any finger prints.

"This door has been opened with a key!" announced the chief, examining it carefully. He tramped upstairs and got the key from Dawson's door. Locked Kerry's door with its own key, and then unlocked it with Dawson's key. Then he stood back and looked at the two dismayed women.

"There you are!" he said significantly. "Better get that lock changed before that guy gets back again! But I don't guess you'll need to hurry. I think it likely he'll stay hid for a few days anyhow after this."

Mrs. Scott scuttled down to her telephone and somehow managed to get a new lock on Kerry's door, late though it was.

While Kerry was at work putting her room to rights, and going carefully over everything to make sure nothing else was gone, Mrs. Scott was down in her kitchen getting a nice little supper.

"Just a cup o' soup and a wee bit salad to hearten you," she explained as she brought it up on a tray, and Kerry was cheered by the kindliness and companionship of the good woman.

As the policeman had prophesied Dawson did not return that night. Mrs. Scott, having reflected all night on the fact that Dawson possessed a latch key to the front door, had the front door lock changed the first thing in the morning. When Dawson did return—if Dawson did return—he would not find it so easy to get in.

Two days went by and no Dawson, and then came a letter from a New Jersey town, saying he had been suddenly called away for a few days. It enclosed a New York draft to pay for his room for another month. Mrs. Scott sat down and looked at it for a few minutes and then she summoned her policeman and laid the matter before him. He looked wise, nodded his head and said:

"Jus' what I thought!" and went mysteriously off with the letter.

17

MEANTIME, Kerry had duly inquired for Holbrook the next morning and found that he had not been well and had gone off on his vacation. That meant two weeks at least before she could tell him what had happened. Meantime a lot more things might happen. However, she was probably foolish about it. What, after all, *could* happen?

The days went by and Kerry was very busy. The proof of her father's book was coming off the press, and she was spending her days going carefully over it, correcting, and revising in places. This work made her as happy as anything material could do, and she went back to the house every night dead tired.

She had ceased to look for a letter from McNair. He had forgotten her, that was all. That was to be expected. What was she to him save a casual stranger whom he had helped to find the way of life? She had great reason to be grateful to him always for the peace that had come to her heart. There was no more tempest and rebellion. She had accepted the fact that she was here on the earth as a sort of college to fit her for the heavenly home, and that she was to look for her joy hereafter, not here. Yet unconsciously, always when she entered the hall, her eyes went to the table where the mail was put. There were only two other lodgers, one in the second story back, and one in the third story back. One was a dressmaker who went out by the day, and sometimes came home very late at night, a sad oldish woman. The other was a trained nurse who had been off on a chronic case ever since Kerry had been there. She had never seen either of them, but there were frequent letters for both which lay on the hall table sometimes when she came in. But there was never anything for her.

One night about ten days after the ransacking of her room Kerry came in a little later than usual and found Mrs. Scott watching for her.

"Come in a wee bit," she said, "I want to talk to you, darlin'. Here's a bite of hot scones and honey I've saved for ye, and a hot bit of meat I had left. You're lookin' peaked and white. I doubt you don't eat enough in them restaurants! Just the same thing day after day and all taste alike."

Kerry accepted the supper gratefully, for indeed she had not stopped to take more than a milk shake on her way home. She felt too tired and warm, for the weather had been unusually hot that day.

"And now," said Mrs. Scott when she had set out a supper fit for a king on her little kitchen table with its white cloth and delicate old china, "now, darlin', may I ask ye a personal question?"

"Why surely," said Kerry opening her sweet eyes in surprise, "you certainly have a right after all you have done for me."

"Well, then, darlin', why don't ye answer my boy's letters?"

"Letters?" said Kerry. "What letters? I've had no letters!"

"Oh, yes ye have, darlin'," said Mrs. Scott studying the girl's open face with a puzzled air, "I saw the letters myself, took 'em in and noted the handwritin'. I never forgets handwritin', not especially when it belongs to one whom I honor and love as me own. And I saw his name right up in the corner of the envelope, Graham McNair, Los Angeles, California. Three letters there was, two in one week, and one the next week, and I laid 'em all neat on the hall table like I always do, and they was gone soon as you come home, for I went out in the hall to see each night after I heard you come in. I says to myself, I says, she'll be tellin' me a message from him, forbye, or mebbe a bit of what he said to her, but never a word did you say. And then I thought, well, why should she? She counts me a stranger, of course. But I was that happy knowin' you had a letter from him whom I love as if he was my own, and that's true!"

"Why, but you dear Mrs. Scott! I never got a letter from Mr. McNair, just that telegram you brought up to my room that second morning after I came. He said he would write, but he never did. You must have made a mistake. It must have been somebody else's letter."

"Oh, na, I made na mistake," said the woman lapsing into a Scotch word now and again in her excitement, "It was him all right, and it was you. Three letters! The first one was in a government envelope with a stamp made on it. I remember them each. One was a long envelope—long and narrow. The third one was big and square."

"Well—but—" said Kerry bewildered, but Mrs. Scott cut in again.

"The reason I dare to ask is, my boy has written ta me. He says would I please find out if anything is the matter with you, or if you just didn't want to correspond with a stranger. He says he meant no harm, but perhaps you feel he was not properly introduced. Perhaps you think he was forward in writin' at all."

There were tears in Kerry's eyes now, and her voice shook.

"Oh, but, Mrs. Scott, *my dear!*" she insisted, "I never got any of those letters at all! Never a one. I looked and looked at that hall table every night hoping one would come. I wanted at least to be able to write and thank him for all that he had done for me, but I had no address. I never realized you might have it or I would have asked you. But surely, Mrs. Scott, you wouldn't think I would do such a mean thing as not to answer his letters. Why, he's a prince of a man, of course. I felt honored that he was so kind to me, and helped me. What a terrible ingrate I would be not to notice his letters. I thought he had been too busy to write, and likely had forgotten me by this time."

"Forgotten ye, nothin'. As if any man with eyes in his head could forget that hair, and them sweet eyes, and them lips—"

"Oh, Mrs. Scott!" said Kerry growing rosy, and the tears dashing down over her hot cheeks. "But where—oh where—! If there were letters where are they? Could they have fallen down behind the table?"

"I'm not that dirty, me darlin'," said Mrs. Scott indignantly. "That table is pulled out twice a week and dusted. No, it's somebody has took 'em, that's what!"

"But let us go and look!" pleaded Kerry jumping up and running out to the hall.

Mrs. Scott came with a flash light, and together they stooped and searched the floor and the corner.

"There's a big crack behind the baseboard!" said Kerry poking in it with a hair pin, "but there's nothing behind there."

It was then that Mrs. Scott's sharp eyes spied the bit of white sticking out from under the linoleum.

"The spalpeen!" she said suddenly and pounced down upon it, ripping up the edge of the linoleum in a hurry with strong angry fingers. "The spalpeen! So that was what he was doin' and I never thought of it after!"

"Who? What?" said Kerry eagerly as Mrs. Scott fished out a long white envelope.

"The spalpeen!" said Mrs. Scott ripping up some more of the linoleum, "I come out in the hall one day and seed him down on his knees a workin' away under this table, and as soon as I come out he gets up and he says, quite polite. 'I dropped my pencil under the table and I was after it,' says he.

And I, fool that I was, thinks nothing of it until now. Why, they might a lain there till doom's day and we never known if you hadn't insisted on coming out to look. And me that proud of my dustin' I wouldn't look!"

But Kerry was not listening. She had gathered the envelopes to her heart, one after another as Mrs. Scott fished them out, and was now half way up the stairs.

"You will excuse me while I read them, won't you Mrs. Scott, dear," she called back, filled with sudden compunction.

"Sure I will, me darlin', an' think nothin' of it, but it's the last time I take in a lodger without references. The very last time!"

Kerry, up in her room was opening her letters with fingers that trembled with eagerness. Joy was surging over her in waves, that threatened a sweet engulfing.

Kerry had just sense enough left to look at the dates on the postmarks and get the first letter first.

It was brief, and evidently written at the station just as the train was leaving:

> My dear Miss Kavanaugh:
>
> Words and time fail me in trying to tell you how disappointed I am that I have to leave in this sudden way without time even for explanation. It is too late to try to get you on the telephone, or I should have had at least a word with you. But please understand that nothing but absolute necessity would take me away just now, and I shall return as soon as I possibly can. Meantime guard yourself carefully, don't take risks, and consult with Mr. Holbrook if anything unpleasant arises. Get Mrs. Scott to show you the way about the city. She will be delighted I am sure. I begrudge the privilege to anyone else.
>
> I am praying that the heavenly Father may be very close to your realization, and that His peace that passeth understanding may be yours. It is good to know we can

meet at the mercy seat. I rejoice that you know my Lord Jesus. Praying that all best blessings may be yours. I shall write from the train. Let me know at above address how you are prospering please.

Yours,
In Christ Jesus,
Graham McNair

The second letter was longer, and went more into detail concerning the business that carried him away so summarily. It contained advice about her new life in the strange city, where to go, what to do for her own refreshment, a list of churches and other places where she would be likely to hear real spiritual preaching and teaching, the address of a book store where she would find helpful books, suggestions about where to go for good music.

It was pervaded all through with a brotherly care for her that filled her with contentment and made her feel as if he were right there beside her talking to her. It touched also on the man Dawson. He said he hoped sincerely that she would have no further trouble with him, and that she was scarcely likely to as he would be afraid of arrest if he tried to put over any more tricks, but in case she did have trouble the matter should be at once put into the hands of the proper authorities, and Mr. Holbrook would surely be willing to assist her in that. In case of any sudden emergency of course she would call the nearest police.

This advice gave Kerry relief, because she had feared that perhaps she ought not to have let Mrs. Scott go quite so far in what she had said to the policeman. Perhaps it might only complicate matters.

The third letter was not so formal as the other two. It began "My dear Kerry." She caught her breath, and her eyes grew starry. She felt like a starved person with food suddenly put before her. Her eyes greedily picked up the words from the paper so fast she could hardly gather the sense.

Do you mind my calling you Kerry? You have been that to me in my heart for a good many days now, in fact ever since the night on shipboard when you gave yourself to my Lord Jesus—the night the storm came up!

Dare I go a little further and tell you that you have become very precious to me? I had not meant to write a thing like this. It ought to be told, quietly, when we are face to face. I ought perhaps to have waited a while till you knew me better. Yet, during these days that the train has been hurrying me away farther and farther from you I have come to think that perhaps you have the right to know it now.

You may not feel that way about me, of course. I can hardly expect it, certainly not at such short notice. But days are so uncertain, and with all these miles between us I want to tell you, that whether you can return my love or not, I hold you deep in my heart as the most precious thing that earth has left for me. Next to my Lord Jesus, Kerry, I love you, dear.

There, now I have told you, and perhaps, if you do not like it, I may have cut myself off from this charming friendship which we had begun, but somehow I could not keep it longer to myself. You are too bright a treasure, and there are too many out seeking such treasures as you. I had to let you know at once.

I am not asking you to decide anything now about the future, although all that a man can give to a woman my heart is giving to yours. I would not hurry you nor worry or disturb you in any way. If you can not feel that you can promise me yourself to be my dear wife, yet; if you feel that I am too precipitate, will you not at least let the matter rest in very dear friendship until I can come back to you and ask you again face to face? Of course what I want is your assurance, but you may not yet know your own mind on this, so do not feel that you must decide anything in haste.

I await your answer with almost childish eagerness. Dear Kerry, your beautiful face is ever before my thoughts. I commend you to our Father's keeping daily, almost hourly.

With deeper love than I know how to write,

Yours,

Graham McNair

With this letter in her hand Kerry sat for a few minutes, just staring down at the lovely words, her face glorified with her joy. Then suddenly she sprang up, the letters still in her hand and clasping them to her breast she dropped upon her knees beside her bed:

"Oh, my dear Father-God," she prayed, "I can never never thank Thee enough for this wonderful joy, this wonderful love, that Thou hast sent me!"

Then she went to her desk and began to write. Soon she appeared downstairs with a folded paper in her hand and her hat on.

"Could you tell me where to find the nearest telegraph office, Mrs. Scott?" she asked shyly. "I'm going to send a telegram."

"Oh, I'm glad you are, dearie," said the good woman with quick intuition. "The lad will be so relieved to know you are all right. I'm glad you won't keep him waiting a whole week for a letter, he's such a dear lad. But you'll not be needin' to go out to telegraph, darlin'. You can phone in your message right from here. I'm just runnin' out next door for a minute now, and you can have the telephone all to yourself. Give him my love, dearie, and I'll pay for part of the message. Tell him Martha sends her love."

The canny old lady seized her hat from a closet shelf and took herself off in a whisk of time, and there was Kerry left with her glowing cheeks, and her starry eyes trying to say those wonderful mysteries into the telephone to a sharp-voiced tired operator. She managed the address all right, reading carefully from her paper, but over the message she choked, and lost her voice several times, and had to be snapped up from Central with a sharp "What? Please repeat that."

> Your letters just reached me to-night. They bring greater joy than I have ever known. With all my heart I say yes. I do not need to wait. So sorry to have seemed indifferent. Am writing. Martha sends love and I send great love.
>
> Kerry

Then with radiant embarrassed face Kerry hung up the receiver and went upstairs to write her letter.

Kerry mailed her letter on the way down to the office next morning, and went on with her work, singing paeans in her heart. For even the hot dusty avenue seemed to her like a way paved with joy that morning. But perhaps if she had stayed to look at the morning paper before she left Mrs. Scott's she would not have felt so much like singing.

She had not been at her desk more than half an hour when she was summoned to the office to see Mr. Holbrook.

This was quite unusual as Holbrook was a busy man, and seldom had time for intimate contact with the employees in the office. Also, this was the first intimation that Kerry had that Holbrook was at home again.

He greeted her in dignified silence, and there was something in his glance that sent a quiver of premonition through her heart. He motioned her to a chair and closed the outer door of the office.

"Miss Kavanaugh," he said and his kindly tone was almost severe, "you did not tell me that you were engaged to be married!"

"Oh!" said Kerry, her cheeks flaming into color, "why—why, it only just happened—last night. I would have—I have had no opportunity. It was all so unexpected—! But—" and a bewildered look came into her eyes, "I don't see how you knew about it. No one knows but Mrs. Scott. Unless—are you a friend of Mr. McNair's? But even then—Why I only sent him an answer last night."

"Mighty quick work, I should say," remarked Holbook dryly, "haven't you seen the morning papers, Miss Kavanaugh?"

"No!" said Kerry sharply sitting up straight in alarm, "what could the morning paper possibly know?"

For answer Holbrook handed her his morning paper, folded with the second page out, and in the very middle at the top of the page Kerry saw her own face looking out at her, a clear good likeness, and just below it in a smaller oval, another picture of herself and her father standing together with the lace-like architecture of the great Rheims Cathedral in the background.

Large headlines caught her horrified gaze.

Brilliant Daughter of Noted Father Plights Troth to Well-known Scientist! Miss Kerry Kavanaugh, daughter of the late Dr. Shannon Kavanaugh, one of the world's greatest scientists, soon to wed Henry Dawson, Ph.D., author of "The How and the Why of it!" and writer of scientific articles. Professor Dawson has already made great attainments in his chosen line, and promises to follow in the footsteps of his noted father-in-law-to-be.

There was more of it, a half column, but Kerry did not read it. The letters swam and danced before her horrified eyes. She lifted her blanched face to her employer and there was no mistaking her misery.

"Oh, how could anybody be so wicked!" she said with white lips. "Oh, how terrible! What shall I do?"

"Do?" said Holbrook stooping to pick up the paper that she

had dropped from nerveless fingers. "Do? Didn't you allow this to be put into the papers? Didn't you furnish the pictures? Isn't it true that you are to marry this man? And isn't he the Dawson whom you warned us against?"

Kerry was stung into action.

"He certainly is, but I am not going to marry him. I would rather die!" she said with vehemence. "He has been dogging my steps ever since I came to the city. He had the impertinence to tell me that he intended to marry me the first week I was here, followed me to the park where I was walking and insisted on talking to me, then when I ran away and took a bus I found him in the hall of the lodging house waiting to finish his sentence when I arrived there. How he knew where I was living I have no idea, but he came and took a room on the floor above me. I managed to keep out of his way for several weeks, but a few days ago I went home one night and found all my belongings pulled out of my trunk and desk and bureau, and two of my father's books and these snapshots gone. I called in the police, and then I tried to see you the next day and tell you, fearing he might try to use the books in some way that was not legitimate. But you were gone—and—Oh!"

Kerry suddenly covered her face with her hands and groaned.

There was silence in the office for an instance and then Holbrook spoke again, still in a cold tone of voice:

"Then you didn't know that this man, Dawson, has written an article for one of the biggest Scientific sheets published in this country, and that he says he was your father's closest friend and co-worker, and that he claims to have rewritten and finished your father's book? You didn't know that he has in that article told the story of your and his romance, begun while you were quite a little girl, and that he quotes from your father's own words in several instances? You didn't know that it was scheduled to come out in the middle of this month?"

Holbrook was watching Kerry with a mingling of compassion and doubt in his eyes, as she lifted her gaze to him once more. If her face had been white before it was ashen now, and it seemed as if her lips were powerless to speak.

"No, I didn't know," and it seemed to her that her voice sounded like one dead.

"But didn't you tell me you were engaged, when you first came into the office? Didn't you admit it?"

Then did Kerry's joy, like a new tide of life, flood into her heart, and into her face in radiance as she remembered.

"Oh, yes!" she said, "I—am engaged! But—not to that creature! I am engaged to Mr. McNair, the man who came here with me the first day, and whom I introduced to you down in the reception room."

"Ah!" said Holbrook with relief. "Ah! That's a different matter! Well, I congratulate you! But now, what shall we do about this? What is your wish in the matter? Of course I've stopped the publication of the article. I have a friend over there in the office of the magazine and he happened to mention that they were publishing such an article and I asked to see the proof of it. He sent it over to my house last night. You see it mentions several things with regard to your father's book which are not true, and which we could not permit, but when I saw the paper this morning I did not know what to think, Miss Kavanaugh!"

Then Kerry struggling with her tears, went carefully over the whole story from the time she left London, and by the time she was through Holbrook's eyes were full of sympathy and he was blowing his nose, and dabbing at his eyes as freely as if Kerry had been his own Natalie.

In a kind and fatherly way he talked it all over and promised to telephone at once to the office of the paper and see that the announcement was corrected. Also to telephone to the police and have them recover the photographs if possible.

When they were through talking Holbrook asked her to go out to lunch with him.

"Oh, if you'll excuse me," she said shyly, "I'd like to go

right away and send a telegram to California. I am afraid Mr.
McNair might somehow get hold of this. Doesn't the Associated Press telegraph news all over the country? Couldn't
they get this? Of course they wouldn't do it on my account,
but having my father's name connected with it, wouldn't
they perhaps put it in California papers?"

"It's quite possible," laughed Holbrook. "Run along, little
girl and set your lover's mind at rest, and then meet me
downstairs in half an hour and I'll have the notice ready and
tell you what the magazine and newspaper people said."

So Kerry sent her telegram, took time to telephone to Martha Scott who was probably worrying her heart out if she had
read the paper, went to lunch with the head of the great publishing house, and then came back to her desk and worked
overtime to make up for it.

It was growing dark when Kerry finally put on her hat and
started to the door. It had started to rain, and the air was chilly
and mean. Kerry had on a thin dress and no wrap.

Ted had made it his business to hover around going in and
out while she was working, pretending that he was doing
overtime too, but really reluctant to leave her alone with only
the janitor and the scrub women.

"Good night!" said Ted cheerily, as she came out of the
cloak room and started toward the street door.

"Good night, Ted," called Kerry with a lilt in her voice, as
Ted disappeared into the back room where he kept his motor
cycle, for he lived far out in the Bronx.

Ted emerged from the little side entrance with his machine,
just as Kerry stepped out from the big door.

A shabby old taxi was drawn up in front of the main door
of the house, or—was it a taxi? Ted stepped back into the
shadow to see who it was.

The driver came toward Kerry and took off his cap.

"Is this Miss Kavanaugh?" he asked in a gruff tone, not at all
mannerly, Ted thought, for such a flower of a girl as Miss
Kavanaugh.

Kerry answered "Yes," brightly. All her tones were full of gladness to-night.

"Well, I was to say Mrs. Scott sent the taxi because it was raining. She didn't want you to walk home in the rain."

Kerry paused, astonished, looked at the shabby cab, then with a laugh and "Oh, that was kind of her!" she stepped toward it.

Ted, watching from his shadowed doorway thought he saw a hand reach out and pull the girl in, heard a scream! He was sure he heard a scream! Could that have been that Mrs. Scott inside to surprise her? Could it have been her hand that pulled her in, and perhaps frightened Miss Kavanaugh for a minute? That was probably it. A poor joke, he thought. But why did that driver seem so hurried? And was that a frightened white face he saw at the window? A hand waved for an instant, then pulled away? Was that his name he heard called in muffled tones as if the voice were being smothered? "Ted! Help!" Did he hear that or was it his imagination carved out from the screech of the passing trolley just then.

"Ted! Help! Help!"

The words rang in his brain.

The cab was half a block away by now, its wicked little tail light winking like a red berry in the distance. What was the matter with his engine? Oh, why in sixty couldn't he get it started? There, that cab had turned the corner to the left! Ah! He was off! Was that it there, just turning another corner? Could he make it before the lights turned and stopped him?

On he flew, trying ever to get near enough to look inside the cab, realizing very soon that the cab was not going in the direction in which Miss Kavanaugh lived.

Sometimes the traffic blocked them both, and Ted could almost have got off and stepped up to the cab and looked inside, only he dared not desert his machine, for in a moment they would be off again and he would get farther separated. Sometimes, the light would change just as Ted came up to it, and the cab would ride far out of sight around a corner, but by this time Ted had learned its license number and could always recognize the right car.

Once he came on a mounted policeman riding along to his location.

"Hey, Chief!" yelled Ted, as he slowed by him. "Send a cop after me. Kidnaping ahead! That cab there! Girl yelled for help!"

He dared not stop to be sure the officer understood, but he thought he saw him nod his head, and a little while later he thought he heard the chug chug of a motor cycle coming on behind. He began to think of some of the things Miss Kavanaugh had said to him now and then, those noon hours when they went to a cheap cafe together, about his mother who was still sick, and about praying and trusting God. He tried to frame a crude prayer in his heart as he thrashed along through the crowded streets. Farther out where the traffic was less he had all he could do to keep up with the cab which was rattling away at a great rate now that the road was clear. Did they see the cop coming, and were they trying to get away? They never would connect him with Miss Kavanaugh. He hadn't brought out his machine till they were well under way.

Thinking his wild boy thoughts, exulting in the adventure, playing the game as he used to play ball on the school yard diamond, Ted rode on.

A little child leading a crippled old lady tried to cross the street, and Ted had to slow up to let them by. Then, looking on ahead, he saw that the cab had gone to the middle of the next block and stopped! A door flung open and light streamed across the pavement. It was a squalid neighborhood. The very atmosphere seemed foreign and menacing, and Ted could not hurry because of the old lady and the little child ahead. Would he get there in time? Yes, there she was! And she was struggling. She was calling, wasn't she? His engine made such a noise he could not tell. He rode up with a boom and a crash, and jumped from his machine to the sidewalk!

18

WHEN Kerry stepped into the shabby cab and felt her wrists seized she was so frightened she could not make a sound at first. But as the driver slammed the door and sprang to his seat, she remembered Ted and screamed for help.

She was not sure that her voice had been heard for it was almost immediately smothered in a dusty woolen cloth that was stuffed into her mouth. She tried to struggle free from the hand that held her, and the rag that was choking her, but she accomplished nothing, and finally sat back limp and waited, trying to pray.

"God! God! Father–God!" she cried in her heart. "I'm yours! Won't you please take care of me! You've promised! I'm trusting you!"

Finally, as she remained limp, the rag was removed from her mouth and the grip that held her around the waist was relaxed.

"Now!" said the hard flat voice which she at once recognized, "if you've decided to act like a sane person, I'll let you free, but I warn you that just as soon as you move or make any loud noise or try to attract attention to us, you'll be bound and gagged! Do you understand?"

Kerry did not answer. She was trying to steady her nerves and think what to do.

"And now, if you are calm enough to listen, I'll tell you that there's nothing in the world for you to be afraid of. Nobody is going to injure you in any way. If you behave yourself everything will be all right."

Kerry still kept her mouth shut.

"I may as well explain before we get to our destination, so that you will understand what you are to do, that we are now on our way to get married. Did you see the announcement in the paper this morning?"

Kerry did not answer. She did not even look at the man in the dim light that came in from the street.

"We are going to a friend of mine. They understand all about it, and another friend of mine is coming to marry us. It will all be done quite regularly and in an orthodox manner. You needn't worry about that, and the notices that go in the paper to-morrow morning will be entirely conservative and socially correct. I have looked out for all that. You will find I have taken every precaution to make you happy!"

The flat voice talked on and on. Kerry began to feel herself floating away, as one that dreams and feels a nightmare gripping his throat, yet is unable to cry out!

Mile after mile that cheap old worn out car bumped over the road, out and out and far away from the city that Kerry knew, no land marks anywhere that she could recognize.

Would the hard flat voice never cease? Could any hell be worse than to be married to that man? Hear him talking about his plans, telling what they would do after they were married!

Perhaps she was dying. She was not conscious of breathing! Well, if she was dying they could not do anything to her! They could not marry a dead person! God! God! Father-God! In the name of Jesus! Help!

"Get out of here. We've got there!" announced that flat, hard voice and she was jerked into an upright position. Then she wasn't quite dead, after all. But perhaps if she stayed asleep they would think she was dead.

"Hurry! Quick! Two motor cycles are after us hot! And one of 'em's a cop!" she heard a strange voice say. Was that the driver?

She was out on the sidewalk now, dazed, being urged toward an open door, a dirty uninviting door, but her feet would not carry her.

"Hurry!" said the hard flat voice. "You will be sorry if you don't do as I say now! Afterwards everything will be all right!"

But she stood there unable to move. There was noise and din and clatter, and great silence, and suddenly she heard Ted's clear voice.

"I'll take care of this baby. You take the driver, cop!" and the hurrying Dawson tripped as neatly as ever a toe felled an adversary and sprawled at her feet. She heard a shrill whistle ring out and saw more shining brass buttons appear from around a corner. Ted's arm was about her now, and he was leading her into the street where stood his shining motor cycle.

"Stay there a minute, Kid," he said as if she were a little child, "I gotta finish that baby," and he rushed back to the sidewalk where Dawson was just arising dazed and looking around him.

Kerry had a vague vision of a taxi driver and a policeman with a gleaming gun between them. She could not see what was going on on the sidewalk, but presently she heard a large unwieldly body dumped with a thud into the back seat of the taxi, heard the policeman call to Ted. "Here, put these bracelets on him, Kid. Better to be on the safe side. Handkerchiefs and greasy rags aren't always very strong." Heard the snap of steel. Heard more steel snapped on the wrists of the driver.

The door that had sent out the long streaming light was shut. The light was gone. All the lights in the house were out.

The house looked dark and unoccupied. She looked at the forbidding windows and thought stupidly that that was the house that was to have sheltered her wedding. A few minutes more and,—if Ted hadn't come! But she would surely have been dead. That awful choking in her throat! That terrible burden on her heart! She couldn't have stood it another minute. Ted had come just in time.

Ted was coming to her now. He was putting her on the mud guard behind him, and they were riding away. He was asking her if she could hold on. It was raining but she did not care. She was laughing and saying she was all right, and all the time it seemed like a dream. Taxi, Dawson, that dirty rag in her mouth, a wedding, and Dawson. Oh, God, how you saved me! Her thoughts were fear and laughter and a great peace. She did not know what had become of Dawson and the driver in their steel bracelets, or the cops. It did not matter! God had come in time. He had sent His angel, Ted.

Hours afterward, it seemed, after they had shot through the rain in the dark, and her brain had cooled off, and her mind was quiet and full of peace, she sat in Mrs. Scott's kitchen eating milk toast and tea, and Ted was telephoning to his mother all about it, telling her that Mrs. Scott was putting him up, it was so late, and after all that had happened they needed a man in the house that night. As he talked on telling details, Kerry learned that Dawson was spending the night in jail, and she drew a deep breath of relief.

Kerry did not go to the office the next morning. Mrs. Scott and Ted had a conspiracy, and kept her asleep, and Ted went down and told the news, going straight to headquarters and leaving nothing untold except the royal part that he had played in the drama. It remained for Kerry herself to do that when she got back. But about noon there came to Kerry from the office the biggest bunch of roses she had ever seen, and before night a telegram arrived from California in a sweet and mysterious code that only those two who had walked the deck together could understand.

The next day Kerry went to the office with shining eyes thoroughly rested.

For three whole days she walked on air, and beauty radiated from her as she passed. The office watched her and rejoiced, for by this time they all loved her.

Then, one night, Kerry went home, and found her mother sitting stiffly in Mrs. Scott's poor little prim parlor. And her house of dreams fell about her feet.

She was still the same old Isobel, though she was attired in a Paquin model of printed blue chiffon softly patterned with feathers. It floated and curled about her feet and her lovely hands, in draperies that only an artist in materials could achieve. Her hat was chic and becoming, her fingers were flashing with jewels, and about her throat was a necklace of exquisite star sapphires. Her wrist watch flashed with a circlet of tiny jewels. Kerry thought she had never seen her look so young and so very beautiful, yet there was something about her that was unpleasantly startling. Her lips were too red, too perfectly pointed like a cupid's bow, her cheeks wore too soft a hue like an apple blossom. There was something artificial in the very arrangement of her hair! Why! Her hair had been bobbed!

"Mother!" said Kerry with a sudden glad hunger in her voice. Then, startled:

"Mother?" with a furtive glance about. Was there always to be some one from whom she had to run away? One enemy was safe in jail for the time being. Must she turn her attention now to hiding from the other?

"Where is—?" the question broke from her lips involuntarily.

"Sam? Oh, he isn't here. You needn't worry! I've left him!" said his wife, getting out her handsome handkerchief, and preparing it for dainty use.

"You've—*what*—? Mother!"

"I've left him, Kerry! Oh, you needn't look so startled, it's what you wanted, isn't it? Now, when I've made this sacrifice mainly on your account don't go to blaming me for it. I might have known you'd be old-fashioned of course. But anyway, I've done it, and I've come to you."

"But Mother, what do you mean? Has he—has he been unkind to you?"

"Oh, no, not unkind. No, I wouldn't say that. He's always good natured enough, but he will get drunk and I just can't abide his getting drunk. You see he promised me before we were married that he wouldn't drink any more but now he doesn't seem to remember about it at all, and I think it's so ungentlemanly. I guess I must be old-fashioned too, living so long with your father, but it doesn't seem quite nice. And he has so many friends I can't stand. They talk loudly, and they joke at me. There's one who is fat and has a red nose, and not a bit of taste. He's known her a long time and she thinks that gives her privileges and I can't abide her. So I decided to get a divorce. It's not at all difficult nowadays. Sam insisted on coming back to America to look after his estate, and I couldn't stand it down there, such an old house and no modern conveniences at all. So I pretended I was coming up to visit you, but I've really decided to go to that place out west for a little while, they call it Reno, I think, and stay there till I can get my divorce and then you and I can live together nicely on my alimony. I mean to insist on a large alimony."

"Mother!"

"Now, look here, Kerry, you needn't go to 'mothering' me. I knew you would make a fuss at first but I've made up my mind, and you know it's no use to talk to me—"

"Mother! Come upstairs. We don't want anyone to hear you talking that way!"

"Now, you're being rude as usual. What am I saying that anyone may not hear, if they have the impertinence to listen?"

"Come, Mother," pleaded Kerry.

"Oh, well, I suppose we might as well go to a more private place. Haven't you an elevator? I thought every house in America had elevators in these days. Mercy, what a narrow staircase. Couldn't you find a pleasanter stopping place? It looks quite ordinary to me."

"Mother, please!" said Kerry in distress lest Mrs. Scott would hear her. "Such a dear little woman owns this house and she has been so very good to me."

"Well, why shouldn't she, I'd like to know? You come of a very good family on both sides, though your father of course was eccentric. But I always say—"

"Mother!" said Kerry in desperation struggling with the key. "Won't you please wait till we get in my room before you talk any more?"

The lock gave way at last and Kerry ushered her mother in and closed the door.

"You haven't even kissed me!" declared Isobel. "I don't believe you're in the least glad to see me."

"Oh, Mother!" cried Kerry and took her beautiful, elegant little mother into her arms, burying her face in her neck.

"Oh, look out, child! You're always so impulsive! You'll ruin my wave! I saw a place quite near the station and stopped in to have it done before I hunted you up, it was so warm and I was so untidy from traveling."

"But you haven't told me how you found me," said Kerry, drawing back and trying to steady her nerves and keep on a safe topic.

"Oh, that was easy," laughed the mother. "Sam found a notice of your father's new book in a magazine and he called the publishing house on long distance and found out your address. He was expecting to come along, only I came away without him."

"You don't mean that he is coming here!" said Kerry with a frightened look, and backing up against the wall like a wild thing at bay.

"Oh, not now," laughed her mother. "You needn't put on any hysterics. That was before we had our quarrel. I said he simply should not invite that coarse fat Russian woman that he met in Cairo to visit us, and he said he had already done it. I cried all night and he only laughed at me and called me Baby. I was furious and came away the next morning on the earliest train I could get, leaving a note that I was not coming back."

Kerry sat down opposite her mother.

"Listen, Mother dear," she said gently, "it's very good to see you of course, but I must make you understand that if that man tried to come near me I shall simply get out and go where no one can find me. There is no use talking about it to you. He is your husband now, and it is too late, but I feel that I cannot be near him. I have my own reasons, and you perhaps could not understand, but that is how it is."

"Oh, well," laughed her mother, "you always were stubborn of course, but there is no need to bother about Sam any more. I'm done with him. We'll take a ducky little apartment somewhere near the park and have a couple of servants and—"

"Look here, Mother!" said Kerry sternly, "you will have to understand right at the start that I will not live in any apartment that is rented or bought or furnished by your husband, or by money that he has given you. And if you want to stay with me we'll have to put up with very plain things. You have only a small allowance yourself, you know, and I am making even less now."

"Well, dear me! Why quarrel!" yawned Isobel, "I'm tired to death and hungry too. Don't they have any service in this sordid place? Can't you ring and have a nice little supper sent up?"

"No," said Kerry sadly, "I can't! There isn't any service and there isn't any bell to ring, nor anybody to answer it. If you are rested enough we can go out to a restaurant and get supper, or if you are too tired for that I'll go out and buy some sandwiches and a bottle of milk and some ice cream. How would you like that?"

"What? Eat in this little room? Why, you haven't any table, nor dishes. Mercy Kerry! You remind me of the horrible days in those dreary hotels in London. I couldn't think of it. Come, we'll go to a good restaurant or a roof garden and have one really good time to celebrate being together again. You call a taxi and we'll go at once. I'm simply starved."

"Mother, dear. I'm afraid I can't afford a roof garden, and anyway I'm not dressed for such a place, and we would feel out of place."

"Not a bit of it!" said the mother cheerily. "We're going. Slip on your best evening things and come on. It won't matter if you haven't evening things. Tourists go to those places in their ordinary garments, just to look on. And as for affording it, I've got plenty of money along. I'll pay for it."

"Mother, look here!" said Kerry sternly. "I meant what I said. I will not go anywhere, nor do anything on money that you got from Mr. Morgan. If I can't afford things I'll go without them, but I will not be beholden to him. If you want to spend his money on yourself I can't prevent you. You married him. But if you mean what you said about leaving him I should think you would not want to touch a penny of his. I shouldn't in your place."

"No, you wouldn't!" said her mother with a sneer of contempt. "You're that way. You'd rather your mother went around in rags and slept on a hard bed, and ate fourth rate cooking and got sick. Well, my lady, you can just understand that I won't!"

It began to look as if they would not get any dinner that night, till all at once Kerry heard steps upon the stairs and a tap at the door and there was Mrs. Scott with a dainty tray on which was a tempting array. Fried chicken, little broilers, hot biscuits light as feathers, home made currant jelly, a pot of tea and heaping dishes of luscious red strawberries."

"I thought your mother might be tired, darlin'," she said in a low tone, and Kerry thanked her gratefully, and could have thrown her arms around her neck and cried on her shoulder.

"Oh, you are very good, Mrs. Scott."

But Isobel had heard the "darlin'."

"What impudence! Attempting to be intimate with you! 'Darlin'.' You shouldn't allow it!"

"Mother!" said Kerry, her eyes blazing indignation, "she will hear you. Listen, Mother, she has been wonderful to me. She is a real lady if there ever was one. And when I was in trouble and had no one she did everything for me—!"

"Well, it was your own fault that you were in trouble! If you had stayed with me you would have had plenty and so would I. Think of it, Kerry, each of us a whole apartment to ourselves and everything imaginable into the bargain. Sam would have been content enough if you had come. He says he just longs for young life and he has to have it. Why, Kerry! I thought you said you didn't have service. This chicken looks really very tempting, and those biscuits. They're almost like the beaten biscuits that Sam's cook in the south made yesterday for me. Suppose you ring—oh, I mean go down and tell her I wish she would send up a nice fruit cup to begin with. I always like an appetizer. It won't take her long to prepare it, and she can take the chicken down and keep it hot till we've eaten the fruit cup. What do you suppose she has for dessert?"

"Mother," said Kerry gently locking her door firmly and coming over to stand beside Isobel, "you don't understand. Mrs. Scott owns this house, and only rents out her rooms. She does not take boarders, nor serve meals. She is only doing this to be kind because she loves me and she knows I love her, and she wants to please my mother."

"Oh, I suppose she thinks I'll take a room here too, does she? Well, she's much mistaken. I wouldn't live in a sordid place like this for anything. It's unspeakable! We'll find another place the first thing in the morning."

Kerry sat her lips firmly, and sitting down opposite her mother with the tray on the desk between them, began to serve the chicken.

Isobel ate hungrily, and seemed in better humor afterward.

"It's really very good for such a place as this," she commented. "Now, have you spoken to her for accommodations for the night? I suppose it's too late to go anywhere else now. What other rooms has she got?"

"There are no vacant rooms here, Mother, every one is taken. You will have to stay here with me to-night."

"But, Kerry, you know how I hate rooming with anyone. You know I must get my rest."

"I'm sorry, Mother, there isn't any other way," said Kerry sadly. Life was getting more and more complicated.

They went to bed at last, and Kerry crept to the far edge of the bed and held herself rigid till she knew by her mother's steady breathing that she was asleep. Hour after hour she lay there and faced facts.

Here was her mother, dependent upon her. Not for an instant would she give in to that idea of her mother living on alimony, not if she meant to live with her. Never would she be under obligation to the man who had wrought trouble between them. It was all too evident that the marriage had not been a happy one. Castles and yachts and diamonds could not bring happiness. Kerry's duty loomed large.

At last she came around to the place that had been hurting her all the evening. McNair. She could not marry McNair and put the burden of a silly mother-in-law like that upon his life. She would not. She must send him on his way. She must give him up!

For hours she wrestled with herself, and the tears poured down and wet her pillow. Was God like this, demanding of her all she had? At last, toward morning she began to pray "Oh, Father, God, I've been very rebellious. Please, please forgive me. I'll do what you say. I hand over my life to you entirely, to do what you will with me. If this wonderful lover is not for me, please give me strength to give him up. Please bear me up and help me to do the right thing." And finally she slept.

Isobel was not awake when Kerry left for her work in the morning. She left a note for her mother suggesting a restaurant nearby where she might get luncheon, and saying she would be home as early as possible and they would go out for dinner together.

Kerry went to her office sadly, with blue shadows under her eyes. The lilt was gone out of her voice, but there was a sweetness and a gentleness about her that all her associates noticed and remarked upon. And when she smiled her face lit up with an inner light of the spirit.

But Kerry found an irate Isobel when she got home at night.

"Leaving me all alone in a strange city when I came on purpose just to see you!" she reproached.

"But Mother, you knew I had a position. I have to work for my living, you know, and now it will have to be for both our livings, so I shall have to be twice as careful to keep my job."

"Your job! The idea! The perfect idea of a girl educated as you have been, with a father like yours, talking about a job like any common workman's daughter. Why, I thought your father left you that book and I thought he always said it was going to make us rich!"

"Mother dear, there will be an income from the book by and by, a royalty, but nothing now before it is published. And it will not make us rich. Not what you count riches. But we can get along."

"Well, that's just what I always supposed," sneered Isobel, "that the great book would turn out to be a very small matter indeed! And you are just like your father, wanting to keep me down to the grindstone, scrimping and turning to keep alive. I never saw such an ungrateful daughter!"

There followed days of agony for Kerry. Days in which her mother searched for apartments, and dragged her to see them at night, only to find they were away beyond all possibility in the matter of price. Days in which Kerry carried about with her the consciousness that she had sent her letter of renunciation to California, and that soon McNair would know the worst, and it would all be over between them.

Nights in which Isobel cried herself to sleep, and Kerry tossed and turned until near morning, and then slept fitfully and got up to drag through the heat to the office again.

Several times during that awful period Harrington Holbrook came up to the city and begged Kerry to come out to the house and get cooled off. And when she told him her mother was with her he urged that her mother come too. But Kerry declined almost fiercely.

All too well she knew that Isobel would take to life at the Holbrooks, would preen herself and demand attention, and put them both under obligation. But though she declined and did not even tell her mother of the invitation, she thanked the boy gratefully, and sent him on his way feeling that at least one girl had not succumbed to the lure of money.

There came a day when Kerry knew that her letter must have reached California. It came on the top of an evening in which she and her mother had had a stormy debate about apartments. Isobel had found one just to her taste away up town where the best abodes were to be expected, and the price was simply out of sight.

Once for all Kerry told her:

"Mother, I am willing to give up my life trying to make you happy, but I cannot and will not take a place that I cannot pay for. If you and I stay together it has got to be with the understanding that we live within our means. I have told you what I can pay, and I am sure from what I know of prices and locations that nothing as good as this room can be found for the money. For the present even with your own income which father gave you, this seems the best place to stay. When the book begins to bring in royalty, or I get a raise perhaps, we'll talk about something better, but not before."

Isobel cried all night that night, or thought she did, which answered the same purpose, and Kerry went to her work ill prepared for the day, and praying constantly for strength and guidance. Strength, more strength to bear what might come from California in a few days, or worse still what might not come, for silence would be even worse than pleading.

About half past eleven o'clock a messenger boy arrived in the office with a telegram asking for Miss K. Kavanaugh.

Kerry's hands were trembling so that she could scarcely sign for the message. He had sent it to the office so that she would get it as soon as possible! He had been so kind and thoughtful. Her heart thrilled with appreciation of his thoughtfulness.

She tried to read the telegram quite casually for she could see furtive interested glances among her fellow workers, but the words leaped at her from the paper like old friends come to cheer her.

> Ruth 1:16, second clause to end of verse. Am starting to-night. Meet me at Pennsylvania station, Ladies waiting room, near telephones, Saturday 3 P.M. Dearest love.

> Graham

Kerry went to the reference library and took down the Bible, turning to the Book of Ruth. As she read the old, wonderful words a look of exultation came into her face.

"Intreat me not to leave thee, or to refrain from following after thee: for whither thou goest, I will go; and where thou lodgest, I will lodge: thy people shall be my people—"

She closed the book and went back to her work, her eyes full of a misty sweetness, and her heart answering with the last phrase of the verse:

"And thy God my God!"

19

THE week dragged by in much the same way that the last ten days had gone, exccept that Kerry was no longer utterly beaten. In spite of the heat and her mother's plaints, in spite of her perplexity and doubt, there was a lilt in her heart that crept into her voice again and all day long whenever she had a quiet minute by herself, her heart was crying out: "Oh Father— God. You're going to let me see him again! You didn't take him away without that! Oh, I thank you! I thank you!"

Saturday she was almost happy, as she dressed quietly not to waken her mother.

She longed to make herself fresh and suitable with a new garment for this occasion, but reminded herself that it would not do. Isobel would think her inconsistent in her talk about money if she spent even five or seven dollars on a little bargain dress. So she did her best with her old dark blue crêpe de Chine, and a freshly washed collar and cuffs of cheap lace which she had carefully dipped in coffee grounds and ironed down in Mrs. Scott's kitchen the night before.

She had not told Mrs. Scott of her lover's coming. It seemed too sacred to speak of even to her who loved him.

And besides, she could not tell her all—not yet anyway.

But Mrs. Scott was canny. She knew all that went on around her. She knew the child was passing through her chastening victoriously. She knew that some kind of struggle was going on within her, and that some light had come in her trouble. She knew that lilt when she heard it.

"What time do you get out from that horrible grind on Saturdays?" questioned Isobel from the bed suddenly, as Kerry was tiptoeing around just about to leave the room, supposing her mother was sound asleep. "Can't we go somewhere and have a little pleasure this afternoon?"

There was something pitiful in the voice. Kerry turned a guilty frightened gaze toward the bed. Was even this joy of meeting her lover for the last time to be denied her?

"I might get home by—four o'clock perhaps," she said hesitating. "It might be later," she added honestly. "But perhaps—this evening!"

"The very idea!" said Kerry's mother indignantly, "keeping you working all the afternoon on Saturday, no half holiday! I never heard of anything so mean! And at such a paltry salary too. I shall go down and speak to that Mr. Holbrook myself this afternoon about it. It's a perfect imposition."

"Mr. Holbrook won't be there this afternoon, Mother, and besides," said Kerry in a troubled voice, "I'm not always busy Saturday. I'll probably be free next week, and we'll go off somewhere and have a real picnic. Perhaps we'll take a little boat trip somewhere. They don't cost much."

"As if I'd care to go on an old common sight-seeing boat, when I've sailed the Mediterranean in my own yacht!" sneered Sam Morgan's wife.

"Well, I'm sorry," said Kerry, and went out, her morning saddened by the little dialogue.

Yet nothing could quite take away the joy of anticipation. He was coming! He was coming! He was coming! The cars that rattled by sang it, the trucks boomed and clattered it, the trolleys hummed it, the very newsboys on the street tuned in with phrases of their own, and seemed to be rejoicing with her. There might be a sad ending to the meeting, but—he was coming!

The morning went slowly and it was hard to keep her mind on her work. She kept going back to that wonderful telegram, and rejoicing over the reference he had included in it. She would not let him do it, of course, but it was wonderful to think he should offer. She thrilled anew every time she thought of it. Of course he had no idea what it would be to live with her mother. Kerry had no illusions. She was facing facts. She loved her mother but she knew that she was a silly, vain, spoiled, complaining, selfish woman. It was a daughter's duty to bear without complaining, but she had no right whatever to drag a man she loved into that kind of life and of course she did not intend to do it. Over and over again she told herself this tale.

At last the release from the office came, and just in time for her to meet the train, for truly it did happen that day that an extra rush on account of delayed printing made it necessary for all proof readers to remain beyond their usual time.

Kerry took a taxi to the station at the last minute, and came breathless to the waiting room where he had told her to be.

Five minutes later she saw him coming toward her. What a man he was, even more attractive than she remembered him, his smile gleaming out before he reached her, sending her heart into quivers of joy, sweeping away all resolves, all reasons, everything but just the breathtaking fact that he was hers, and he was willing to take her in spite of all drawbacks, willing to take over her trials as well as herself.

She got up and stood trembling for his approach.

"Silly," she told herself, and beamed at him, her eyes like stars, her cheeks glowing, all the worry of the weeks banished, just gladness in her face.

There before all the hurrying crowds and the staring multitude he stooped as if he had the right and kissed her, drew her two hands within his for an instant, and looked deep into her eyes. Then, as if he had fathomed her love and was satisfied, he said, "Come, let us find a place where we can talk," He searched out a quiet corner which had just been deserted by a large family and there they sat down.

"Now first," he said smiling, "get this! I don't intend to be shaken, nor turned down nor rejected. I'm going to be worse than Dawson. If I can't get you any other way I'll kidnap you, and I'll do it better than he did. I'll really get you for keeps, and there won't be any Ted around to help you out either for I'll suborn him first."

"Oh, but I mustn't let you," said Kerry firmly, "I love you for it, but I mustn't. You don't know my mother. I love her, but she is an unhappy woman and she makes everybody around her unhappy. I hate to have to tell you that, but I would rather tell you than have you experience it and blame me for letting you in on it."

"So you think I would blame you, little girl, do you?" he asked, suddenly grown serious.

"Oh, no, I know you wouldn't! You never would! But in your heart you could not help feeling I had not been quite square with you. Truly you cannot understand how hard it would be for you."

"Would it make it harder for you if I was there to help share the unpleasantness?" he asked tenderly.

"Oh, no!" she said with a deep drawn wistful sigh, "only that I would blame myself for letting you be there."

"Well, then, put that idea out of your head. I *want* to be there. I want to know and experience what you have been through and have to pass through, because only so can you and I be thoroughly one. I have found that we learn to know Christ only as we are permitted to share in His sufferings; only in that way can we be one with Him in His resurrection and triumph. And I think it is so, in lesser degree, in our earthly relations. Unless we are one in our troubles and unhappinesses, and bear them together, how can we possibly be one in our joys? I say it reverently."

"Oh—you are wonderful!" said Kerry. "You make it almost seem right!"

"Of course I do!" he said joyously. "Now, come, lead me to my new mother, for I'm going to love her as you do whether she is disagreeable or not."

Kerry laughed.

"She's not unpleasant to look at," she admitted, "she's very beautiful. Everybody admires her."

"One would know that to look at her daughter," said McNair drinking in the beauty of the lovely face before him.

"Oh, I'm not beautiful!" said Kerry incredulously, "I'm nothing at all like mother. She is lovely!"

"Well, I'll tell you whether you're more beautiful after I see her," said McNair smiling, "but we won't tell her. Come now, let us go and get this over with, and then, dear, you and I are going out to get married. Yes, I mean it," he said as he saw protest in Kerry's eyes. "I'm running no more risks. I'm going to have the right to stay by you whatever comes. And we're going to get your mother so interested in our wedding that she won't have time to be unhappy any more. This is our job now, yours and mine, to take care of her, since the man she has married seems not to be able to make her happy."

Before she could protest longer he had her in a taxi, and they were threading their way through traffic toward Mrs. Scott's. As they went McNair went on planning.

"We'll let your mother choose where we are to live. We'll have to give up a honeymoon for the present perhaps, but we're going to have a good time anyway. What's a wedding trip! Why, we can make our whole lives into one!"

"You are wonderful!" said Kerry, her face full of deep joy and reverence. "I never knew that a man could be like that! Only my father! He never thought of himself! And to think—

why! I told my heavenly Father this very morning that I would give you up, and here I'm letting you go on and do this. I'm not keeping my promise to God!"

"Dearest, did you never know how God delights sometimes to give us back the treasures we have laid at His feet? I'm not calling myself a treasure, but our united love is, I'm sure of that, a God-given treasure. Now, here we are! Let's remember we are one, and whatever one wants the other wants too. And this is our job now, to make that beautiful little mother happy!"

He helped her out and Kerry went upstairs to call her mother, but when she got there she found the room empty.

Startled, she looked around and then ran down to ask Mrs. Scott if she had seen her.

That good woman was wiping happy tears from her eyes with her kitchen apron and rejoicing over the dear lad who had come back again from afar.

"Your mother went out," said Mrs. Scott. "Yes, she come in here, and said she was going and she'd left a note on the bureau for you. She said you would understand."

Kerry rushed upstairs again to find the note, foreboding in her heart. What had her beautiful little mother done now? She unfolded the note hurriedly.

> Dear Kerry:—I'm going back to Sam. I can't stand this kind of a life. I wasn't made for roughing it. Sam has just telegraphed that the Russian lady and her friends have left and he is meeting me in Philadelphia, and he thinks we had better take a trip to Bermuda on the yacht. He's had my private cabin refurnished in orchid. You know that always was so becoming. I shall have one done in jade green for you whenever you decide you'd like to join us. I'm sorry to desert you this way, but it's your own stubborn fault. You're like your poor dear father, and I can't stand hardships. Perhaps some day you'll find out that it's better to take what

you can get and not be so squeamish. Good-by, I'm going. Don't work too hard, and do write me a line now and then.

Lovingly, Mother

Kerry read this letter in a daze, read it over twice, gradually taking it in that the trouble was lifted. Her mother, it was true, had gone back to Sam Morgan and separated herself from her, but the way was made clear now for her to live her own life. Had God done that too? Was it all in His plan?

She went down presently, a kind of wonder in her face and asked what time her mother left.

"Why the telegram came soon after you went out," said the woman, "and I should say it was about an hour later that she went. She had me to call the taxi, and asked me for a cup of coffee. She didn't leave any message except that there was a note for you on the bureau and that she had been called away."

"She has gone!" said Kerry looking at McNair with troubled eyes.

"Where?" asked McNair, accepting the note she handed him to read.

"Gone back," said Kerry, "just as she came, inconsequently. Just as she went in the first place."

"She's a bonnie wee lady," said Mrs. Scott, saying nothing about the way the bonnie wee lady had ordered her around at the last, and demanded her assistance.

McNair read the letter slowly and then handed it back to Kerry who stood by anxiously.

"It is all a part of the Father's plan," he said with a look of more than tenderness, "it will work out all in His good way, and when the next climax occurs we'll be together to stand by her." The smile that went with the words swept all of Kerry's difficulties aside, and thrilled her with a joy such as she had never dreamed could be. Her face broke into radiance.

"And now," said McNair, "when can we have our wedding? Would an hour be too soon? I want to belong!"

"But what about my job?" said Kerry suddenly remembering her obligations. "I can't just leave right out of the blue like that!"

"Well, no, I suppose not. But I'll be lenient. We'll put that up to Holbrook, and let it work out the best way for all concerned. I want what you want. Need we bother about that to-day? We have all day to-day and to-morrow. We might even get in a preliminary wedding trip before Monday if we tried."

"Well, you've got to give me time to get a wedding supper ready," said Martha Scott anxiously, "I'd never forgive myself if I couldn't do that for my lad and his bonnie lassie."

"All right, Martha, we'll eat it if you'll cook it, but don't make it too elaborate. Just some of your nice flap jacks would do, or corn fritters. I haven't tasted any like them since you left us."

"Bless his heart! Hear the lad. Well, I'll run right out to the store and get a few things and I'll have it ready by the time you are."

"I've got to have a new dress!" said Kerry. "I can't get married in this old rag."

"Now, look here, lady," said McNair, "you can't get any delays on that score. I've waited ages already, and I'll give you only two hours, and that is all. I'll have to get the license and the minister, and if I thought I could do it sooner I'd make it less. If you can conjure a new dress in that length of time all right, but anything longer I object to. I've seen you in several different kinds of dresses, but I never saw you look prettier than you do at this minute—and—"

Just at that moment the back door slammed. Mrs. Scott had discreetly taken herself to the store, and McNair folded his hungry arms about Kerry and gathered her to his heart for the first time.

Half an hour later they parted from each other in the shopping district and Kerry dashed into a store and selected two dresses, one a little white silk, the other a lovely green ensemble with a creamy fur collar which she had admired that morning as she passed the window. Two pairs of slippers, a little green hat, a pair of gloves and some hastily selected lingerie completed her trousseau, and she took another taxi back to the house, with just fifteen minutes left to dress for her wedding. In Martha Scott's funny stiff little parlor Kerry stood up in her simple white frock and was married by the minister of the church that she and McNair had attended together that first night in New York. Martha Scott in her best black dress, with her hands reverently folded at her waist stood adoringly by and beamed on them both, her dear lad and the bonnie lassie. And she was canny enough not to remark: "It's a pity your bonnie little mother couldn't have stayed for the wedding." Martha Scott did not need to be told such things.

After the wedding supper, which was excellent in every detail even to a piece of old black fruit cake, hurriedly iced, that Martha Scott had kept put away ripening for months, they went unhurriedly away to a quiet unfashionable little town on the coast that had been the delight of McNair in years agone. There they spent the first Sabbath of their married life. It was a holy and a blessed time to them both.

"I'm so surprised," said Kerry, Sunday evening when they came in from attending a sweet little country service in the local church, "to find there is real happiness on the earth. Ever since I was a little girl I've thought that people could not really be happy on the earth. But I've been perfectly happy to day. The memory of it will be like a beautiful jewel to possess always and carry to heaven with me when I go."

"You blessed child!" said McNair taking her into his arms. "Please God, I shall make it my business to see that you have many more days of happiness if we are spared here. And the best of it is that we are both expecting to spend eternity in the same place!"

They took the very early train into town Monday morning that Kerry might get to her desk on time. The morning papers arrived as the train came in, and McNair bought one of a sleepy village boy who had come down to get them to distribute.

"I wonder how our friend Dawson is," said McNair as they settled themselves in the train. "You don't suppose perhaps we should send him announcement cards do you?"

Kerry giggled and gave a little shiver.

"I'm so glad," she said, "that now I have somebody to stand between me and him."

A moment later McNair turned to the inside of the paper and exclaimed.

"Look here! I guess you won't need to be protected from Dawson for some time to come. Read that!"

Kerry leaned over and read:

NOTED CROOK CAUGHT AT LAST!

A literary and scientific crook Henry Dawson, Ph.D as he signs himself, for whom the secret service has been quietly combing the country for the past three years, has been neatly rounded up and brought to justice by a fifteen-year-old boy from the Bronx, Ted Gallagher by name, employed in the publishing house of Holbrook, Harris and Company, publishers of technical books.

Henry Dawson Ph.D. will be remembered as the so-called scientist who sold synthetic bones of a prehistoric beast to the Museum several years ago, for a fabulous sum, professing to have dug them up himself. The bones were afterwards found on investigation to be hand made, and the account of his finding them manufactured out of whole cloth. In fact, there was no such spot as the place he described. Later Dawson stole the manuscript of a book of poems and published them under his own name, and the next year got possession of a book on Electricity by one of the professors in the State

University and attempted to do the same thing, but was discovered before the book was actually in print. He succeeded, however, in getting away with the advance royalty, forging a check incidentally. Later, he forged a check for a hundred thousand dollars in the name of J. D. T. Wilkinson of California, since which time Dawson has been wanted for any one of these misdemeanors. His latest enterprise has been an attempt to marry the daughter of the late Dr. Shannon Kavanaugh, perhaps the greatest investigator of the Einstein theory and various other subjects. A few days ago Mr. Dawson, without the knowledge or consent of Miss Kavanaugh, announced his engagement to her in our papers, together with a statement that he had helped to prepare for publication Dr. Kavanaugh's new book which is to be released for sale this week.

Dawson attempted to kidnap Miss Kavanaugh in a hired taxicab as she came out from the publishing house in the early evening. Young Gallagher heard her scream, as he was about to leave the place on his motor cycle, and followed her; succeeded in tripping Dawson as he got out of the cab, called a policeman and captured the kidnaper, then rescued the lady on his motor cycle.

Dawson's case was rushed through without preliminaries, and he will be under strict confinement for at least twenty-one years for forgeries, to say nothing of his minor offenses.

Kerry lifted startled eyes to her husband's face:

"And I've been worrying a lot lest I ought not to have let that policeman know about my room being ransacked!" she said. "Oh, God has been good to me! He's worked it all out for us."

"Indeed He has! Been good to us both!" said McNair. "And He always does work things out if we let Him have His way. But to think I went off and left you in the same house with that snake! Oh! I should never have forgiven myself if anything had happened to you! What was business beside your safety?"

Kerry went demurely to her desk at the office that morning, with only the big blue diamond on her finger to call attention to the modest band of platinum it guarded.

Everybody in the office was so excited over the account in the paper that at first nobody noticed the rings. It was Ted who saw them first, as Kerry put up an unthinking hand to push back a wave of the red-gold hair that would persist in falling over her forehead.

His eyes got large and his jaw dropped, as he looked, till the others followed his gaze and stared too.

"Oh, gee!" he said. "Look what! She's pulled a wedding after all. I don't call that fair. You might have rung us all in on that!"

"Well, it rather took me by surprise myself," smiled Kerry. "You see Mr. McNair came on sooner than I expected, and when he heard what had happened he thought he'd put me in bonds so I couldn't get strayed or stolen again. By the way, he's coming around this afternoon at quitting time, Ted, especially on purpose to thank you for rescuing me! And he wants to meet you all!" she added, smiling about upon her fellow workers!

"You're not going to leave us?" they asked anxiously, for everybody in the office loved Kerry.

"Not right away," she assured them happily.

Mysterious whisperings floated around among the office people during the day, and there was much exchanging of money. Even the heads of the firm had a part in the conspiracy, but Kerry noticed none of it. She was too busy and too happy. Her father's book was coming out that day, and she almost felt as if too many beautiful things were happening at once for her to fully enjoy them all.

Late in the afternoon McNair called for Kerry in a shiny new car which he explained to her later he was using on trial.

The entire office force gathered about to be introduced, and while they were all there, Holbrook himself with them, Ted stepped forward and blurted out an invitation.

"Miss Kav—I mean Mrs. McNair—excuse me—why— we're pulling a party to-night at the Ritz and in the name of the office I invite you and Mr. McNair to be among those present. At least if you aren't, there won't be any party!" he finished bravely, amid the shouts and laughter of the entire group.

So Kerry went to the party looking her loveliest in her white wedding silk with a string of real pearls around her neck. They had belonged to McNair's mother, but he had not had time to get them out of the bank before the ceremony Saturday evening.

It was a real party indeed, flowers and sumptuous foods, but no liquors. Strange to say young Harrington Holbrook had been the one to taboo that.

"She doesn't like it," he said emphatically in his father's office where the committee was arranging things, "won't even drink a cocktail!"

"I should say not!" seconded Ted who by right of his recent rescue was on the committee by common consent.

Everybody was there, even Mrs. Holbrook and Natalie, who now that Kerry had become a heroine of kidnaping and married a stunning new man without anybody's social assistance, were quite disposed to be chummy, and affect a former friendship. Kerry even overheard Mrs. Holbrook telling the head proof reader that Harrington was broken-hearted that he hadn't found her before McNair came on the scene.

They had a beautiful time with merry speeches, and when it came time Ted made the speech of the evening in his own characteristic boy language, presenting in the name of the office a handsome sterling silver tea service, rare in workmanship and exquisite in simplicity of design.

Kerry made a shy little speech and Graham McNair spoke a few witty and grateful words, and then Ripley Holbrook arose. A waiter brought in a white satin cushion, and on it lay a copy of Shannon Kavanaugh's new book, bound in leather, hand tooled, and with a hand-illuminated inscription from the house of Holbrook for Shannon Kavanaugh's daughter, in token of the great service she had rendered in the preparation and publishing of the book.

Late that evening when they were back at Martha Scott's where they were to stay until they should find a house, McNair brought out a package wrapped in brown paper and handed it to Kerry.

"Kerry, little girl," he said tenderly, "this is your real wedding present. I forgot all about it yesterday, but I've been keeping it for you a long time."

Kerry opened the package, and found books, books in rare old bindings with a strangely familiar look. She picked up one and exclaimed in wonder and joy! It bore Shannon Kavanaugh's signature on the fly leaf.

"Where did you find them?" she asked, her eyes shining with pleasure. "My dear, dear books! Oh, how I hated to sell them! But how did you know—! Why! you were in the book shop the day I sold them to old Mr. Peddington, father's friend! And you bought them! You dear! You're wonderful! They will be doubly precious to me now. But how did you—why did you—happen—?"

"I didn't happen," said McNair with a dreamy tenderness in his eyes. "I knew perfectly well what I was doing. For you see, I fell in love with you that day, my darling!"

About the Author

Grace Livingston Hill is well-known as one of the most prolific writers of romantic fiction. Her personal life was fraught with joys and sorrows not unlike those experienced by many of her fictional heroines.

Born in Wellsville, New York, Grace nearly died during the first hours of life. But her loving parents and friends turned to God in prayer. She survived miraculously, thus her thankful father named her Grace.

Grace was always close to her father, a Presbyterian minister, and her mother, a published writer. It was from them that she learned the art of storytelling. When Grace was twelve, a close aunt surprised her with a hardbound, illustrated copy of one of Grace's stories. This was the beginning of Grace's journey into being a published author.

In 1892 Grace married Fred Hill, a young minister, and they soon had two lovely young daughters. Then came 1901, a difficult year for Grace—the year when, within months of each other, both her father and husband died. Suddenly Grace had to find a new place to live (her home was owned by the church where her husband had been pastor). It was a struggle for Grace to raise her young daughters alone, but through everything she kept writing. In 1902 she produced *The Angel of His Presence, The Story of a Whim,* and *An Unwilling Guest.* In 1903 her two books *According to the Pattern* and *Because of Stephen* were published.

It wasn't long before Grace was a well-known author, but she wanted to go beyond just entertaining her readers. She soon included the message of God's salvation through Jesus Christ in each of her books. For Grace, the most important thing she did was not write books but share the message of salvation, a message she felt God wanted her to share through the abilities he had given her.

In all, Grace Livingston Hill wrote more than one hundred books, all of which have sold thousands of copies and have touched the lives of readers around the world with their message of "enduring love" and the true way to lasting happiness: a relationship with God through his Son, Jesus Christ.

In an interview shortly before her death, Grace's devotion to her Lord still shone clear. She commented that whatever she had accomplished had been God's doing. She was only his servant, one who had tried to follow his teaching in all her thoughts and writing.

Don't miss these Grace Livingston Hill romance novels!